All she wanted was a quiet, normal life...but you don't always get what you want.

Lilian Quinn came to this remote town to start a new life. No one knew she had escaped from Custodes Secreti, a secret organization dedicated to using people with strange abilities for their own ends. All she wanted was a quiet, normal existence. Even if it meant living a lie.

Matthias Romulus was content to be the Alpha werewolf of the local pack, until he bumped into Lilian. Powerfully drawn to her, he stepped in to help her when the Custodes Secreti tracked her down. He didn't know she was trained in much more than waiting tables.

With Lilian's murderous ex-boyfriend coming after her and secret agents on her trail, the strange dreams she's been having are only the beginning. Matthias has problems of his own with his pack giving ultimatums. Can a psychic woman and an alpha wolf come together to resolve the issues of their hearts—and the issues of their continued survival?

I0677553

Books by Isolbael Liu

Moonlight and Magick

Published by Kensington Publishing Corporation

Moonlight and Magick

Isobael Liu

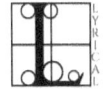

LYRICAL PRESS
Kensington Publishing Corp.
www.kensingtonbooks.com

Lyrical Press books are published by
Kensington Publishing Corp. 119 West 40th Street New York, NY 10018

First Electronic Edition: May 2010
eISBN-13: 978-1-61650-148-8
eISBN-10: 1-61650-148-0

First Print Edition: May 2010
ISBN-13: 978-1-61650-883-8
ISBN-10: 1-61650-883-3

Printed in the United States of America

To my husband, Spike, and my daughter, Pixie-Brat, who supported me while I wrote this book. To Lynn, for being my best friend, even if you live a billion miles away. To my parents, who always encouraged me to write.

I love you all.

Prologue

It was a scene repeated many times over in her young life. Lilian couldn't remember a time when John wasn't hitting Jane, the woman she called Mama, but it'd never been this bad. She watched as it went on and on, screaming as John kicked Mama, as he yelled and cursed.

It didn't look like he would ever stop.

She couldn't take any more. The world seemed like it turned upside down and sideways, making her tummy ache. There was a buzzing in her ears, like hovering bees. She dragged herself to her feet, gaping at her stepfather and the now unrecognizable form of her mama on the floor of their home. All Lilian could see was the blood, the bright red splatter decorating the floor and the wall. She could hear the squelching noises made with each blow.

The buzzing grew louder and louder until she covered her ears.

Lilian took in his reddened face, blood stained suit, and watched as the monstrous expression turned to confusion. He'd noticed the objects around the room, circling the two of them.

Vases, jewelry, pillows, her mother's hairbrush, items no heavier than her parents' bedside lamps, flew through the air, collided with one another, and smashed against the walls. She watched as they flew at John, striking him again and again.

He turned and gawked at her in horror.

"You freak. I knew something was wrong with you. Spawn of the devil!"

Lilian was taken by an inner calm, unafraid. Even though tears dripped from her cheeks and ragged, uneven breaths tore at her lungs, it was like she was watching from the outside. Not part of the chaos happening in the room.

Her stepfather grabbed his chest as his face twisted in a grimace. He gasped aloud, trying to breathe, but couldn't. His skin went from red to white, and to a pale blue. Several moments later, he fell onto the floor, a horrified expression in his dulling eyes.

Lilian looked back at him as he took his last breath.

The moment he died, everything dropped to the floor and became still, silent. Her shaking hands fell to her sides and she bolted out of the room to her secret hiding place.

What had she done?

It took two days before anyone came to the house. Lilian, weak, exhausted, and hungry, heard the sirens approaching, which later became voices downstairs. There was the sound of mumbling in the distance, coming from below, but she remained hidden.

The voices grew louder, clearer, and called her name. Curling up into a tighter ball, she pulled the blankets around her until hidden away, safely concealed.

The voices went away, but returned some time later, accompanied by the sounds of moving objects.

The closer they came, the more still and tense she became, like a baby deer hiding from hunters in the tall grass. She heard boxes shuffled and old trunks scraped across the wooden floor. The dresser was next, and soon her blankets were carefully pulled aside.

"I found her!" a man called, and the sound of hurried movements followed.

A hand touched her cheek, warm against her cold skin. She jerked back and opened her eyes.

"She's alive!"

A collective cheer came from the rescue workers and her body jolted. Her heart raced, and her breathing became rapid and shallow.

Everything went black.

Chapter 1

Hawk's Point was known as a waypoint for hikers and campers who braved the Mount Rainier National Forest. It was a small town Lilian had wandered into a couple of years ago, and immediately fell in love with. It was perfect. No one knew about her past or her true identity. This was her chance to start over, live a simple life, away from the larger cities. Seattle, especially.

The residents of her new home recognized her as Lilian Quinn and accepted her as a welcomed member of their tight knit community. Regardless if everyone knew what skeletons lurked in their neighbors' closets, they didn't know her secrets.

She found a job working at the local diner, which paid little, but she didn't need to be rich. As long as it paid her bills and there was a little extra, she was happy.

Taking orders from a few of the tables outside, she heard the loud rumbling roar of motorcycles. Dishes and glasses rattled on the tables. Lilian glanced up to see a small gang of about ten bikers riding by. She spotted one of the members as they passed. With his mirrored sunglasses, she couldn't see much other than a masculine face and black hair long enough to hang mid way down his back in a ponytail.

She chuckled to herself and bent to hear the customer's order, scribbling onto a small notepad, as their engines cut out. From the distance of the sound, Lilian assumed they had parked at the Motel 6. A few of the customers, however, kept their eyes on the strangers, and conversations shifted to the activities of the gang members.

Going about her duties, she heard from the lunch crowd what the bikers were doing; getting off their bikes, gathering around and stretching, which resulted in various debates over why. She smiled faintly in amusement at the patron's musings, went inside to turn in the orders and pick up plates from the hot table to deliver. It took her a few minutes, as she served the tables and filled glasses, before heading back outside.

A wave of nausea and a sense of trepidation hit her as she stepped onto the terrace, causing her to pause and survey the area. As Lilian scanned the patio, she saw the two men seated at the far table, in dark suits and sunglasses. While sunglasses were par for the course on such a beautiful day in Hawk's Point, suits were not.

The men sat themselves in such a way one could face and watch customers and servers moving about the alfresco area, the other faced out to the street to watch the coming and going of passersby.

Lilian knew they were trouble, but for whom? If they were here for her, she couldn't run. She had to continue as if nothing was wrong.

After delivering food, she picked up two menus and a pitcher of ice water. Pasting on a smile, she approached the table. "Good afternoon." She set their menus down and poured water into their glasses. "Can I get you anything to drink besides water? Iced tea or soda?"

"Lilian Powell?" He kept his tone soft, but still meant business.

Lilian shook her head. "I'm sorry, my last name is Quinn. Wrong girl." She tapped the menus on the table. "I'll be back to take your order in a few."

Before they could say anything else, she walked away, checking on the other diners and refilling water glasses until she made it back inside, hurrying into the kitchen to escape the prying eyes of the two strangers .

"What's the matter, *chica*?" Maria tossed a basket of onion rings into the fryer.

Maria was one of her closest friends, as close as she could be while Lilian still retained her carefully guarded secrets.

"There are two men in my section who're just freaky. I think they might be government agents," Lilian replied.

"Government? Cool! Bet they make some major money. Are they cute?" Maria asked as she flipped burgers on the grill.

Leave it to Maria to think of money and good looks rather than wonder why they were here.

"I didn't pay attention." Lilian checked her watch.

Damn, still thirty minutes to go before clocking out.

"Well, take a peek when you go back out and let me know, girl! I ain't getting any younger!" Maria shooed her out.

Those men gave her the heebie-jeebies. Still, Lilian couldn't hide in here or they'd become suspicious. On her way out, she picked up a pitcher of ice water in one hand, a pitcher of iced tea in the other, and turned to use her hip to open the door. Motioning to one of the other waitresses that she had the iced tea, the door flung open. She cried out as she stumbled. She turned her body to try and catch her balance, but collided into what felt like a brick wall.

There were a few gasps of shock and some masculine guffaws. Wondering what or whom she'd collided with she turned and stared into the face of the biker she'd noticed earlier. He was soaked. The water and the iced tea drenched the front of him, from chest down.

At least she had a better view of him.

He had a masculine face with a dimple in his left cheek, passably handsome in a rugged, outdoorsy way, and yes, the dark hair. He was tall, probably a good four inches taller than her, and from the way the now wet t-shirt clung to his torso, a nicely built frame, but not an overzealous bodybuilder. He grabbed onto her to keep her from falling, and she could feel the strength in his hands, though his hold was gentle.

"That'll cool ya off, brother," a man called out and laughed, joined by the others of the gang.

A low growl emanated from the drenched biker, too low for anyone else to hear, but it rumbled through the man and into her. Lilian's eyes widened in shock, mortified. She jerked back from the man, or tried to, stammering out an apology.

"Please, I'm terribly sorry. I'll pay for your meal, of course. I didn't expect the door to not be there." Her words tripped and stumbled over her tongue and she kept trying to pull away from him, but he refused to let her go.

"If you stop a minute," he drawled, "I can let go of you without you flying down the street."

Lilian fell silent, blinking in surprise. It was true. His hold on her kept her upright, but she kept pulling away and if he did let go of her, she would go flying just from her momentum. She glanced up at him, but with his sunglasses on, couldn't see his eyes. There was a wry twist to his lips, not quite a smile, but not a grimace either.

Lilian went still and he let go of her upper arms.

"There," he said.

She stared at her reflection in the sunglasses. He lifted a brow at her, the corner of his lips tilting up into a smile. She blushed and backed away a couple of steps.

"Don't scare her off, little brother," another of the gang said. "I'm hungry and thirsty."

"The way she's looking at him, you'd think he just told her she's on the menu," said another.

Lilian looked away from the man in front of her and made a quick, visual foray around the outdoor section. The biker gang took up residence at the empty tables, her appointed station now filled to capacity. Dismayed and nervous, she snapped her gaze back at the one in front of her.

"Could we have some menus?"

Lilian blinked, nodded, turned and ran back into the diner as though the hounds of hell were nipping at her heels. Hounds of hell, no, but the guffaws of the biker gang followed her inside.

She glanced over her shoulder and saw him looking toward her, having not moved from the spot he stood before. Uneasy, she looked away and headed to the front desk.

As if the two suited men hadn't been enough, now she had to deal with this?

It wasn't a personal threat she sensed. If Lilian had been in some form of danger from him, she'd have known. Still, something about him made her feel uneasy. What? Because he was in a motorcycle gang, or maybe because he was a stranger and strangers, especially strange men, made her uncomfortable?

Opting to err on the side of caution, she handed the menus off to one of the other waitresses, trading with her so Lilian could watch over the interior tables.

Thirty minutes later, with her shift over, she removed her apron and tossed it into the hamper. She picked up her small purse and clocked out. With a final wave to Maria and fellow waitresses, she used the back door with the hopes of escaping the notice of the suited men and the bikers. Unfortunately, her plan didn't work so well. As Lilian stepped out of the parking lot and onto the sidewalk along Main Street, one of the suited men stepped into her path and stopped her.

"Miss Quinn."

Lilian heard the wry tone in his voice as he said her name and knew he doubted her.

"Yes?" she asked.

"We'd like to speak to you. In private."

The second suited man crossed the street to join them. Lilian knew if she went anywhere with them, she'd disappear.

"I'm sorry, but I don't have the time. I have some errands to run."

"I don't think you understand." The man reached into his jacket's inner pocket.

Lilian tensed, wary, and shifted her stance so the two men couldn't position themselves to box her in.

The man withdrew what looked like a white card and turned it to show her a photograph of her as a child, after the "incident". The blood rushed from her head and a sinking feeling filled her gut.

"Maybe you'd like to try again with your name?" he asked.

Lilian glanced up from the photograph to the man. He still wore his sunglasses, but she didn't need to see his eyes to read his mind. Very carefully, and with the lightest of touches, she scanned his surface thoughts. *"Run. Run so I can chase you. When I catch you, I'll punish you. I'll pin you down and show you..."*

She immediately pulled her mind from his, nauseated. "I'm sorry, but who are you? Where did you get that picture?"

She quickly but carefully scanned the second man's thoughts, which were easier on her senses. *"Stephan's description was exactly like the picture shows. She's the right one. She's obviously lying about her name. Why are we wasting our time here?"*

Neither man replied to her questions, but it was obvious they intended to get her to confess her real name. However, she was spared any further attempts with the arrival of the biker gang.

"There you are," the biker leader called out. "Come on, we'll be late."

Lilian and the suited men looked over at him. His friends flanked the leather-clad man, and despite the friendly tone he'd used, all were tense. She quickly scanned the surface thoughts of the leader. *"Help her. Those men are up to no good. Don't trust them."*

As she stepped toward him one of the suited men grabbed onto her arm. A mistake. The biker gang exploded into action and rushed toward them. The suited man released her and she was pulled into the arms of the gang leader. He led her some distance away.

"Let go of me." She struggled to free her arms.

"That's not very nice," he quipped. She could hear the amusement in his tone. "I just saved you from who knows what and I don't even get a thank you."

Lilian found herself blushing, yet again.

"Thank you. *Now*, let me go."

He chuckled before changing the subject. "What's your name?"

The distinct sounds of fighting emanated behind her, but a quick glance over her shoulder revealed nothing. Deciding they must have dragged the fight into the alley, she turned to look back up at the man.

"Lilian Quinn. Who're you?"

He grinned at her. "Matthias."

She heard a loud snarling sound from the alley, but when she turned to look, Matthias used his hold on her and kept her from looking. Was he trying to distract her from seeing something?

"Why are they harassing you?"

Lilian looked back at him, frowning. "Why do you want to know?"

He lifted a brow at her. "I asked first."

She studied his face. Every logical fiber told her not to trust him. Still, he and his friends did come to help her when she needed it.

"I can't tell you. I don't even know who you are. Please let me go."

Matthias released her and she took a step back from him.

"Thank you." She rubbed her arm.

"You know why those men are after you, don't you?"

She sighed. *The man is infuriatingly persistent.*

"Yes, but I'm not going to tell you why."

She could feel him studying her, but those sunglasses hid his eyes. What color were they? Lilian tilted her head slightly as she studied his face.

"Why are you staring at me?" Amusement colored his tone.

"You were staring first," she said.

"Was I?"

"What color are your eyes?"

A faint sense of satisfaction came over her when she saw his brows lift over the rim of his shades.

He was spared from answering by the return of his friends. The men joked a bit back and forth, teasing one another about their lack of practice, but the words didn't sink in. Instead, her attention was drawn to the crimson color. A couple of them had bloody noses and others had scraped knuckles. Even from where she stood, in the darkened parking lot of the diner, the blood stood out like a bright beacon. Time seemed to slow, and then stop as she stared at them.

Long buried memories crashed down on her and she couldn't help but relive the night her stepfather had murdered her mother. All she could see was the crimson splatter left in the wake of his brutality.

Lilian backed away from the approaching group, but ran into Matthias. Feeling weak and lightheaded, she turned to face him.

Her knees threatened to buckle and she stiffened her muscles. She had to get out of there, away from the blood and the reminders of her past.

Matthias reached for her, but she jerked back from him. He frowned, but before he could speak, Lilian turned and bolted for the entrance of the diner.

* * * *

It had taken a couple more hours before she braved leaving the diner to head home. She'd gotten a ride with a customer who lived near her home. As they left the diner, she glanced around for signs of the suited men or of Matthias and his gang, but neither were to be seen. Overly cautious, Lilian knew, but she had to remain vigilant.

Once home, she checked and locked the doors and windows before taking a hot shower to soothe her frazzled nerves. She took her time, washing off the taint of fear and loathing from her skin. By the end she relaxed, her mind clearer.

Twenty minutes later, she was enjoying a cup of chamomile tea when her phone rang, shattering the peaceful silence.

"Hello?"

"My pretty Lilian. I've missed you."

Lilian's heart jolted and then pounded back to life as pain coursed through her chest.

Stephan.

She didn't believe in coincidences, just as she didn't believe Stephan's call had nothing to do with the presence of the suited men in Hawk's Point.

"Miss me?" he asked.

Goosebumps rose along her skin and the hair on the back of her neck tingled with chilling fright. Lilian said nothing in reply. She couldn't. There wasn't enough air in her lungs to say anything.

"Do you remember the last time we were together, my darling? Do you remember how much I hurt you? Do you remember the blood?"

Lilian slammed the phone down. Her stomach heaved and threatened to empty its contents as she struggled to breathe, to keep from panicking.

Memories flooded into her mind's eye, reliving every moment in supersonic speed. Stephan's smile, cold and unfeeling, superimposed over the memories, the physical abuse, the hospital visits, the blood stained towels. He'd been so kind in the beginning, but slowly changed. He'd begun to abuse her, mentally, verbally, and at the end, physically. She had planned to run away and leave him. Once he discovered her plans, he took away all her money and the ID she had, and threatened to turn her over to the police for murder.

The final straw had been when she found the printed email giving him directions of how to hold her for the agents to pick her up. It had been a shock to her and the idea of returning terrified her. In the many times her mind accidentally brushed against his, never once did she pick up the thought of him knowing the truth about her. Lilian didn't know how he'd found out about her past, or if perhaps he'd been a trap set by them all this time, but after two years with Stephan, she left that night.

She went through her house one more time before she retired for the night. She was tempted to pack a bag and head into town, just in case, but her own home was her haven, for the moment, and so she stayed. When she lay down in bed, curled up beneath the covers, Lilian knew sleep would be fleeting, if it came at all.

* * * *

She could hear the hounds baying in the background. Looking around, she saw no trail, no landmarks she recognized, but knew she had to run. Lilian had already been running, her heart beating hard in her chest, and was out of breath. Still, she knew if the hounds caught up with her, they would tear her apart.

She crisscrossed the ground quickly, her feet barely touching the soil, leaping over fallen logs and ducking low branches in order to escape the death at the jaws of the hounds and spear of the hunt master.

How did she know this?

Even with her speed and agility, Lilian knew the hounds were gaining on her. It was only a matter of time before they caught her, and when they did, they'd tear her apart. She stopped and looked around, for a way out, a place to hide; anyplace she could wait out the hunt. There was nothing, only the dark forest which stretched out before her in every direction.

Suddenly, there was a flash of white in her peripheral, a glowing white, almost ghostly. She turned her head and saw a white stag. It stood tall, the top of her head reaching its shoulders, and had a proud head, heavy with antlers as wide as the beast long. As she watched, it pawed the ground and waved its great head at her.

"There is not much time, my child. Come with me."

She was surprised when the stag spoke to her, not aloud but in her mind. Even though she hadn't heard its words, there was an urgency and she nodded.

It turned and ran, Lilian following behind it. As she did so, she heard the baying of the hounds and the enraged bellow of the thwarted huntsman.

Lilian jolted awake, heart pounding.

Chapter 2

Lilian slept little. Going through the motions of starting her morning, she was anxious and jittery. After the umpteenth time of reminding herself to breathe and calm down, she plopped herself onto the floor and sat cross-legged. She cupped her hands together and brought them to chest level, as though holding a book. Looking into her palms, she mentally focused on the issues at hand.

The *Custodes Secreti* agents were a problem.

She'd have to go away again. If they found her here, they wouldn't leave her alone until she disappeared or joined them.

Ever since her first experience with them, Lilian had managed to keep her abilities reined in and under strict control. She didn't want to alert anyone sensitive enough to pick up on psychic vibrations, nor did she want to alert CS agents of her whereabouts. Her gift to sense when someone nearby used their abilities was another reason why CS wanted her on their side.

What about Stephan? His re-entry into her life was *definitely* under the heading of "not a good thing". She was certain the sudden appearance of the CS agents and Stephan was no coincidence. How did he get her phone number, anyway? However much as she hated speaking to the local law enforcement, she knew she'd better do it soon, before things escalated.

Lilian stood and stretched; her mind more organized than earlier. She still had to address the nightmare and what it meant, but she'd need the library.

* * * *

Armed with notebook, pencil, and a stack of books on dreams, Lilian tackled the project like a defensive lineman on a quarterback.

Her first entry was the white stag. She looked it up and found the stag symbolized male sexuality, virility, grace, agility, regeneration, and growth. She scribbled the info into her notebook.

The next entry was forest. She went over the notes and tried to put them into perspective. It could mean she wanted to escape to a simpler life, which made sense considering the agents and Stephan were after her.

Again.

However, when she looked up the entry for woods, Lilian found it signified a return to an aspect of oneself which was innocent and spiritual. Hounds, in dreams, indicated something or someone may be "hounding" her and being unable to run away from it until the issue or person is confronted.

Hmm. This most assuredly fits my life right now.

To hear howling referred to loneliness or solitude. Ahh. Now *that* was interesting.

Lilian sighed and sat back in her chair. So, what did it mean? What was it *supposed* to mean?

* * * *

Matthias was waiting for her at the diner when Lilian arrived for her shift. Anticipation fluttered through her at the sight of him, but she nixed it. She wasn't here to date, nor was she looking for any attachments.

He met her at the entrance, still wearing his sunglasses and dressed in black jeans and a t-shirt.

She saw his lips tighten as she chose to ignore him, walking past him to the door of the diner. He reached out and touched her arm.

"Lilian," he said, "what's wrong?"

Well, gee, where to start? "I'm going to be late for work."

"We need to talk about what happened last night."

"Look, thank you for helping me out—" she started.

"But?" he interrupted.

"But I like my life the way it is, peaceful and without…" She tried to find the right words.

He drew back a bit. She didn't need to see his eyes to detect the surprise that came over his face. Lilian turned and reached for the door, but he grabbed her hand and turned her around to face him.

"Those men, what do you know about them?"

The blood rushed from her face and her heart stuttered. "Why?"

"Oh, no, you don't. You're going to answer my question."

She tensed and narrowed her eyes on him. "I don't have to answer any question you ask me, Matthias. Now, either release me, or I'll start screaming. You can deal with the police."

A black eyebrow quirked up over the rim of his sunglasses at her outburst and his lips tilted in a smile. She couldn't help but glance at his lips, just like she couldn't help the little tingle of awareness which shot through her when she did.

"I don't know why that amused you." Lilian tried to pull her arm from his grip. "Let go of me!"

"Answer my question."

She pressed her lips together and fell still, glaring up at him. She could see in the reflection of his sunglasses how her eyes darkened to stormy gray. As her anger grew, she watched her eyes darken even more, until they were almost black. She closed her eyes, and dragged ragged breaths in to try and calm herself.

Must not lose control.

"You have to let me go," she whispered. "Please."

His grip loosened and she backed away until she hit the diner's wall. She leaned back, laying her hands flat against the wall so her palms were pressed against the bricks. She concentrated on the tactile sensations, of the rough edged clay blocks, the coarse mortar which held them together, the overall warmth from the sun's rays.

When Lilian opened her eyes once more, she was much calmer. Matthias stood nearby. He must have watched her the whole time because she could read the suspicion on his face.

"Are you all right?" he asked.

"Yeah." A weak smile followed her reply.

"You don't look it."

"Thanks."

"You aren't human." He studied her eyes.

"I am too!" She stood up from the wall.

Before she could try to get to the door, Matthias used his body to pen her, crowding her until she was pressed back against the wall once more. While he didn't pin her to the wall, Lilian couldn't escape either.

"You're not human," he reiterated.

"Don't be an idiot. What else would I be?" She cringed at the sound of her breathless voice.

"Those two men are after you for a reason. You're something more than human."

He really is rather handsome, in a nosy, pain in the ass sort of way. She couldn't stop herself from watching his lips move as he talked.

"Stop that," he growled under his breath.

Lilian jerked her eyes up from his lips to his concealed eyes. "What?"

"You're staring at my mouth."

She was aware of the sudden warmth in her face and knew she was blushing.

"If you wanted to kiss me, all you had to do was say so."

Lilian pushed at him. "You're a jerk. Move."

He leaned his head down toward hers but she jerked back, only to crack her head against the wall.

"Ow!"

Matthias pulled back from her to stand upright and reached for her head, his fingers delving through her hair to feel the back of her head. His touch was incredibly gentle, and, damn it, she liked it.

"Want me to kiss it and make it better?" he asked.

"Stop it. I'm going to be late for work and you're not helping."

He chuckled. "I'll pick you up after your shift."

"No need."

"You think those men are finished with you?"

"Did your gang kill them?" she asked.

"No."

Not that it mattered. The organization would send others.

Matthias must have read something in her face because his fingers tightened in her hair, holding her in place.

"You know more than you're letting on."

Damn, damn, damn!

"Lilian, you have to let me help you. Those men weren't just human. How do you fit in with it all?"

Lilian sighed. "This isn't the place to talk about it—"

Matthias suddenly kissed her. Her eyes widened and her breath caught in a soft gasp. His hands tilted her head a bit. His lips moved over hers and her eyes fluttered closed as she gave in to the gentle demand. Her hands moved up of their own accord, her fingers slid through his hair to his ponytail, pulling it free from the binding. One hand remained holding him by the hair, the other came up and pulled his sunglasses up and off. He growled then, and used his body to pin her to the wall. Fire exploded in her veins and she moaned as he deepened the kiss, his tongue delving into her mouth to caress her tongue.

Matthias tasted wild, reminding her of pine forests and the earth. Lilian loved the taste of his mouth, his kisses. She squirmed against him, and he pulled her closer so that his arousal pressed against her.

This time, when he growled, she not only heard it, but it reverberated through her. In her mind, she heard the howl of a wolf.

"Hey, get a room, will ya?"

Ice water couldn't have been more effective than hearing the amused tone in Maria's voice.

Lilian jerked her mouth from Matthias's, her eyes flying up to his. Gold! His eyes were a molten gold color, heated with passion and possessiveness.

"Lily, come on! You're gonna be late!"

Lilian released his hair, and tried to push him back, but he was an unmovable force.

"Please," she whimpered.

He laid his face against the crook of her neck and with a languid inhalation, dragged in a breath through his nose. He exhaled and stepped back.

"I'll be waiting for you after your shift." He gave her a pointed look.

Lilian nodded and rushed toward the diner door where Maria waited.

* * * *

Lilian wasn't sure if her shift took forever to end, or went by way too quickly. Either way, she was very aware of Matthias's presence— watching her. He took a seat in the outside dining area and positioned himself so he could watch her, as well as their surroundings.

When her shift did end, she wanted to crawl into a dark corner and breathe. The butterflies in her stomach didn't just flutter; they staged an all-out air raid. So much so, breathing became difficult, made even harder whenever he looked at her. Even with his sunglasses on, she knew when his eyes fell on her. It made her edgy and nervous. Her tray would shake, the ice in the pitchers rattled, and he'd smile.

Those were the times she imagined his reaction if she dumped the ice water over his head. The image made her smile and put her back on track.

But, all good things must come to an end, she told herself.

Wait, this wasn't good. Matthias was waiting for her.

She sighed and clocked out. Maria, still in the kitchen, grinned whenever she looked at her, but said nothing. Of course, Maria didn't have to say anything. Her expression said plenty. Lilian blushed and looked away.

Matthias met her at the back door to the diner, and she tried to ignore the way her breath caught in a soft gasp at seeing him there, but wasn't very successful.

"Ready?" he asked.

Lilian nodded and looked around the little lot. After the previous evening, she was a bit leery of the agents returning.

"Your place?"

She looked at him in surprise. Her place? No way. She wouldn't be able to handle her emotions with him being in her home.

"I don't think that'd be very…"

"Safe?" He gave her a knowing grin.

In so many more ways than you think.

"Someplace more neutral," she said.

He pondered a moment and then nodded. "All right." He took her by the arm, walked with her out of the lot and around the corner where a rather large motorcycle was parked.

Lilian dug her heels in and balked. "No way."

Matthias looked at her. "What?"

"There's no way I'm getting on that *death trap* with you."

He shook his head. "It's not a death trap."

"Yes, it is. I've seen the news. There's not enough metal around me and there's only two wheels."

"Scared?" he asked.

Lilian narrowed her eyes. "Of your motorcycle? You betcha."

He laughed and before she could even think about darting away, he had her over his shoulder in a fireman's carry, strolling toward his bike.

Lilian shrieked and started to struggle. "You jerk! Put me down!"

Matthias swatted her on the butt, and leaned down to deposit her on the seat with a threat. "If you move, I'll kiss you again."

She froze to ponder his words, and wondered what the downside was. He chuckled, rearranged her legs so he could swing onto his motorcycle, and straightened the bike up. Her heart dropped out of her chest. She wrapped her arms around him, and held on for dear life.

"Lilian, you need to relax a little."

She heard the amusement in his voice.

"We could just walk to the park, you know," she suggested in a hopeful tone.

"I have a place in mind." He put the key into the ignition and pressed the starter button.

The motorcycle roared to life and he revved the engine. Lilian buried her face against his back.

She had no idea where he was taking her and knew she ought to be wary, but all thoughts went out of her brain as she inhaled his scent. A heady aroma, it reminded her of the forest on a summer evening, warm and earthy, alive. She closed her eyes as she breathed in and out, taking in his scent. It calmed her, made her almost forget she sat on a moving death trap with a man she barely knew but had made out with, going who knew where. When Lilian did remember, she jerked upright, causing the motorcycle to wobble a little. She shrieked in alarm and threw herself back against Matthias. He chuckled, patting her hands as if to reassure her.

Like that was going to happen.

After what seemed like an eternity, he slowed and turned off the main road. The uneven feel and crunching sound made her think it was a gravel drive of some sort. She wasn't entirely sure, since she refused to look up. When they finally came to a stop, Matthias killed the engine.

"You can let go, sweetheart," he said.

There was definitely some amusement in his tone as she released him.

"Stop laughing at me!"

Lilian sat upright, looked around, and gaped as she realized he'd brought her home.

She scrambled off the motorcycle and spun around to face him, furious. "I told you no. How do you know where I live, anyway?"

"I asked around, found your mailbox when I drove by, and figured this was your place. Anyway, we're not in your home and I see no reason why we can't talk out here." He shrugged and smiled.

"Oh! You insufferable jerk!"

He swung himself off the bike and stood. She refused to take a step back, even if he was just a bit intimidating.

"Tell me about the men, Lilian."

"No."

He lifted a brow. "No?"

Lilian looked around as she mentally went over her options. Could she run to her house and get inside before he caught up to her? No. Feasibly, she could fight him, but did she want to hurt him? No. Would it hurt to tell him, considering he was now involved? No.

Lilian realized she didn't have much of a choice now and her shoulders drooped in resignation. "Fine. They're from an organization called *Custodes Secreti*. They're...a secret group that gathers information and beings more enhanced than the normal human."

He removed his sunglasses and stared at her. "And they're after you, why?"

Lilian backed away a couple of steps. "Look, Matthias, I really don't want to get into this with you. I don't know you, and I'm not sure I trust you."

Not entirely true. Intuition told her to trust him. She could just read his mind to find out more, but with the agents so close, she didn't want to give herself away by using her abilities.

"You're just going to have to," he said.

Okay, so maybe she trusted him, but she sure as hell didn't like him. She'd just ignore the fact his mere presence made her tremble and his eyes made her feel like melting.

Lilian glanced away from him, and looked around until her gaze fell on her house. It wasn't very large, just two bedrooms and one bath. It could be considered more a cottage. It needed new paint, she noticed in a distant manner. The white paint was peeling off the siding and the trim faded. Still, it was her home and she didn't want to have to sell it in order to move again.

"Lilian," he said.

She looked back at him. "We better go inside. It's going to take a while to talk about."

Lilian turned and walked away. Fishing her keys out of her pocket, she stepped onto the little porch. Her hand trembled as she put the key in the lock.

Lilian hated telling anyone about herself. She had been so careful about keeping her secrets, but she should have known her past would catch up with her, and someday it would all come out.

She turned the key, expecting to hear the usual click of the door unlocking. When it didn't happen, she frowned and withdrew the key.

"What's wrong?" Matthias asked.

"My door's unlocked."

Matthias moved her behind him. "Stay back."

His tone was calm, but she heard the thread of steel behind it. Turning the knob with care, he opened the door at a snail's pace, and his head tilted as though listening to the sound of it opening. When the door opened a crack, he paused and looked over his shoulder at her.

"Maybe you should go stand by my bike."

Lilian shook her head. "No way."

Matthias appeared as though about to argue. Instead, he looked back through the open door. His body blocked her view, and she knew he did it on purpose. She poked him in the back to remind him of her presence.

"Move. I need to see."

"No, you don't." He lifted an arm to block the doorway, like a gate.

Before he could stop her, Lilian ducked beneath his arm and hurried into the house. She needed to see what he was trying to keep from her.

This was her safe haven, and if something had happened to it, she needed to know. Plus, she wasn't about to let him, a veritable stranger, dictate to her what she could and could not do on her own property.

Her eyes widened in horror as she took in the sight of what had been once an ordered and comfortable living room. Her furniture was broken, tossed about like trash. Tears rose up in her eyes and she had to blink them back, forcing herself to look around. Her pillows and cushions had been slashed, the stuffing spilling out. She switched on the lights, and the damage to her home became abruptly clear. As did the message on the wall, written in red.

Remember the pain, kitten.

As though in a stupor, she made her way closer to the wall, her mind not taking in the message as much as the red liquid used to write it.

Paint? Please, let it be paint.

She reached out with a shaky hand to touch the ink but Matthias grabbed her hand, pulled her away.

"No, Lilian. We have to call the police."

She looked away from the wall and glanced around yet again at the destruction. It was then she saw the dead cat. If it hadn't been for the blood, she would have thought it to be a stuffed animal, but in the bright light, the blood was a brilliant crimson.

Lilian stood rigidly. She could hear Matthias call her name, but couldn't make herself move. She could only stare at the carcass of the poor cat, slaughtered for the message on her wall. Even when he threw her over his shoulder and carried her outside, she could not react, could not protest. When he set her down, her knees gave out and she fell to the ground, with a faint sob. He crouched over her.

"Look at me," he said.

Lilian shook her head, refusing, and instead drew her knees up and wrapped her arms around her legs. She rocked back and forth, still sobbing.

"Lilian," he snapped.

She looked at him, startled, expecting to see a raised hand to strike her, or an angry expression on his face. There were neither. "I'm going to call the police," he said in a calm tone. "This has to be reported."

Lilian nodded and he pulled out his cellphone. He kept his eyes on her even as he dialed 9-1-1.

"Yes, we need the police. There's been a break in and vandalism at…"

His voice faded from her hearing as the reality set in. Someone had broken into her home and destroyed her sense of safety.

Run! Get away!

Lilian burst into motion, scrambled to her feet and ran into the woods as fast as she could, away from her home, and Matthias. She didn't know why, where the feeling of urgency came from, she only knew she had to get away. Heart pounding, ragged breaths, mind foggy and unable to think clearly, she just ran.

"Lilian!" Matthias yelled.

She didn't stop. Away from the road, deeper into the shadowy depths of the pine forest surrounding her home, she ran.

Her right palm began to burn, but she continued to run, not stopping to see what it was. Matthias caught up to her, wrapped his arms around her and jerked her to a stop. She screamed and fought him, struggling against his hold, but he refused to let her go and pulled her close to him. She had little leverage to struggle, to fight. Lilian fell into him and cried. She dragged deep, broken breaths as she sobbed. He held her close, rubbing her back.

After some time, when her sobs had died down and she could breathe without the ragged tearing of air into her lungs, Matthias leaned back a bit and tilted her chin up so he could look at her.

"Are you okay?" he asked.

She took mental stock of herself before she nodded. "I'm fine now." Lilian lifted her right hand and rubbed at her burning palm.

Matthias took hold of her hand and turned it over. There, in the center was a mark, a symbol of some sort with four circles, overlapping in a way to create a four petaled flower in the center.

"How did I get that?" she asked.

"You didn't know you had it?"

"I've never seen it before."

Matthias studied the symbol, tracing it with a finger. "It's familiar. I'm not sure why though."

He pulled her close to him again and held her as she leaned against him, taking comfort. Neither said anything for some time until they heard the faint sounds of sirens in the distance.

"We need to get back," he said.

* * * *

The next couple of hours went by in a hazy blur. If it hadn't been for Matthias, she doubted she'd have made it through the questioning.

She was very careful about not mentioning the CS agents. However, she did give Stephan's name to the police as a potential suspect.

After what seemed like forever, Lilian just couldn't handle it anymore.

"Look, I'm tired, I'm scared, and I'm done with the questions. You know where to find me if you want to interrogate me further, but right now, I want to find someplace safe, curl up into a ball and cry. So, if you gentlemen will excuse me…" She turned and walked away.

Matthias rattled off his number to the officers where they could reach him, jogged after her until he caught up, and walked her toward his motorcycle.

"Do you need a place to stay?" he asked.

"I'll get a room at the motel."

"I have more than enough room at my place."

Lilian glanced at him. "I don't think it's a good idea."

"You're afraid of me."

She spun around to face him, furious. Her hands clenched into fists and a surge of adrenaline hit her. "Why, yes, I am! Of course, I am! I don't know you and now you're constantly around me. Why shouldn't I be suspicious of you?"

"Because I'm not here to hurt you. I might be the only person you can trust."

"It's not that easy," she said, walking once more.

Her heart raced in her chest. She closed her eyes and took a ragged breath.

"I know, but you aren't willing to even try," he said.

"By staying at your place? Of course, it makes perfect sense. My house was broken into and vandalized. I have men after me, an ex-boyfriend stalker after me, and now I have a stranger who thinks it's perfectly fine for me to go to his house, despite everything going on, so he can prove he can be trusted."

He lifted a brow. "Don't forget we kissed."

Lilian felt her face heat. "You're a jerk."

"I can help you."

"I don't need your help. I'm going to have to leave town anyway."

"Running isn't the solution."

"Thank you. Why didn't I think of that?" she asked in a biting tone.

"You still owe me some answers," he pointed out.

"I'm still not going to your place."

Matthias sighed. "Fine. Have it your way. However, we can't walk all the way into town."

"It's not very far," she said. "I walk it every day."

"Get on the bike."

Lilian wanted to argue with him. The motorcycle, while sexy and conjured images of rebels and freedom, still felt unsafe to her. However, between his stony expression and her emotional exhaustion, she opted to give in without a protest and climbed onto the back of the bike.

"It'd serve you right if the cops ticketed you for no helmets," she sniped.

Matthias laughed as he started the bike. Before she could poke him for laughing, he took off. Lilian grabbed onto him and buried her face into his back, nixing any other witty retorts she might have come up with.

* * * *

After checking her into the motel, they walked over to the diner. She had refused to get back onto the motorcycle, and she refused to allow him into her motel room. He had grinned at her, and she glared back, but neither said anything.

Finding a booth in the back corner, they each ordered a meal and drank iced tea as they waited. An awkward silence enveloped them. Watching him fidget with the salt and pepper, she sighed.

"All right, already. We better talk," she said.

He nodded.

"Where to start?"

"You could start with why those men are after you."

Lilian nodded and went silent, trying to put her words into some semblance of order.

"Like I said before, they're members of a secret organization called *Custodes Secreti*. They're an off-branch of what used to be the Knights Templar. When the Knights were declared heretics and rounded up for extermination, escaping members took Templar treasures for safekeeping."

She took a shaky breath. She knew the next part would be a little strange to the uninitiated.

"A small group ended up with paranormal items. Books, scrolls, magical items, those sorts of things. When they discovered what they had, they began to study the possibility of magic and supernatural beings." Lilian took a sip of her iced tea, giving her time to think about her next words.

Matthias, much to her gratitude, stayed silent and just listened, letting her speak at her own pace. She watched his facial reactions to gauge how much to tell him. So far, he was open and receptive to her explanation.

Odd.

"When I was ten years old, my stepfather murdered my mother in front of me. He beat her to death. I killed him."

Matthias looked surprised. Before he could say anything, she hurried to continue.

"At least, I think I killed him. The coroner said he died of a massive heart attack brought on by his stress and his overexertion when he beat my mama to death. I never told them that as he was dying of the heart attack, things were flying around the room and pelting him. After he died, I ran and hid in the attic. It took two days for them to find me."

Matthias reached over the table and took her by the hand, holding it tight enough to be reassuring, but not confining. She studied his face expecting disgust or at the very least, disbelief, but there was neither.

"I spent a couple of weeks in a mental hospital. I had stopped talking, withdrawn into myself. When I did manage to come out again, I started developing odd abilities. I knew what the attendants were thinking. I could make things move with my mind and I could communicate with others without speaking.

"When word got out what I could do, they isolated me away from the other children. They started running tests. Soon, I was being sent to other hospitals for more tests. After a few months of this, everything changed. I had new handlers, and they took me to a different location. I found out the group was called the *Custodes Secreti*. They apparently paid a hefty amount for me." Lilian couldn't help the bitter note to her voice.

"Between the ages of eleven and eighteen, I became their guinea pig. They ran several examinations, both medical and psychological. I learned to control my abilities, use it at will, or when they wanted me to. I was given an education as well as physical training, combat training, and encouraging me to use my telekinesis to aid in combat."

Matthias frowned. "You were being trained to be an enhanced soldier."

Lilian gave a faint smile. "Yes. Project Knight."

"Project Knight?"

Lilian paused when their orders were delivered. She smiled at her co-worker, Peggy, who gave her a pointed look, flicked her eyes toward Matthias, and looked back at Lilian with a wink and a smile.

Needless to say, everyone would hear about it. She knew there would be an interrogation about the biker gang leader she "dated".

Matthias released her hand as the plates were set down. He smiled at Peggy, thanked her, and picked up the ketchup to add to his fries.

Once Peggy had refilled their drinks and left them alone, Lilian continued.

"I said the CS was a branch of the Knights Templar. Actually, I'm not entirely sure the Knights Templar is aware of them. They came from the original Templar, so while they shared their roots, I doubt they're affiliated with one another now. Anyway, Project Knight, spelled with a K, is a branch of the CS specifically for the training of agents and knights, specialized for the retrieval of either rogue agents or the acquisition of new members."

Matthias paused in eating a fry, a brow arched in question.

"Yes, acquisition, as in willing or not." She sipped her drink as she watched him eat.

The man was a veritable bottomless pit, or starving, from the way he scarfed down his burger and fries. Was he even chewing his food? She slid her plate over to him, not hungry. Matthias glanced at her in question, but she shook her head in amusement.

"Anyway, I escaped with a few others. I think I was eighteen or close to it. Once we were off the compound property, we scattered and I have no idea if any of them made it. I lived on the streets for a while before I decided I wanted a life, like those I had read about in books. I looked for work, but no one was willing to hire me. I had no identification, no proof of citizenship, no address, nothing."

Matthias slid the plate back toward her. "Eat."

Lilian shook her head and picked up a fry, using it to wave at him as she spoke. "You are not my father, so you can't tell me what to do." She nibbled on the fry, taking her time before speaking again. "And then I met Stephan."

Matthias studied her with the mention of Stephan's name.

"Tell me about him," he said.

Chapter 3

Lilian explained how she had been harassed by a few of the local street punks. Stephan stepped in to rescue her and after finding out she had no place to go, no job, nothing, he took her in. He helped her find a place to live, and a job as a waitress in a small bar. It wasn't much, but she earned the money which supported her. It had given her a sense of accomplishment.

Stephan also helped her access her inheritance and the money went into a bank account, which collected interest. It was a sizeable amount left to her from her mother's estate and Lilian had used some of her inheritance to have her name changed. Little good it did.

"He was someone I trusted," she said.

"But?"

"He was the first person I trusted, and he took something from me I'm not sure I know how to get back."

Lilian couldn't tell him. Not everything. Just saying his name brought back the ugly memories of the pain, and fear of being hurt again. Trust was something she couldn't easily give anyone, not after Stephan. Their relationship might not have been sexual, despite Stephan's desire otherwise, but he had still hurt her, physically and mentally.

"The message on the wall," Matthias said, "reminding you to remember the pain. Did he abuse you?"

Lilian refused to look at Matthias. She didn't want to see the pity in his eyes.

"I found a printed email from the CS giving him instructions about how to get me to a meeting place. Somehow, he had found out about me and was going to help them. They were going to pay him a reward. I ran away. Everything I had, which wasn't much anyway, I left behind, and just ran. I went to a lawyer, had my name changed, had my bank account transferred to my new name, and eventually came here, fell in love with the town and never left."

"Why didn't you use your abilities to stop him?"

"Because…I was afraid to." Lilian sighed and continued. "If I did use my abilities, anyone associated with the CS could locate me easily. If I had used my gift, I might have known what Stephan had planned. I could have escaped him, but the agents were another story."

"But he's tracked you down, as well as the CS agents."

Lilian looked at him and nodded.

Matthias gestured to her uneaten burger and gave her a pointed look. She shook her head and pushed it back to him. He was silent as he ate her burger.

In three bites, no less.

How did he *do* it? Lilian picked at a fry.

Matthias finished eating and wiped his mouth with a napkin. "You can't keep running. It's too late now anyway."

Lilian blinked. She'd told him she was a trained soldier, had special abilities, was wanted by a secret organization, and he comes up with *that*?

"I know," she replied in a near whisper, "I just don't know what else to do."

"Fight back. You have abilities and you must have some friends here."

It was said in a calm manner, without accusation or derision, but she flinched anyway.

"It's not so easy. No one here knows and I kept it that way on purpose."

Matthias sipped his iced tea, and then set the glass down. "You've lived here for how many years and haven't allowed yourself to trust anyone?" He picked up a fry and took a bite, only to make a face and pick up the saltshaker.

Lilian bristled. Tension shot up another notch and she hated that his words made her feel defensive. "I don't appreciate the attitude, Matthias. You have no idea what I've been through and you have no right to judge me."

He gave her a conciliatory smile. "I'm sorry. I didn't mean to sound judgmental. I just don't understand why, when everyone here seems to know and like you, you don't trust them." He sprinkled salt onto the fries.

"I'm not even sure I trust you," she said.

"Yes, you do. Otherwise, you wouldn't have told me anything."

Lilian glared at him. "I've been known to make grand mistakes of epic proportions."

He grinned. "I can help you."

"Make epic mistakes?"

He laughed and shook his head. "No, with your problems."

She leaned back in her seat and eyed him. "Why would you want to?"

He eased back with a smile and she narrowed her eyes at him as she studied his expression. He was up to something. She could see the glint of amusement and mischief behind his eyes.

"I don't need your help." Lilian started to slide out of the booth.

Matthias was in front of her before she realized it. When she stood up, they were almost nose-to-nose. Well, her nose to his chest since he had a few inches on her.

She tensed. *How did he move so fast?* She hadn't even seen it coming; his body language hadn't revealed anything to her.

She froze in place when he leaned down to whisper near her ear. "You need my help."

Lilian shoved him back a couple of steps. "What I need is for you to move away from me. You're crowding me and I don't like it."

It was *mostly* true. He was crowding her, but for some reason, rather than dislike it, warmth spread in her body.

He chuckled, just loud enough for her to hear, and moved back. Peggy took that moment to arrive.

"All done?" she asked.

Lilian nodded and gave Peggy a weak smile. "Yes, we're done. Just put it on my tab, all right?"

"I'll pay for dinner," Matthias said.

"No, you won't."

Peggy looked between the two of them. "Umm. Okay. No problem, Lil. I'll make note of it." She hurried away.

Matthias made a soft rumbling noise, beneath his breath.

Lilian lifted a brow, then turned and headed for the exit. She knew he followed, and closely, because she could feel his body heat emanating from him against her back, and her skin prickled with awareness of just how close he was. As she reached for the door, one of his hands shot out and held the handle before she did. She stopped so he could open the door, but when he didn't, she glanced back over her shoulder at him.

"We have more to discuss," he whispered.

"No, we don't. I'm tired. I want—no, I need a hot shower and then some sleep. I have a house to clean tomorrow."

"If the police release the scene and let you go back," he said.

"They better. It's my house. I need clothes."

Matthias opened the door, pushing it wide enough to let her pass. He used his body to herd her out of the diner and into the night air.

"It might take another day or two for them to finish investigating," he reminded her.

Lilian sighed. Of course, they would. It wasn't like on TV where they came in with high tech gadgets and finish so the victim could get on with her life. No, they had to make it hard for her.

"I'm sure they'll give you permission to grab some stuff," he said.

She shook her head. "No, it's okay. I'll pick something up. If worse comes to worse, I'll get a ride into Enumclaw or Bonney Lake."

"If you want, I can take you."

"Not on that motorcycle of yours."

He chuckled and walked with her back toward the motel. "I have a truck."

"Where do you live anyway?"

There was a hesitation on his part. Matthias looked unsure, as if he didn't know whether to tell her or not. Anger hit her, hot and hard.

"I caved and told you about me, but you can't even answer one simple question of mine in regards to your life?"

Matthias started to speak, but she shook her head. "Forget it." She stormed down the street, toward the motel. She just wanted to lock herself away and collapse.

"Lilian, wait."

By the time he caught up to her and had grabbed her by the arm, a loud, piercing whistle split the night. Matthias pulled her to him as he turned his head toward the sound. Lilian's temper flared and she started to pull from his grasp as she found herself manhandled yet again by Matthias.

He called out in another language. It sounded like Latin to her, but not exactly the same. His call was replied to in the same language. She tried to peer around Matthias to see, but he kept her against him with one arm, and adjusted his movements to hers.

Three of Matthias's friends approached. She recognized their faces from the diner and the rumble in the alley with the CS agents. They smiled at her, but when Matthias growled, they looked away from her and at him instead.

They continued to speak in their language, and it sounded rather serious. She tried to put some space between her and Matthias, but he wouldn't let her move very far from him.

Lilian had had enough. She stomped on one of his feet and with a shift of her body, kicked a foot out, catching his legs. She swept them from under him. Matthias lost his balance and went down to the pavement. Unfortunately, he didn't release her so when he went down, she did too, and landed on top of him with a soft *oomph*. The others burst into laughter as Matthias lifted a brow at her. She thumped him hard on the chest.

"You were *supposed* to let me go!"

He gave her a crooked smile. "I rather like how we ended up."

Lilian blinked and scrambled to her feet as the blood rushed to her face, heating it. The guys continued to laugh with relish.

"I'm so glad you found it hilarious." She glared at them.

"Can't remember the last time the Alph–*oomph*!" one said, interrupted when another elbowed him.

She looked between the two of them.

Matthias stood up and she turned to him. "What's going on?"

He sighed and gave her a shrug. "I suppose I should tell you."

Lilian started to back away. "So, you *are* hiding something. I knew it. I should have known better."

"Wait, let me explain."

The guys sobered and watched the two of them carefully.

She lifted her branded hand, as if to ward him off.

"No, stay back, Matthias. I mean it. I don't want to hurt you."

He held out his hands, palms upward. "Lilian."

One of his friends moved in a quick motion and she took her eyes off Matthias to look at him. It gave Matthias the chance to dart in and grab her. She reacted as she was trained, to strike at a vulnerable spot on his body, and in this case, a punch at his throat.

Matthias snarled and grabbed her wrist before the blow could connect. He turned his body and carrying on with the momentum, spun her around. With a jerk, she found herself back against his firm, muscular chest with her wrist in one of his hands and his free arm around her throat in a sleeper hold.

Lilian hissed in anger and gave a struggle, but he merely tightened his arm in warning. "Enough."

Since he had her arm already extended, he forced her to turn her hand over, palm up, to show the brand.

"Look at this," he told his friends. "I want this mark traced."

One of the men came forward and studied her palm. She tried to jerk her hand away, and turn her palm down, but Matthias wasn't having it. Tears welled up in her eyes.

"It looks familiar," the man said.

"I thought so too," Matthias replied. "What do you know of it?"

The man shook his head and she could see he was trying to remember, but nothing came to mind, it seemed.

"All right. Tiberius, you look into it. Lukas and Augustus, I want you two to look into *Custodes Secreti*. Check the archives. Also, check for offshoots of the Knights Templar. I want everything we can find on them."

The three men gave a nod, a salute of some form by the formality of the movement, and hurried off.

Lilian was still tense in his hold, but she didn't fight him. "Are you going to let me go now?"

"Are you going to remain calm and not attack me?"

"I warned you, but you pushed it!"

He leaned down and nuzzled her neck. "I want you to read my thoughts."

Oh, hell, no!

"I don't think so." Lilian shook her head. "No way."

"Scared?" he asked as he nibbled along the line of her neck.

She tried not to tilt her head for him, but it proved difficult.

"Hell, yes." She shivered. "Matthias, stop it."

"Read my mind," he urged.

"No." She tried to struggle out of his hold, but failed and fell still again.

"What do you know about shape shifters?" he asked.

Lilian frowned. "Like werewolves?"

"There are others besides werewolves, but yes."

She remained silent for a few long moments. Should she? He did invite her to. If she kept it light, only surface thoughts, it shouldn't cause any ripples.

"Let me see your face."

Matthias hesitated before he loosened his hold so she could turn and look up at him. He stared at her with a serious expression. She reached up with her free hand as he hadn't let go of her right wrist, and placed it against his cheek. She narrowed her eyes on him, and with a light touch, brushed his mind with hers.

On principle, Lilian was careful not to use her telepathy. She didn't want to know what others were thinking. Most of the time, though, it was just a pain to read minds. Most people didn't *think* in an organized manner. Their thoughts were jumbled and went in all different directions, at different speeds. If she wasn't careful, she'd suffer migraines. Not only from pushing her abilities, but also having to deal with the confusion.

However, as she touched Matthias's mind, she gasped in astonishment. His mind was nothing like a normal human's. He didn't even have the typical thought patterns for a human. He thought in pictures and emotions, and oh God, those pictures and emotions were a bit…*explicit,* with a capital E.

Lilian's nerves tingled and her heart stuttered, but pushed on. Beneath those rather hormonally driven emotions were images, memories in pictures. Sometimes scenes, but usually flashes of remembered things like a wolf pack, moonlit nights, the forest, and hunting prey.

She jerked her hand from his face, wide eyed as she stared at him. Was she feeling confusion or awe?

He still held her, but she could see the expectant look on his face, in his eyes.

"You're…a werewolf?" she asked.

He nodded. "Yes."

"The Alpha. He was trying to say Alpha when he was interrupted."

Matthias gave a weak grin. "Yeah."

"And you can change into a wolf?"

Okay, that's a stupid question.

"Yes," he said. "Want me to prove it?"

"No! I mean, no, I believe you."

"Do you want to talk about it?" He watched her carefully.

"Not particularly. The whole thing's a bit daunting."

"It's no different than you and your abilities."

"I don't turn into a wolf. Can you do anything else?"

"I have three forms. Human, wolf, and a hybrid form, or war form. It's the typical wolf man form you see in the movies, except, we're a little bigger."

"How big?"

"About eight feet or so."

Okay, that's one hell of a big wolf.

Lilian tried to pull her wrist from his grip. "Let go, please."

Matthias released her in a slow, languid manner. She took a deep breath and slowly exhaled.

"You okay?" he asked.

"Not so much, no." She shook her head and started for her motel room. "I think I need to be alone. Too much going on."

He didn't follow. "Let me give you my number in case you need anything."

Lilian waved him off. "Good night, Matthias."

* * * *

She lay in a field of grass. The sun warm on her skin and bright, even with her eyes closed. She could smell the sun-kissed, earthy scent of grass and soil.

A howl pierced the peace and she opened her eyes. In the distance, a pack of wolves took their leisure near the forest edge and she stood up to watch.

They were playing with one another, mock battles and games of tag and tug of war with a stick of some sort.

A black wolf paused and looked over at her, its golden eyes bright, and its ears perked toward her. The others paused and looked over as well.

The dream changed. Daylight turned to night. Shadows stretched over the landscape, but the wolves were there. She could see their shadowy forms as they melted amongst the trees. Her right palm began to hurt and she brought her hand up to look. The brand glowed a dull pink and burned with the scorching heat of molten metal. She rubbed at it, but the pain didn't subside.

A howl broke her worry and she looked toward the noise. The black wolf watched her.

"Come play," it invited her. "Come run and play!"

Lilian smiled and broke into a run toward the majestic creature. Before she had gotten halfway, her body changed. At first, it was painful as her muscles stretched, her bones elongated, but the pain became an afterthought compared to the sheer freedom of shifting to another form. By the time she reached the black wolf, the change completed and instead of her human form, she stood there as a white wolf.

The black wolf bounded around her and they both ran, moving through the woods as though they were a part of the shadows, the forests, and the earth.

Senses keen, she smelled not only the forest, but also the earth they tore up from their claws, and various other beings whose scents floated in the air currents. She could hear his heartbeat, the way he drew in air as he ran beside her and the rhythm of their paws as they hit the ground. She could see the world through the wolf's eyes, pupils dilated to catch every nuance of the moon's light as they ran through the woods.

Freedom!

A large, white creature stepped into their path and caused them both to come to a sudden stop, scrambling for purchase on the soft ground. As she looked, she saw the white stag. The black wolf snarled and put himself between her and the majestic creature, his hackles raised.

"You are not this," the white stag said.

At least, she thought *it spoke.*

The black wolf snarled again and gave a mock lunge toward the stag, in warning. The stag lowered its head and waved it, brandishing its huge antlers in response.

"Wait!" Lilian called out, surprised when she found herself in human form again.

"Come with me," the stag told her.

She shook her head. "Who are you?"

The stag lifted its head and looked beyond her.

A sudden, loud knocking woke Lilian up from her sleep. She jerked upright, her heart pounding. She slid out of the bed and pulled on her clothes. When another knock echoed through the motel room, she made her way to the door, careful to make no noise. Staying low, she made sure she didn't block the peephole.

The doorknob jiggled and Lilian looked around for another way out.

Or in.

* * * *

Matthias wandered the streets of Hawk's Point, too antsy to return to the pack and he didn't want to leave Lilian alone, not after everything that'd happened.

She had a right to be angry with me.

He hadn't intended to tell her about himself, even after she revealed her own story. He also realized there must have been more to the story about Stephan, something she held back.

Had Stephan abused her sexually as well as mentally and physically? Why wouldn't she tell him what happened? Of course, he was still a stranger to her, in her eyes, and he couldn't blame her for not revealing everything.

He debated heading back to the motel but knew she wouldn't have been thrilled about his presence after she'd sent him away.

There was something about her that made him want to protect her. He didn't exactly know what, but it had started the moment he laid eyes on her at the diner, when she had spilled the cold water and iced tea over him. Her look of horror had been priceless and made him want to kiss her.

When they had kissed, he wanted to wrap his arms around her and drag her to the ground. The wolf inside him fought his control, demanded he take Lilian as his own, mate with her, claim her as his, but the man refused, tightened the leash and chained the beast.

Even now, the wolf inside him demanded he return to her, carry her kicking and screaming to his den and bind them together. Never before had his wolf-self made its desires known like this. Before, it was either because of hunger, or self-preservation, but not for mating. Still, Matthias wasn't a rash man, and he wouldn't allow the beast inside to rule him. He may change into an animal, but he wasn't, nor ever would be, an animal.

Yet, he found himself making his way back to the motel.

As he rounded the corner, he came to a stop. Outside Lilian's door stood two men he didn't recognize. Dressed in suits, one of them fiddled with the doorknob. Matthias growled low in his throat and pushed forward with every intention of knocking their heads together.

As he approached, one of the men turned, lifted a pistol and fired at him. A high-pitched, *phewt* sound was followed by the whine of a bullet as it whizzed by. Matthias dodged back behind the corner.

Enough!

Matthias took a deep breath and charged around the corner, toward the men. He went for the one with the pistol who kept firing at him. When the burn of a bullet pierced his right shoulder, Matthias jerked and gave a loud roar. His muscles stretched, bones snapped and popped as his body shifted forms. By the time he had shifted to his war form, he reached the pistol-wielding agent, and Matthias swiped at the agent with a huge paw tipped with razor sharp claws. Flesh tore and blood spilt as the man screamed and dropped the pistol. The second agent spun around to face the battle. Lilian's door flew open and the agent went flying into the parking lot.

Matthias spun toward the third form before he realized it was Lilian, and gave a soft huffing sound. The second agent got to his feet and as he drew his weapon, she made a swiping motion with a sweep of her arm. The man's pistol went flying out of his hand and toward her.

Matthias swung a paw at the pistol and knocked it out of the way so it clattered to the pavement. He looked at her and growled. She narrowed her eyes at him, her silver gaze slashing at him in anger, but she turned her attention to the agents, who were trying to escape. One clutched his arm to his chest and ran in a not-so-steady manner. The other just ran, leaving his partner to make his own way.

Matthias started to give chase, but she stopped him.

"No, leave them be!"

He paused and looked back at her, ears perked.

She stared at him, a surprised look on her face, as if she'd just realized what he was, what he looked like. When he took a step toward her, she jerked back, so he stopped.

"Matthias, I hope?"

He nodded his huge head and took another step toward her. Again, she jerked back and he stopped.

"This is very weird," she said. "Can you, umm, change back, please?"

Matthias huffed and closed his eyes as he concentrated. His form changed and shifted, and he groaned as his wound burned. When he resumed his human form, he staggered. Right away, she wrapped an arm around his waist.

"You're hurt." He could hear the worry in her voice.

"It'll heal soon enough," he replied, as he tried to shrug off the pain.

"Come inside." She looked around. "I only hope no one saw anything."

"They won't remember it."

Matthias let her help him inside her motel room. He could have easily walked inside without her help, but with her worrying he was going to milk it for all its worth.

"What do you mean no one will remember?" She helped him to sit on the edge of the bed.

"If we're seen in our war form, unless they're special in some way, not human, they won't remember."

"How convenient." She hurried to the bathroom. "Don't move. I'll get a towel."

Matthias waited until Lilian left the room to smile. He hadn't wanted her to think he was amused by her concern. Not so much the concern, but it had been her bossiness which tickled him. Her bossiness and lack of fear of him, despite knowing he turned into an eight-foot monster with teeth the size of her fingers. She also seemed to have forgotten about her aversion to the sight of blood. Because of her worry for him? He grinned.

He removed his ruined shirt, and flexed the muscles of his chest. Matthias winced as the muscles pulled at the wound, but he knew it was already knitting. Within minutes, his body would eject the bullet on its own. Lupine's wounds healed from the inside out, to push out any foreign objects like bullets.

Lilian made a *tsking* sound as she came out and saw him. "Stop messing with it." She used a warm, wet washcloth to clean around the wound.

"Lilian, I'm fine. It'll heal. There won't even be a scar in a couple of days." He watched her as she fussed over him.

She looked at him and he could see the worry in her eyes.

"What if it gets infected?"

"Unless the wound was made with silver, it won't get infected. We're hard to kill." Matthias smiled at her, but sobered to ask, "Are you all right? Did they hurt you?"

Lilian shook her head and looked away to finish cleaning the blood from the wound.

"I'm fine. They didn't get the chance to do anything."

"You can't stay here." Matthias reached into the pocket of his jeans and pulled out his cellphone. "They know where to find you and it's hardly safe here."

"I won't be safe anywhere. They'll just track me down and try again."

He dialed his phone and lifted it to his ear, giving her a frown. "I know of one place."

She looked at him and shook her head. "Oh, no. I won't go to your place."

Lilian stood, but he grabbed her wrist. He spoke into his phone, in Roman Latin, the language of his people, and soon hung up.

"What did you just do?" she asked.

"Called for a ride. I know how much you dislike my motorcycle, so I called for the truck."

"I'm not going home with you, Matthias."

"Yes, you are."

Matthias watched as her cheeks went pink with her growing anger and her silver eyes darkened to a stormy gray. Did she know how desirable she was when she looked like that?

"Like hell I am!" She tugged her wrist free from his grasp.

"What are you afraid of?" he asked. "If you're worried I'll try something, well, I probably will, but we won't be alone. I have my pack there. If it'll make you feel any better, you can have a chaperone."

Lilian narrowed her eyes at him.

"Honest. I have family. My mother."

Her eyes flared open wide. "And here I thought you crawled out from under a rock."

"Funny."

She smiled. "I thought so and the answer's still no."

His acute sense of hearing picked up the sound of the truck engine as it pulled up. Matthias stood up, grabbed his shirt, and walked to the door. When he opened it, he turned back to look at her. She was standing where he left her, frowning.

"Come here," he said. He kept his voice soft and gentle.

"Why?" She stared at him with suspicion.

"You have to lock the door behind me," he said as he quirked a brow at her.

Lilian scowled as she walked over to him and the door.

"Do I get a kiss good night?" he asked.

She pointed outside. "Go. Goodbye and good riddance."

Matthias smiled. Before she could react, he had a hold of her arm, jerked her toward him as he bent down, and tossed her over his shoulder. Lilian shrieked with anger as she beat on his back with her fists and kicked her legs out. He gave her a swat on her upturned butt, sharp enough to sting, and carried her out to the waiting truck.

Tiberius climbed out of the truck with a grin on his face. All of a sudden, he went flying away from the truck. He snarled in anger and surprise as he hit the pavement hard.

"That wasn't very nice," Matthias said to her, his voice calm with a bit of male amusement. "You could have done this the easy way and just came with me. Oh, no. You had to be stubborn and willful. Now I'm kidnapping you."

He opened the passenger door as Tiberius was getting to his feet. Although he was glad she hadn't tried to use her abilities on him, he was sure it was because she might have hurt herself in the process. Tiberius had made a better target.

"What the hell?" Tiberius demanded.

"Explanations later," Matthias replied. "Let's just get back home."

Lilian renewed her struggling as Matthias tried to put her into the truck.

"Let me go! Put me down, Matthias! I'm going to report you to the police! Kidnapping!" she screamed.

Tiberius shook his head. "You are your father's son, my brother."

Matthias chuckled. "It's the Roman DNA."

Matthias waited until Tiberius got back into the truck, behind the steering wheel and tossed Lilian in beside him. He quickly followed, sliding in so she was trapped between the two men.

As the truck drove away, she remained silent, fuming. Again, he was grateful she didn't try to use her abilities.

* * * *

He watched as the wounded male carried Lilian out of the motel room. He was very careful to remain in the shadows, to keep his thoughts centered and normal, in case she tried to scan the area. She hadn't wanted to go, he saw, but had little choice.

Of course, this meant getting to her would be much more difficult with the shape-shifter involved. He'd have to wait and see how this ended up and how he could get close to her.

He had little time, as did she.

Chapter 4

"The master is not going to like hearing about this."

The two failed agents stood in defeat as they listened to the Prior. They both knew it had been sheer luck they had an excuse, as flimsy as it was. As agents, they weren't expected to defeat powerful supernatural beings. With the CS aware of the Lupines being present and involved, Knights would be sent to retrieve or eliminate the target.

"We're sorry, Prior, but we didn't know the Lupines would interfere. He was shot, but as you can see…" the one said as he indicated his doctored wounds.

"And the target did use her abilities," the other said.

The Prior nodded slowly as he pondered the implication. "She was not using her abilities before," he said.

"She's coming of age," said a low, gravelly male voice.

The men turned to an open door and bowed as the tall figure stepped into the room from the shadowed doorway. They had missed his presence, camouflaged by his black attire. His blue eyes, bitter cold, were steady on the agents and they fought to stand still beneath his piercing gaze.

"Master?" the Prior asked.

"Never mind. It matters little. What does matter is that she's brought back to the fold before the next full moon," the pale man said as he looked at the two agents. "The Lupines are involved?"

"Yes, Master. He intervened when we tried to take her from her motel room. That was when she used her abilities to attack us."

The pale man narrowed his eyes as he thought it over. "Before, she was content to bury them, but now she feels as though she needs to protect herself. Given that and the impending Chrysalis, her abilities are growing stronger."

"The Chrysalis, Master?"

"She is not human," the pale man replied. "Send two Knights for her this time. Kill the Lupines if need be, but she is to remain unharmed."

"Yes, Master," the Prior replied.

* * * *

Lilian sat up when they reached the compound. They were connected to a high privacy wall, at least eight feet tall, and made of stucco. Two rather capable looking men guarded the entrance, dressed in black jeans and black shirts. The moment the truck pulled in, one went to get the gate, and the other came over to the driver's side. He peered in, and seeing Matthias, he saluted and signaled to the other. Tiberius pulled the truck onto the grounds.

Her jaw dropped in astonishment. Stunned by what she saw, when Matthias exited and pulled her out after him, she didn't even think to struggle. She couldn't take her eyes off the Roman style palace and villa.

Lilian glanced at Matthias, who smiled at her.

"What the hell is this place?" she whispered.

"My home. You are welcome here. What is mine is yours."

She studied his face before she turned to stare at the columned entryway of the villa. She could see the large fountain in the center of the courtyard and splashes of color from the blooming trees and flowers livened up the otherwise formal appearance.

The entryway was lined with eight pairs of marble columns, and an archway connected each of the corresponding pairs. On either side of the entryway were doors, four on each side.

Matthias led her through the palace, giving her a brief tour, pointing out the key rooms she should know the locations of, such as the dining hall, the meeting room, the kitchen, and the servants' quarters. He also showed her where to find the bathroom.

Not just any bathroom, however.

Matthias opened a door and led her in and the hot, humid air took her breath away. In front of her sat a sunken, tiled bathtub which could very well fit ten people. Already filled with steaming water, it didn't look deep enough to swim in, only about waist high if she stood up in it.

"The water is heated naturally through piped hot springs. It's filtered on a constant basis. The toilets are there." He pointed to the right of the sunken tub, where there were three toilet stalls located. "If you need towels or other supplies, there is the storage closet." Matthias gestured to a large room at the end of the stalls.

He led her out into the hall again and closed the doors. Leading her down the hall, he stopped outside a room. "This is my suite."

Turning to the left, he pointed out the next two sets of doors on the right. "Guest rooms. This will be your room."

He walked her to the guest room nearest his suite and opened the doors. Lilian gasped. *It's beautiful!*

She stepped in and stared at the huge canopied bed, surrounded by gauzy, netted curtains. The room was white with blue accents. The closet was larger than her bedroom at her own house. A sitting area near the window completed the suite. The room was calm and soothing. She turned and smiled at Matthias.

"I love it."

He smiled at her and nodded.

"The room further down the hall is green and white, the room beyond is Tiberius's suite. There's a guest room after his suite, then the library, which connects to the meeting hall. Everyone else has a suite which lines the outside of the villa."

Lilian didn't know what to say. It hit her that Matthias was important and wealthy. She trembled, overwhelmed.

"Who are you, Matthias? What is all of this?" She turned to look at him. He stepped toward her, but she took a step back, keeping distance between them. Matthias frowned, but did not pursue her.

"Perhaps we could sit? I'll explain." He gestured to the sitting area.

Lilian nodded. She made her way over to one of the chairs and sat. She trembled and exhaustion had set in, but she needed to hear what he had to say.

Matthias waited until she sat before he walked over and took a seat. "I guess it's my turn to talk."

"Talk…just talk?"

He looked at her with a rather devious, yet charming smile. "Unless you had another suggestion?"

"Get your mind out of the gutter."

He grinned. "It wasn't in the gutter. It was in the bed."

Lilian couldn't help but laugh. He was being rather cute and oh-so-charming.

"Well, get it out of there too. We're just talking."

Matthias nodded and leaned back in the chair, looking comfortable and relaxed. His golden eyes steady on her, to the point she had to look away from him.

He was silent for so long, she glanced back, finding him staring at her, his golden eyes blazing.

"What do you know about the Lupine?" he asked her, his tone calm.

She shook her head. "Not much."

"I'm going to tell you a story. I want you to listen."

Lilian gave a careful nod.

"Do you know the history of how Rome was built?"

She nodded again. She had learned this myth while in training with *Custodes Secreti.*

"The twins who were suckled by a wolf. Romulus built Rome, becoming the first king after he killed his brother."

Matthias smiled. "That part is nothing but a story to conceal the truth. The truth is Lupa suckled the abandoned Romulus and Remus. It is said her milk gave the boys the ability to shift into wolves and they grew up among the wolf pack. They were found by a shepherd and taken in, raised as humans. They retained the ability to shift."

He leaned back in his chair.

"Romulus and Remus were competitive, always trying to outdo each other. Remus, more hot-tempered than his brother, was jealous of Romulus, who was more thoughtful, even tempered.

"Eventually, they married, sired children, and built Rome. Legend has it Romulus slew Remus as Rome was being built, but Remus merely took his family and left after a bitter quarrel between the brothers. This split the Lupa, or Lupine, line into two factions. The Romulus clan and the Remus clan."

Matthias smiled proudly.

"Romulus went on to build Rome and sired more of his kind among the Sabines. This line has always been known as natural leaders, judges, politicians, generals, as well as warriors.

"Remus took his family and people away and settled in Germania, co-mingling with the early Norse tribes. Personally, I think it explains why the Vikings were so hot-tempered and yet excellent warriors."

Lilian stared at Matthias. She wasn't altogether sure whether to believe him and his story. Werewolves in ancient Rome, werewolves having started ancient Rome, was a bit hard to accept. Of course, when one considered what she could do, she supposed it wasn't so farfetched.

He smiled at her. She was rather thankful for the silence. How was she supposed to process what he told her? How was she supposed to react to what she just learned? Her thoughts were going in circles and she couldn't still any of them in order to think.

Lilian lifted a hand to brush back a lock of errant hair from her face and saw how her hand shook.

Nope, not going to happen, no thinking tonight.

Lilian stood. "Well, good night."

Matthias looked surprised, but stood up as well. "Lilian?"

She lifted a hand up to ward off any more words. "It's late. Actually, it's very early and I'm exhausted. You should get your wound looked at before too long, just in case. I need sleep and I need to be alone."

Lilian kept eye contact with him and he must have seen she was telling the truth. Matthias nodded.

"If you need anything, I'm next door. Don't hesitate to knock," he said.

She gave him a faint smirk. "Don't hold your breath."

"I didn't mean that." He grinned. "But since you mentioned it, that too."

"Out!"

Matthias laughed before leaving.

* * * *

Lilian was running in the forest again. Her heart raced, while her breathing came in ragged gasps. The baying of the hounds could be heard in the distance, but they were getting closer. She had to keep moving before they caught her.

She jumped over a fallen log and a distant part of her marveled at how agile and graceful her movements were . It felt as though she'd been running for hours and yet her legs were strong and her body, exhausted, continued on.

Without warning, the ground gave way beneath her and with a cry, she fell into a large hole. It was deep enough and large enough there was no climbing out. She remained where she fell, trying to catch her breath as a desperate look around yielded nothing.

"Finally," a male voice said, deep and gravelly in tone.

Lilian gasped in surprise and looked in the direction of the voice. She couldn't see what he looked like hidden in the shadow, but could tell he was tall.

"You've given us a merry hunt, little one, but the hunt is over."

"Who are you?" She stood up and faced him.

"The huntsman," he replied, giving her a mocking bow. "And you are the prey."

"I'm no one's prey. You're just a nightmare."

He laughed and the sound grated on her nerves, like rocks being rubbed together. "Oh, child. How innocent you are."

Lilian allowed the anger to wash over her and lashed out, using telekinesis to throw him back. However, she was surprised when he didn't move other than to wave a hand. A net was thrown over her and the weight of it dragged her down to the floor.

The burning began. It was a dull ache at first, and grew until it was as though flames were consuming her. She screamed and struggled, but as the moments ticked by, her strength waned, both from the pain and what caused it. Her voice grew hoarse from screaming.

"Yes," the shadowed man hissed. "You are definitely the one."

Her vision darkened, but not before she saw the white stag as it ran toward the huntsman. The huntsman yelled something in a strange language, and while it might have been almost lyrical to her, with his voice, it sounded evil and malevolent.

Lilian lay there, unable to move, her eyes closed, and she could feel her body shaking. From a great distance, she heard her name being called. The net was pulled from her, and she opened her eyes to gaze up at the white stag.

"Wake up, daughter!"

Lilian jolted awake and the movement caused a whimper. The bright light in her room assaulted her eyes.

Movement in her peripheral vision made her jump and turn to confront the threat. Even seeing Matthias wasn't enough to calm her.

"Shh." His tone was soft and soothing. "You were screaming in your sleep. I couldn't wake you."

She nodded as his voice washed over her. Still, she trembled from the aftermath of her nightmare.

He reached out and picked up one of her hands. He frowned and touched her cheek. "You're freezing."

Lilian turned her face into his palm. The warmth of his hand was a blessing and she wanted more, needed more. "Please, Matthias. I need…"

What exactly did she need? Heat? Warmth? Comfort?

Matthias didn't question her. He crawled into bed and drew her into his arms, against him. She could feel his body tense from the cold, but he pulled her closer to him.

"Do you want to talk about it?" he asked in a gentle tone.

Lilian couldn't reply at first, but as his body heat warmed her and the trembling eased, she sighed. "I was being hunted. He caught me and threw a net over me. I started to burn."

He turned her in his arms so that her head was pillowed on his arm as he lay on his side, looking down on her. He brushed some damp hair from her brow.

"Is this the first time you had this nightmare?"

"No. Well, yes. The first time he caught me. Usually, I'm escaping, running through the woods and a white stag helps me."

She noticed him go still.

"Tell me about them," he said.

"What's wrong?" she asked.

"Reoccurring dreams have a meaning," he explained. "Maybe something in your dreams is trying to warn you."

Something or someone?

Matthias played with her hair as she thought it over. Her muscles relaxed and the cold faded.

"They're pretty much always the same. I'm running through the woods, chased by hounds and a huntsman. Just before I'm caught or lose strength, a white stag appears and helps me."

"How does the white stag help?"

"He either encourages me, runs with me, or puts himself between me and the huntsman. Tonight, he chased off the huntsman and removed the net covering me."

"Tell me about tonight's nightmare."

Lilian squirmed a bit, trying to get closer. She stared up at him, into his golden eyes, which blazed as bright and hot as the sun.

"I was running, but fell into a trap. One of those holes in the ground type of traps."

Matthias nodded.

"The huntsman was there. I tried to use telekinesis on him, but it didn't work. Then a net dropped on me. It started to burn."

"Can you tell me anything about the net?"

She closed her eyes and concentrated on remembering. She had been so caught up in the pain and fear, she hadn't paid much attention to what had caused it.

"Not really, no."

Her eyes snapped open when he nuzzled at her neck and shoulder.

"Matthias, please."

His lips turned upward into a smile against her skin. "What?" She heard the amusement and the playful innocence in his tone.

"This isn't the time or place."

"I'd say this is the perfect time and place," he said. "I'm in bed with you and it's nearly dawn."

She groaned. "You're incorrigible."

"It's the wolf in me." Matthias nipped along her neck in gentle, little bites.

Lilian shivered in reaction to the sensations skittering up and down her nerve endings. He lifted his head and touched her lips with his.

She knew she shouldn't be doing this, shouldn't encourage him, but to be honest, she wanted him to kiss her. She wanted the sensations he caused when their lips met, wanted to feel wanted. It was an emotion Lilian rarely experienced as a child; the *Custodes Secreti* was not there to coddle the children in their program. Sometimes, if she was lucky, one or two members of the administration would show some form of affection, but it only made her realize what she was missing. Stephan had given what she craved, at first, and she had blossomed under his affection, but he changed and hurt her. When she ran away, she had buried the need deep down.

Matthias's kiss deepened, his tongue traced the seam of her lips until he had coaxed her to open them for him. His tongue delved into her mouth and caressed hers, invited her to respond. With a shy hesitation, she did and as their tongues slid against one another, wrestled with one another, desire flamed hot inside of her. She moaned.

He pulled back to murmur against her lips, "*Lilia mea*," and tasted his way over the curve of her jaw, down to her throat.

My Lily. She loved the translation of his words.

She tilted her head back as his lips brushed against the sensitive skin of her throat. Each tickling sensation made her heart beat faster and she squirmed beneath him, restless.

His hand crept along her arm in a slow stroke, brushed against the curve of her breast and she jumped. His fingers caressed, teased the puckered nipple underneath her shirt and she gasped, her back arched, as she invited him to further his explorations. His lips returned to hers and devoured them as he slid his hand under her shirt to touch her breast in direct contact. His body shifted against hers, a leg moved to intertwine with hers. She reached up and wrapped her arms around his neck, holding him close as her body went into meltdown.

The muscles of her stomach twitched and jumped as his hand roamed over her skin until it reached the waistband of her panties. Lilian remembered she had removed her jeans and bra before going to sleep, now realizing how easy she'd made this for him. She tensed, waited to see what he would do. Little by little, he teased the skin along the waistband, and slid upward, dragging her t-shirt with, until he was touching, massaging her breast once more. The cool air in the room whispered across her heated skin and she broke the kiss to gasp and sigh. He kissed her chin, made his way down her throat, skipped over her bunched up t-shirt, and with languorous slowness, brushed his lips over a bared breast, before doing the same to the other.

Lilian squirmed in restless anticipation. "Please, Matthias," she pleaded. "Please."

She smiled just before he took her nipple into his mouth. She gave a soft cry as the heat of his mouth engulfed the sensitive nubbin, and her back arched up from the bed.

All of a sudden, there was a beating on the door, shattering the sensual haze surrounding her. She went still beneath Matthias, who also tensed at the sound, but did not stop what he was doing.

The door burst open and Tiberius stepped in. "Forgive the intrusion, but…"

Matthias released her nipple, snarled something in their shared language.

Tiberius stiffened, jerked upright, and slammed his right hand, fisted, over his heart. "My Lord!"

"Get out!" Matthias snapped.

Even she flinched at his tone.

Tiberius nodded his head once and made his way to the door, but before closing it, he said, "Just wanted to let you know her house is on fire."

The door slammed, leaving a very stunned Lilian and Matthias.

* * * *

An hour later, they stood on the outskirts of her property watching as the firefighters finished putting out the hot coals of what used to be her house.

Lilian took in the scene with a sense of horrific bewilderment. Matthias stood near her, kept an arm around her waist to keep her close to him. She knew it was to comfort and protect her as she had touched his thoughts. She was glad of his presence. If he hadn't been there with her, she probably would have started crying.

Another two hours passed before they were approached by the fire marshal and the police officers on scene. Matthias shifted his weight, as if preparing to fight, but she laid a hand on his arm to stall him.

"I'm sorry, Lilian," one of the officers began. "It's completely gone. They couldn't save any of it."

She gave a brief, weak smile to her friend. "Thanks, Ben."

Ben glanced between her and Matthias. "I know this is going to be hard for you, but…" He glanced back at her. "Where were you tonight?"

Lilian tensed. "If you think I set fire to my own house, you're insane. I loved this house. It was my home."

He flinched. "It's my job to ask. You know that."

Matthias caressed her back. "Lilian."

She took a slow breath in, and, just as slow, exhaled.

"Lilian was with me and my family," Matthias replied for her. "After the vandalism, I took her into town to get a motel room, but when a couple of men started harassing her, I decided to take her to my place for safety."

Ben and Officer Turner studied him. She frowned.

"Matthias has been nothing but helpful. Plus, he was with me tonight, so he couldn't have done it."

"All night?"

Lilian felt the blush creeping over her face. "Yes, all night."

"Not all night, *Lilia mea*," Matthias said. "You were alone, sleeping for about two hours before your nightmare woke us up."

Ben and Officer Turner glanced at one another before they looked back at Matthias. Officer Turner stepped toward him. "If you'd come this way, sir? I'd like to ask you a few questions in private."

Lilian started to protest, but Matthias leaned in and kissed her, shutting her up. Afterward, he smiled down at her.

"It's okay, sweetheart. It's their job."

He walked with Turner some distance away. She wrapped her arms around herself, feeling the chill of the early morning air without his presence.

"How did you meet, err…what's his name?" Ben asked.

"He and his family helped me when I was harassed by a couple of men." She looked to the charred ruins of what used to be her home. "He was with me when we found the vandalism inside my house."

"How long have you known him?"

"Not that long. He didn't do this, Ben. I'd know if he did."

"He could have had a family member, or a friend do it. He wouldn't have had to do it himself."

Lilian shook her head. "No. I'd know."

Ben sighed and looked at the fire marshal.

The marshal shrugged and said, "It was obviously arson. They didn't even bother taking the cans with them when they left. We'll have the cans dusted for prints, of course."

Lilian knew there was a 'but' in there. They'd have a better chance at winning the lottery than them finding any fingerprints on the cans. Still, she nodded and gave him a weak smile.

"Better call your homeowner's insurance and have this reported. They can get the ball rolling for you on getting some things replaced."

"Thank you." She glanced over to Matthias and Turner.

Matthias looked away from Turner, and winked at her. She blushed.

"I hope you know what you're doing," Ben said.

Lilian gave Ben a frosty look. "You might want to investigate a man by the name of Stephan Cavanaugh. I really think he's behind all of this."

"We're already investigating his whereabouts, but no one's reported seeing anyone by that description in town."

"Investigate harder."

Ben stiffened. "I understand you're upset, but there's no need to take it out on me."

Matthias and Turner returned. Matthias wrapped an arm around her, and she leaned against him as she took a shaky breath.

"If you think of anything else, you know how to reach me," Ben said.

"Thank you." She nodded.

Ben, Turner, and the fire marshal turned and walked away.

"I'm sure we can find you some clothes to wear," Matthias said.

"The least of my concerns," she replied, and stood back from him. "I'm tired of this. I'm tired of running and hiding. It has to end."

He studied her face. "I agree."

"Good, because either way, I'm doing it."

"Doing what?"

Lilian gave a faint smile. "We have plans to make."

Chapter 5

"You're not going to find anything in the public library, Matthias."

They'd gone back into town after leaving the charred ruins of her home. She needed to check out of the motel and go shopping for necessities. Matthias had taken her into Bonney Lake, a small town about an hour from Hawk's Point, and to a local one-stop shopping mart to purchase what she needed, change of clothes and toiletries, as well as to place a few calls to her insurance company.

Matthias had suggested stopping by the local library to do some research, but she doubted it would do any good.

"The library here is bigger than the one in Hawk's Point," he said. "They might have better references to look into."

"You don't understand," she argued. "They're a *secret* organization. Not even the government knows what they are. If they have a public face, it'd be set up like the Masons or the Rosicrucians. The whole 'we're training a private army' part isn't public knowledge."

He grinned at her and she sighed. "You're impossible, you know that?"

"I know."

Fifteen minutes later, they pulled up at the Bonney Lake Library. She scanned the general area, and sent out psychic feelers to read the surface thoughts of nearby people. Other than Matthias's overprotective thoughts, she picked up nothing of interest.

The two of them made their way into the library and after getting a computer, they started their research. Matthias wasn't experienced in using a computer and didn't want to learn, so Lilian ended up doing the typing. He scribbled any notes they found interesting.

Two hours later, her stomach growled.

"Break time," she announced as she stood up. "I'm starving, and this is getting us nowhere."

"Maybe we should go into Seattle," he said as he gathered up their notes.

She looked up at him, eyes widened with horror. "Oh, hell no. No way, no how, over my dead body, over your dead body, not even if it's the end of the world and it held the only portal to safety. No."

Matthias grinned.

"Don't even give me that 'I'm too cute so I'll just grin and get what I want' grin. I will not now, nor will I ever, go back there."

Lilian started to turn, but stopped as a thought came to her. Before she could think twice, before he could try to distract her with one of his disarming smiles, she thrust her mind into his.

Matthias sucked in a harsh breath and fell back against the chair at the sudden onslaught. She felt wretched for the pain she might have caused, but this had to be done. She flowed through his mind like a shark after prey, catching mental eddies and currents of thoughts as she sought information from him. She found nothing to suspect him of duplicity. Well, other than being a werewolf and withholding *that* information until forced out, but it was nothing compared to the possibility he might have been undercover for the *Custodes Secreti*, in an elaborate plan to bring her back.

Lilian withdrew and sat back down, expelling a slow breath.

He growled low in his throat, and his golden eyes burned as he stared at her.

"I'm sorry," she whispered. "I had to make sure you weren't trying to trap me."

He glared at her. "What?"

"Stephan had planned to return me to them, take me to a meeting place so he could hand me off to them. I had to make sure your suggestion wasn't a ruse to take me back."

She could tell he was still angry from his closed off expression, but she could see he understood her reasoning.

"I really am sorry, but if I waited to ask, you could have hidden the thoughts, buried the memory. I needed to know."

He nodded, and took a deep breath before releasing a drawn out sigh. "I understand. I just didn't appreciate it."

"Matthias, I wouldn't have done it otherwise unless I felt it absolutely necessary. I really don't like to use my abilities unless I have to."

He nodded again and stood up, motioning for her to get up. "Let's get you something to eat before you decide to attack little old ladies and boy scouts." His tone held amusement, but his features clearly told her he was irked.

She sighed, stood up, and proceeded out to the parking lot. As they turned a corner, incoming library patrons took up the walkway and Lilian moved to one side to give them room. As she did so, her hand touched the wrought iron fencing that blocked the flowerbeds from the sidewalk. She jerked her hand away with a loud cry of pain. At once, Matthias had her hand in his and examined it.

"What's happened?" he asked as he searched her palm.

"I don't know." She frowned. "I put my hand on the railing and the heat stung me."

Matthias laid his own hand on the railing and withdrew it. "It's not hot."

She could feel the mark on her palm as it throbbed with a burning ache. Passersby eyed her, but said nothing as they made their way into the library.

Lilian looked over her palm. The mark had reddened, but otherwise was no different than before. There were no indications of sting or burn. "I don't know."

Matthias started toward the truck again. "Maybe you're allergic to iron." It was said as a joke, but they looked at one another and turned to hurry back into the library.

"Tell me everything you know which seems a little weird about yourself," he said as they rushed into the library and to a computer.

"Well, gee, where to start." She rolled her eyes at him. "There's just a long list, you know."

He gave her a pointed look and all but pushed her into the computer chair. He dropped down into the chair beside her and picked up a pencil and notepaper. "Allergies."

"Umm, well. Lots of different kinds of medicines have an adverse reaction."

He scribbled it down. "What else?"

"Salt," she replied. "Salt makes me sick. Actually, if it's already cooked in something, it's fine, but when added after, or if I touch it, it makes me sick."

Matthias added it to the list. "Wrought iron," he said.

"I don't know. It's the first time that ever happened."

"We could go test it elsewhere."

"You're mean," she muttered as she turned to the computer.

He chuckled under his breath, leaned in to kiss her neck, and whispered, "I'll make it up to you later."

Lilian's face grew warm, and she waved him off before typing a few words into the search engine. Her eyes scanned the results and she lifted a brow.

"What?" he asked.

"Well, according to this, I'm either a demon or a faerie."

He blinked a few times before he looked to the screen and read the results himself. She grinned.

"I'm not either of those, so we can chalk this up to mythology hits. Search engines just find mentions of what you type in. See? This one is for a role playing game with faeries."

He looked at her and whispered in a soft tone. "Considering who and what you're talking to, you might want to rethink the last bit."

Lilian frowned. "Now you're being ridiculous."

"Am I?"

"Matthias, be serious. You can't possibly think I'm either of those."

Matthias studied her face as she frowned at him.

"It's so obvious," he said at last.

"What is?"

"Think about it," he said, his voice edging into excitement. "Your dreams, the white stag, the huntsman and the hounds. The salt and iron weakness, your abilities."

His gold eyes glittered with enthusiasm.

"You're insane. Does it look like I have wings or glitter? Do I look like a freaking Tinkerbell?" Too loud. It echoed a bit in the quiet library.

"Shh!" A few of the patrons hushed her.

She turned and glared at them. They were quick to look away.

Matthias chuckled and grabbed onto her hand. "I can see you're in dire need of some food." He dragged her out of the library and toward his truck.

Lilian tried to pull her hand from his, but he held on firmly.

"Food, then home," he told her. "I want you to talk to someone."

"Who?"

Matthias just about tossed her into the truck. "I want you to meet my family, but I want you to talk to our…" He hesitated a moment before he continued. "Healer, I guess you can call him. Shaman? Spiritual advisor? All of the above."

He shut the door and jogged around to the driver's side, closing the door once seated.

"Why? What's he going to say?"

"He'd know more about the Fae than any library or search engine," Matthias replied as he started the truck.

"Actually, a search engine doesn't give you information…err, never mind." Not the time to go into the finite detail of what the internet is or what a search engine did and didn't do.

He gave her an odd look before he put the truck in drive and drove away from the library. From what she could see, he seemed to be a bit antsy, excited, and it kind of worried her.

"Okay, what is it?" she asked.

"What do you mean?"

"You're like a kid on Christmas morning. Full moon tonight?"

He snorted. "Full moons have nothing to do with shifting. We can shift any time we want."

"So what's with the full moon thing?"

"The full moon makes us feel more primitive. We're closer to our primitive side, but otherwise it doesn't do a whole lot. What about you? Do the moon phases affect you?"

Lilian was taken aback by his question. She'd never even considered the possibility. She shook her head. "No. And it's still a stupid idea."

"Why is it you can accept your abilities and the fact I can change into a wolf, but you can't accept the idea you may be something more than human?"

Because she already felt like a freak; she didn't need it verified in any way. In her eyes, it didn't make her special, it made her a mutant, a freak of nature, and she didn't want it. She just wanted to be normal and have a normal life.

When she didn't reply, he stayed silent, leaving her to her thoughts. She appreciated that about him; he just knew.

Matthias pulled into the drive-thru of a local fast food joint and ordered enough food to feed his biker gang. At least, she thought it would be. Maybe not, she thought ten minutes later, as she watched him mow through five large cheeseburgers *while* driving. She eyed her half eaten burger and shook her head.

When they returned to the—what the hell *was* she suppose to call it? Compound? Palace? What? When they returned, he helped her out of the truck and led her, a hand on her arm, to the courtyard, nodded to people who called out greetings to him. Many of them were in various states of undress, with men wearing what looked like nothing more than white cloth kilts, and women in white slips. Some wore more modern clothing, shorts and tank tops, others had swimsuits, and children ranged from being altogether naked to wearing the same as the adults.

They stared at her, although Lilian could see some of the female population had more than curiosity in their eyes. One woman, with blond hair and bright green eyes, glared at her with hostility.

"Where is my mother?" Matthias asked a nearby man.

"She's in the solarium," came a reply from a female.

Matthias nodded his thanks and led her away, but as they walked down the hall, the blond hair, green-eyed woman approached. She noticed the woman was perhaps only a little older than her, but beautiful. She carried herself with a regal pride.

"Matthias," the woman said as she stepped up to them, her hands extended to him.

Ignoring me, she noted.

Matthias released her to take the woman's hands. "Anoria," he said in greeting. "Lilian, this is Anoria."

Anoria gave her a brief look and dismissed her. "Matthias, will you be here for the evening meal?"

"Yes. I will be here, with Lilian," he replied.

Anoria looked a little peeved but smiled. "Of course. I'll be sure to include some form of simple entertainment for her tastes."

Lilian bristled, offended. Now she understood Anoria's problem. Jealousy, pure and simple, and she knew, without a doubt, her stay here would be rough.

She smiled oh so sweetly at Anoria. "Why, thank you, Anoria. I'm sure it won't tax your brain *too* much to come up with a simple thought."

Two could play that *game.*

Matthias's lips twitched as he looked between the two women. Anoria snapped her gaze toward her, her green eyes narrowing. The two women stared at one another, and a feminine understanding passed between them.

Anoria looked back at Matthias, giving him a rather sultry, come hither smile. It sickened Lilian and she turned and headed down the hall. The only satisfaction she received from it was Matthias excused himself and followed after her, leaving Anoria standing there, alone, fuming. It didn't take her psychic powers to feel the mental daggers shooting into her back.

Matthias wrapped an arm around her waist and walked alongside her.

"She's a bitch," she announced.

Matthias grinned. "Yes, she is. She's Lupine."

Lilian looked over at him and smirked. "Funny, and it's not what I meant."

He pulled her closer to him. "You're a stranger and there's a pack dynamic, a hierarchy."

"Did you and her have something going on before me?" she asked.

"No," Matthias said. "Nothing between us. I'm sure she wishes. I am the Alpha of the pack and it would bring her status up, but I've never had any interest in her in any way." He looked over at her and grinned. "Why?"

Lilian cursed the blush creeping over her face. "Just wondering."

He laughed, turned toward her and pulled her against him, ignoring the stares of the people around them. "Jealous?" he asked.

She glared at him. "Get over yourself."

"He does act like he's arrogant," a female voice said from behind them, "but I assure you, it comes naturally."

Matthias turned to the woman. Lilian tried to pull away from Matthias, but he wasn't letting her go.

"Mother," Matthias said in greeting.

"My son," the woman replied.

When she looked back, she saw a statuesque blonde, with blue eyes. Her skin a lovely shade of cream, sun kissed but not tanned. She wore jeans and a tank top, with golden bracelets and armbands.

The woman looked her over as well and she felt out of place. She tensed and poked Matthias in the gut.

"Would you please let go of me?" she asked, exasperated.

Matthias released her, but kept a hold of her hand. "Mother, this is Lilian Quinn. Lilian, this is my Mother, Helena."

Lilian tried to twist her hand from him as she pasted on a polite smile. "It's good to meet you, ma'am."

Helena smiled at her, her blue eyes twinkling. "And good to meet you. Finally." She gave Matthias a reproachful look before she glanced back at her. "Tiberius has told me about you."

"What exactly did he tell you?" Matthias asked.

"Enough to wonder if I should be expecting a surprise in the next nine months," Helena replied in a sardonic tone.

Lilian blushed. "I'll kill him."

Matthias laughed. "No, no surprises. I wanted to introduce her to you before we speak with Octavius."

Helena nodded but continued to study her, making her feel a bit uneasy and anxious.

"I'm not one of you," she said.

Helena smiled. "I know, my dear. You're something entirely different but I can't place it quite yet."

Lilian frowned. "I'm human."

"No," Helena said. "There's something more to you."

Lilian's heart stuttered at Helena's words. She didn't want to be different. To have a stranger point it out, someone who didn't know her, pick up on it, hurt. She looked away.

"It needn't be a bad thing, my dear. We are all different in our own way."

Matthias lifted her hand to his mouth and brushed his lips over her knuckles. "Mother is right. If you were just Lilian, human, I doubt I would have given you a second glance."

"Even after I spilled iced tea and cold water over you?" she asked.

He grinned. "Well, I might have noticed you for a bit then."

"Is this a story I'd be interested in?" Helena asked with a smile.

"Maybe later." Matthias laughed. "Lilian's going red."

Lilian poked him before looking at Helena. "It was nice to meet you."

"Don't let him walk all over you. Matthias is spoiled and tends to get what he wants far too easily. Make him work for it." Helena winked at her and walked away.

Matthias blinked and shook his head. "I am not spoiled."

Lilian laughed. "If your own mother says you are, then I'd say you are."

Matthias made a gruff *hmph* sound and led her away to find Octavius.

* * * *

The two men walked down the sidewalk of Hawk's Point. Residents, and even visitors to the small town, eyed the men and gave them a wide berth. If the two found it amusing, they didn't show it.

Of the two, one man was dark skinned, dark haired, and dark eyed. Tall and muscular, he had an aura of danger around him. The second was not as tall, nor as dark. In fact, he looked rather pasty, and much thinner, but moved with an oozing slickness. While he didn't have the aura of danger as the first, something about him made people want to avoid him. It might have been the glint in his blue eyes, or the smirk he had on his thin lips. Either way, no one wanted to go near him. Both dressed in the same manner, in black, although the tall, muscular man wore a trench coat, even in the summer heat.

The two of them walked into the town center. Neither of them spoke to one another, but they moved together, as if they knew what they were doing and where they were going.

The diner was slow when they entered. Peggy manned the dining room but when she spotted the two as they looked around, she froze in her tracks. Evil radiated from those two and she didn't want anything to do with them. She jerked around and hurried into the kitchen.

Diners fell silent as they watched the strangers sit down at a booth.

"You have a table, Peggy," one of the older waitresses announced as she came into the kitchen.

"Uh, you take it? I want to take a break."

"No way. I'm off in five minutes."

Peggy sighed and grabbed menus as she headed toward the booth and two freaky men.

"Hi," she said in a polite tone. "Can I get you anything to drink while you decide?" She handed the menus to them.

The pasty man ignored her altogether, but the dark one looked her over. "Whatcha offerin', sweet thing?"

Peggy shuddered and her smile weakened. "Iced tea, some different sodas, or lemonade. Most like the lemonade."

"We'll take the lemonade then," he said with a sneer.

"And we'll take whatever information you have on Lilian Quinn," the pasty man said.

His voice was soft and carried a definite sense of threat.

Peggy took a step back. "Lil's not here. She has the next couple of days off."

"Don't go yet, sweetheart," Pasty whispered.

Peggy tried to take another step back as fear rose in her, but she couldn't move. Her eyes flared open.

"You're not being a very good waitress."

Peggy let out a soft moan as pressure built in her head. With an odd "popping" sensation, the pressure released and memories tumbled out of her brain. She could feel something, or someone, in her head, sifting through the memories like a secretary sifting through a filing cabinet.

Memories of Lilian were extracted from her mind, examined. She could feel the amusement of the one in her mind, and a feeling of lust.

"Pretty, little woman, this Lilian Quinn."

Peggy wanted to run, to get away from the two men, but locked in place, she experienced her mind being tampered with. She gave up her friend's secrets: where she lived, what she liked to eat, who she had been seen with. When Peggy had given everything, she was released and she staggered. Peggy grabbed onto the table to keep from falling to the floor as she sobbed. The two men slid out of the booth and made their way to the exit.

One man watched the two, his eyes narrowed as he studied them. When they had left, he turned his head to look at Peggy and made his way over to her.

"Miss? Do you need help?" he asked.

Peggy looked at him, wide eyed with fear and confusion.

"Come on," he said. "Sit down. You look like you're going to pass out."

One of the other waitresses came over, frowning. "Peggy? What's wrong? What happened?"

Peggy cried. "I don't know. They asked about Lilian and then…"

The waitress wrapped an arm around Peggy and led her to the restroom. "Come on, let's get you cleaned up."

The man watched the two women leave. By the time they returned, the man was long gone.

* * * *

"Alpha!"

Matthias and Lilian were on their way over to a group of young adults, about five in total, when the booming voice rang out. Matthias turned to look and smiled.

"Octavius," he said.

She watched an older man approach. Dressed in a toga, of all things. She wasn't sure whether to smile or not. She had always thought togas were costumes for college frat parties, and seeing someone wearing one seemed a bit odd to her. Although given the place and the people involved, she supposed it wasn't too farfetched.

Octavius extended a hand to Matthias, and they clasped one another by the forearms.

"How goes the class?" Matthias asked.

"They're young, but their minds are eager," Octavius said. "Good children."

"What are you teaching?" she asked, curious.

"Herbalism," Octavius replied.

Lilian gazed into his watery green eyes and they stared at one another for a few moments. She experienced a weak attempt to brush her mind and without hesitation, she slammed down mental barriers to keep out any intruders. She tensed in wariness, and her body instinctively took on a posture of defense.

Octavius nodded. "Class dismissed." He waved the group off and turned to Matthias. "Come, we will talk in private." He looked back at her, nodded, and turned, leading the way.

Matthias gave her hand a reassuring squeeze before he led her after Octavius.

They were taken to a small temple-like structure. When they stepped inside, the scent of drying herbs and burning incense wafted in the air. Warm and dark, with only candles giving off any sort of light, the far end of the temple had a dais on which the statue of a wolf had been placed. Beneath the wolf were two children, both reaching up to suckle from the wolf's teats.

Lupa, the she-wolf who had raised the abandoned Romulus and Remus.

Lilian studied the statue. She could see its eyes were inset with amber stones so when caught in the light, they glittered as though with life. The statue itself looked to be bronze, and old.

She looked at Matthias, who had watched her study the statue. She smiled at him.

"Lupa."

He nodded and lifted her hand to his lips, kissing her palm before he turned to Octavius.

"Octavius, this is Lilian Quinn."

"Miss Quinn." He nodded his head toward her.

"Octavius," she said.

"She is a mystery, even to herself. We have a suspicion, but we'd like to know what she is. She is not fully human nor is she Lupine."

Lilian fidgeted, uneasy.

"The Rite is not an easy one," Octavius warned. "It can be physically and mentally wearing."

"We are prepared," Matthias said.

"Wait!" she interjected. "Maybe I'm not. Maybe I don't want to know."

Matthias turned and took her into his arms. "It's all right to be afraid."

She tried to push him away from her. "Stop, Matthias. I'm not afraid, per se. I just, well, maybe I don't want to know what kind of freak I am."

Lilian tried to get him to release her by bringing a knee up, but he twisted his body out of the way. He maintained his hold on her.

"Lilian," he said. He seemed amused by her attempt at violence. "Deep down, you want to know."

"No, I don't," she snapped. "I'm content knowing nothing. I'm content being normal in this little hole in the wall town. I'm content being nobody!"

"No, you aren't. You can lie to yourself all you want, but I know better. Your nightmares, your hand, your strange allergies, you want to know, you're just afraid to take that step."

Lilian gave up and leaned her head against his chest. "I don't want to verify that I'm a freak, Matthias. I just want to be normal."

"Who's to say you aren't normal?" Octavius asked. "For you, this might be normal. We change into wolves. For us, *that* is normal."

She remained silent for a while, counting the heartbeats in Matthias's chest. Finally, she spoke. "How does it work?"

"We take a walk," Octavius replied with a brilliant smile.

This is so not going to go well.

* * * *

Peggy walked out to her car after her shift. She was on pins and needles, afraid the two strange men would come back, or worse, be waiting for her. When neither happened, she was relieved, but still kept alert.

"Hey, Peggy?" a masculine voice called out.

Peggy gasped, spun around, and pressed back against her car, terrified.

"Whoa, easy. It's all right. Remember me? I sat in your section? I helped you when the two men left."

She panted as her heart tried to regain its normal rhythm. Peggy studied his face and nodded. "I remember."

He smiled. "Good. I was just making sure you were okay. I saw how much they had shaken you up."

She gave a nervous chuckle and glanced around again, as if they might be watching. "If I never see them again, it'll be too soon. I hope they're gone for good."

He gestured to her car. "I'll see you into your car. Do you know what they wanted?"

Peggy eyed the stranger, but he looked nice enough and he wasn't one of the two freaky men who'd been in the diner earlier. She stepped away from her car and opened the driver's side door.

"They were asking about a friend of mine," she replied.

It was the last thing Peggy said, other than a loud cry of pain as she was struck from behind. She fell forward into her car, consciousness careening in and out. The man shoved her over and slid in. With her keys, he started the car and drove off, taking her with him.

Peggy whimpered in fear, her head pounding like a bass drum. She tried to sit up, but when she moved, the man punched her again. Peggy moved in and out of unconsciousness, too dizzy to notice where they were going.

She surfaced from the blackness just before the car turned off the pavement and drove along a gravel road. Peggy could feel every bounce of the car amplified by the pounding of her head. When the car stopped and the engine turned off, Peggy remained in place, except for the trembling. She kept her eyes closed and tried to keep her breathing slow, as if unconscious. The man got out of the car and a few moments later, the passenger side door opened. She shrieked with pain and fear as he pulled her out of the car by her hair. Peggy fell to the ground and scrambled to catch up as he dragged her along.

She opened her eyes and noticed the forest surrounding her, the smell of charred wood close by. The man released her and she tried to turn her body and stand, but dizziness caused her to fall back to her knees. Her vision swam as she struggled to get her bearings, and it took a few moments to realize she was looking at the charred remains of a house. Her eyes widened in horror when she recognized where she was. It was Lilian's yard!

"She shouldn't have run, you know," the man said.

Peggy looked at him with growing horror as he pulled out a large knife. The setting sun glinted off the metal blade as he lifted it. She dragged in a ragged breath to scream.

Her scream was short lived.

* * * *

Matthias eased the semi-conscious Lilian onto a raised platform in the center of the temple. She could hear Octavius mixing herbs and the acrid smell of smoke became strong as the herbs were applied to a burning censer.

"She is all right?" Matthias asked Octavius.

"She's fine, Alpha. Merely in a relaxed state. She can still hear us."

Matthias made a rumbling sound. She brushed his mind with her own. "*Stop it.*"

"*Lilian?*"

"*You know of any other women who can talk to you telepathically?*"

She heard Matthias choke back a soft laugh.

The incense become stronger and she heard the shuffling of steps.

Octavius spoke near her. "All right then, we're ready."

With her connection with Matthias, she knew he moved aside and took a seat on a marble bench nearby, but out of the way.

Octavius touched his fingertips to either side of her temples. Because she had not relinquished her connection with Matthias, she knew he was able to see and experience everything she went through as though with her, a part of her.

Lilian was in a forest, dark and shadowy. She recognized it as the same forest in her dreams and nightmares.

I can't hear anything. I don't feel a sense of danger.

Lilian lifted her head, took a deep breath, and slowly exhaled. . She shifted her form to the white wolf she'd used before. She felt Matthias and Octavius's surprise and she laughed as she began to run.

The sheer joy of it was amazing. The freedom, the sense of being carefree, intoxicating. She leapt over fallen logs, her body instinctive twisting to take the turns, to grip the earth to keep her balance.

With a sudden appearance, the white stag stepped into her path and reared up, its hooves pawing the air. She twisted and rolled to avoid colliding with the beast.

Damn it!

The stag lowered itself back down to the ground and looked around.

"*Something is different here.*"

Lilian shifted to her human form. "Who are you?"

The stag looked at her. "*Do you think you're ready to learn the truth?*"

Lilian sucked in a soft gasp of air as she nodded. "I think it's time."

"*What of your abilities? What number are they?*"

"What do you mean? How many abilities I have? Telepathy, Telekinesis, and Empathy. Why?"

The stag shook his head. "*One more and then you will be ready.*"

"Why can't you tell me now?" she asked, frustrated. "I'm tired of the nightmares."

"*I will say this in warning. Death approaches. Beware. Trust only in yourself and your abilities. All will be explained soon, but not here. Not now. You are not ready.*"

The white stag stepped toward her. "*Let me see your right palm and the mark there.*"

Lilian lifted her palm toward the stag. It reached out with its nose and touched her. Her mark began to burn and she cried out as she jerked her hand away.

"*Lilian!*" Matthias cried out in her mind, and she winced in reaction.

The stag's head jerked up, its ears turned back. It stomped a hoof. "*You are not one of them! You should not be with them!*"

Before Lilian could reply, her vision blurred, followed by an explosion of bright white light. She gasped out loud and shielded her eyes from the intensity. After a moment, everything went black.

Chapter 6

"Well," Lilian said as she sat up. "That was useless."

"Not entirely." Octavius handed her a mug.

"How not entirely?" she asked as she took the mug and sniffed the contents.

"It's tea, drink it." He walked away from her. "First, why did you choose the wolf form when you shifted?"

Lilian shrugged. "I did it before in a dream. Matthias was there in my dream as well. As a black wolf."

Matthias and Octavius exchanged glances before they looked back at her.

"You two have not…" Octavius started to ask.

Lilian narrowed her eyes. "Not that it's anyone's business, but no."

Octavius chuckled. "You are not a Shifter, yet you are able to change your form."

"In my dreams," she said. "You can do anything you want in your dreams."

"You have never changed forms in your waking life?"

"No, of course not."

"Have you ever woken up and been somewhere different, or woken up and suspected you'd been somewhere else?"

"Like sleepwalking?" she asked with a frown.

"In a way, yes." Octavius returned to her side and checked the mug. He motioned toward it. "Drink."

"I don't know what's in it."

He eyed her and she stared right back at him. Matthias stepped up to her, took the mug, and lifted it to his lips. He handed it back to her. She glanced in the mug, noticing the level of liquid had gone down. She looked at him.

"It's herbs to calm you down, strengthen your mind," Octavius said.

"It's safe, Lilian." Matthias reached up and caressed her cheek.

She nodded and took a small sip.

"You did not trust me?" Octavius asked.

She gave him a smile. "I don't trust very many people. I'm not even sure I trust Matthias yet."

Matthias laughed at Octavius's shocked expression. "She jests, Octavius. She trusts me enough to come home with me and meet my family."

"I did not. You kidnapped me."

It was Octavius's turn to burst into laughter. "Like father, like son!"

Lilian looked at Octavius, and at Matthias, her eyes narrowed. "What?"

Octavius let out a hoot of amusement. "Matthias's father kidnapped his mother from the Remus clan. The fallout went on for years!"

Matthias rolled his eyes. "There's always been fallout for some reason or another."

"Why did he kidnap her?" she asked.

"He fell in love with her, but since the two clans are enemies, there was no way he'd be able to convince a mating. So, he planned a raid and kidnapped her."

"I'm going to assume she wanted to be kidnapped."

Octavius snorted, but fell silent when Matthias gave him a quelling look.

"Not at first, no," Matthias said as he looked at her. "It took a while."

"They fought likes cats and dogs," Octavius said.

Matthias gave him another look.

Lilian lifted a brow at Matthias before setting the mug down. "I think I'll get a motel room."

Matthias smiled. "Of course not. It's not safe for one, and two, you already have a room here. Plus Anoria is arranging entertainment, remember?"

Lilian hissed on her exhale. Like she wanted to be around that woman? *Hah.*

Matthias picked her up and headed for the doorway, carrying her in his arms. Octavius chuckled.

"Put me down."

"I like having you in my arms." His words were quiet and said rather simply, but it was enough to cause her heart to stutter.

He smiled down at her and she stared up at him, eyes wide. She remembered what had happened in her room, in her bed, before they were interrupted, and it caused her breath to catch, her heart to quicken. God, he had a beautiful smile. His eyes were like molten gold, the way he looked at her. They burned for her.

It was more than lust, how he made her feel deep down inside. She knew she'd never have the chance to have a normal relationship or a family of her own because of her secrets.

Along came Matthias, who woke up those slumbering emotions. Those sensations defied her wishes to remain buried, rebelled against their imposed imprisonment, and demanded things she wasn't sure she was ready for.

She had no words for how he made her feel. Instead, she connected their minds, shared with him her thoughts, her emotions. Her desires made themselves known to him first and foremost. He stumbled a couple of steps before quickening his pace. She sent him her fears next.

"I'm afraid, Matthias. There's so much going on and I'm not sure if I'm ready."

He stopped walking. "Do you trust me?"

As curious as it was, she did trust him. Something about him overcame her survival instincts. While he could be a pain in the ass, and she had no problem fighting him if need be, she trusted him.

"Yes. I trust you."

His arms tightened and he pulled her up to his mouth to kiss her. Her eyes closed as their lips met and she could have sworn fireworks exploded. Lilian must have sent the thought to him because he gave a soft chuckle before he deepened the kiss, nearly devouring her mouth with his. She squirmed in his arms as she tried to turn her body into him, but the way he held her wouldn't allow for it. She whimpered in frustration.

"I do hope you two aren't going to progress any further than making out in public." The words were spoken with a wry tone.

Lilian felt as well as heard Matthias's growl as Tiberius interrupted them. She broke the kiss to turn her head and glare at him.

"Don't you have anything better to do than to bug us?" she snapped at him.

Tiberius lifted a brow and glanced around. "Oh, sure, but do the others?"

Lilian blinked in confusion and looked around to see what Tiberius was talking about. Her face grew hot when she realized it wasn't just Tiberius watching, but everyone present had stopped to watch in amusement and interest.

Well, except Anoria, who was glaring those daggers at her, yet again. She would have smiled but too mortified, she turned her head into Matthias's chest to hide.

"Maybe your guest would like to refresh herself before the evening meal?" Anoria suggested.

Matthias rumbled in his chest before he replied. "Good idea, Anoria. Thank you."

He set her down on her feet.

"Maybe Mother has something you can borrow to wear." Matthias started to lead her toward the main building.

Anoria hurried to speak. "I could loan her some clothing. I might have a few items she can borrow."

Matthias paused but Lilian knew she'd probably end up wearing something horrible, or worn out in order to be embarrassed or laughed at.

"Actually, I'd feel more comfortable wearing a dress belonging to your mother, Matthias. I'd be honored if I could."

Lilian glanced at Anoria. The woman looked like she had sucked on a lemon and was trying not to spit it out.

Matthias nodded. "I think she'd like it." He led her off again.

She smiled at Anoria before she turned away. In doing so, she saw Tiberius's expression. He was fighting not to smile, let alone laugh. He caught her gaze and winked before he headed off, shoulders shaking in silent laughter.

When they reached the entryway of the main building, Matthias took her to the right and around the outside of the building. From here, she could see doors spaced out along the building.

"These are personal suites of families. Mother has the largest, as befitting her station."

Lilian glanced at him. "Why doesn't she live inside?"

"She didn't want to," he replied. "I offered her Tiberius's suite, and one of the guest rooms, but she wanted her own outside."

He knocked on his mother's suite door when they arrived and a young woman answered it.

"Alpha," she said, bowing her head.

"Diana, is my mother in?"

"No, Alpha. She's visiting."

Lilian wondered who Helena was visiting as the reply seemed to be left hanging.

"This is Lilian. Would you see if my mother has some clothes she might borrow?"

"Of course, Alpha. I would be pleased to do so."

Matthias smiled and turned to Lilian. "I'll be back to get you after you're done. Diana will help you choose something."

"Sure, abandon me." Her tone was teasing though.

Matthias leaned in and kissed her before whispering, "I'll make it up to you later."

Before she could respond to his parting words, he turned and walked away.

* * * *

Diana was a shy young woman, she found out, and didn't speak unless spoken to first. After Lilian had showered, Diana helped her dress in what was called a *peplos*, made from two rectangular pieces of cotton cloth sewn together on both sides with the open sections at the top and folded down in the front and back. Diana pulled it over Lilian's head, shimmying it down her body. It was then fastened with two gold pins at the shoulders. This formed a sleeveless dress, belted with a golden cord at the waist, beneath the draped, folded over fabric. She eyed herself in the mirror, unsure of the gown as it bared her shoulders and arms.

"You look lovely, Lady," Diana said in her soft voice as she finished with Lilian's hair.

"I've never worn anything like this. Are you sure I look okay?"

Diana's smile was soft and sweet. "The Alpha will be speechless," she said. "I doubt he'll be able to take his eyes off you."

Lilian blushed and fiddled with the material.

"Would you like some jewelry to wear as well?"

Lilian's eyes widened as she gasped in horror. "Oh, no, I couldn't! It wouldn't be proper for me to borrow someone's jewelry. What if something happened to it? I wouldn't be able to replace it."

Diana looked confused, but hurried to reassure her. "It's all right, Lady. It's all right."

"Is something wrong?" Matthias asked.

Lilian turned to look at him. He was standing in the doorway of the bedroom. She watched as his eyes widened and jaw dropped. Diana giggled from somewhere behind her.

"It's okay, right?" Lilian asked.

He stepped closer, his eyes roaming over her. "I'll have to beat your admirers off with a stick."

She laughed. "You're the only one I have."

Matthias lifted a brow and smiled. She wasn't sure she liked that smile. It seemed as though it was made of trouble.

"The Lady didn't want any jewelry," Diana said.

Lilian cringed. "I don't want to be responsible for them."

Matthias seemed to be thinking over something, and nodded. "I understand."

Lilian smiled. "Thank you, Diana. You made me look wonderful."

The young woman blushed and looked down. "It was my pleasure, Lady."

Matthias took her by the hand and led her out of the suite. One thing she continued to notice Matthias was a hands-on type of man, touching her, holding her, standing close to her. She wondered if it was a wolf thing.

"Yes," he said.

She looked up at him. "Yes, what?"

"It's a wolf thing," he said with a smile.

"How did…" she started.

Matthias tapped his temple with his free hand. "You're still here."

Lilian blinked in surprise, having forgotten they were still mentally connected.

"It's actually nice," he said. "I like having you here."

She knew he didn't mean just physically.

"I rather like your home," she said. "It's interesting. Different."

"We're a curious mix of traditional and modern, aren't we?"

"Yeah, that's putting it mildly." She grinned.

Matthias led her to a raised platform where carpets and blankets were set down and pillows strewn about. Helena, already seated, had some people around her. She smiled at her and Lilian returned the greeting.

Matthias helped her to sit before he sat beside her, his side against hers. Once seated, people began to find places of their own and a bonfire was lit in the center of the courtyard, in a lined fire pit. When the fire crackled and burned, two people approached. A man carried a large basin and a woman carried a towel. The man knelt before Matthias, who flicked his fingers toward her. The man blinked, shifted his position, and presented the basin of water to her.

Lilian glanced at Matthias in question.

"To rinse your hands," he whispered.

"Oh." She smiled with embarrassment as she dipped her hands in the water. The woman presented the towel to her and she dried her hands as she watched Matthias rinse his hands. When he finished, the towel was offered to him and the couple moved on. Only the people seated on the raised platform were furnished with basin and towel, and once everyone had rinsed their hands, the food was served.

Matthias was served first as befitting his station. A long plate was placed on the blanket before him and as the food came by, it was shown to him. He'd either nod if he wanted some or shake his head. By the time the plate was filled, she was laughing and wiping tears of amusement from her eyes.

"What's so funny?" he asked, grinning.

The others were giving her odd looks, which she ignored.

"No offense, Matthias, but I feel like I'm in the Twilight Zone. I have the urge to pinch myself to see if I'm awake. If you and some of your people weren't wearing jeans and t-shirts, I'd wonder what drug I was on. This is very surreal."

"No offense taken. It's a bit much, I know, but it's a tradition we like to keep. It reminds us of our past."

When put that way, a ripple of pain sliced through her gut and tears rose in her eyes. She didn't have a connection with her past. She had nothing in the way of a family past.

Matthias leaned in and brushed his lips against her temple. "Don't be sad."

Lilian gave him a brief smile. "I have no family, no family past. I have no idea where I came from."

"Your mother never told you?"

"I was ten when my stepfather killed her. I didn't even know I wasn't her biological child until later. No one knows where I came from."

Matthias moved a long plate, trencher, and set it closer to them. He picked up a slice of meat and offered it to her. She gave him an odd look, but when his expression turned to challenging, she leaned in and took the offering. He smiled and moved closer to whisper.

"Roasted lamb, seasoned with herbs and sea salt."

"*It's good.*" She chewed the morsel as he chose another and popped it into his mouth.

They watched one another as they ate. Matthias fed her and she reciprocated by feeding him morsels. He always suckled on her fingers, cleaning them seductively as she pulled away. By the time they were done eating, she was flushed, her body heated and the burning flames of desire raced along her veins. She didn't need to read his thoughts to know what he wanted of her. Of course, whatever he thought and felt, amplified her desire.

When they were finished eating, music began to play and she looked away from Matthias to watch the musicians.

"Matthias!" Tiberius called.

Both Lilian and Matthias turned their heads toward him.

Tiberius approached them and handed Matthias a small, stringed instrument. He winked at her and chuckled as he walked away. Matthias growled.

"You're such a baby," she said.

He smiled at her before he looked down at the instrument. He began to strum it, and plucked at the strings.

"I dream of you. Every whisper which floats on gentle breezes brings your name to me. Every face which passes by brings you to memory."

His voice was soft and sensual and the words were spoken in a seductive tone as he played the little instrument. He didn't sing the words, as the music was more of a background accompaniment to accentuate the mood.

"Every dream I dream is a dream of only you. Every touch we share brings pleasure anew."

Lilian leaned in and brushed her lips against his. He smiled at her and nuzzled her cheek before murmuring near her ear.

"Would you like to go for a walk with me?"

Lilian smiled and nodded. Matthias rose to his feet and extended a hand to her. She took it and he helped her to stand. She adjusted the *peplos* as he started to lead her off.

She could hear the faint whispers of the others and while she couldn't pick out what they were saying, she knew they were talking about her and Matthias. She chose to ignore them. She didn't want their gossip to ruin what she was experiencing right now.

Unfortunately, they didn't get very far before the mood was ruined with the scream of a child. Matthias and Lilian spun around to look for the cause and they both caught sight of the young girl, holding her hands out in pain, screaming and crying.

"*Go! You can heal her!*" She heard the stag's voice in her head.

Lilian didn't hesitate. She released Matthias's hand, gathered up the *peplos* so it wouldn't tangle about her legs, and ran toward the girl with Matthias right on her heels. She pushed her way through the gathering people and dropped to her knees before the injured child. The smell of burnt flesh was strong. She would have normally shied away, but she reached out and took the child by the wrists, holding her with a firm grip.

"*Connect with her, cease the pain.*"

Without hesitation, she sought the girl's mind, delving deep. Pain, sharp and stabbing, hit her hard when the two minds connected. She gasped aloud, tears spilled over her eyes and down her cheeks, but she remained locked with the girl. They shared the pain for a few moments before Lilian found the pain receptors and blocked them, giving them both relief.

A bright, white mist crept and seeped around her and the young girl until it engulfed them. So intent on helping the child, she almost didn't hear the gasps from around her. She only noticed it in a distracted manner, but knew it had to do with her somehow. Still, she didn't let it draw her out of healing the girl's burnt hands. From her memories, Lilian learned the child had been running after her brother and tripped. The wind had been knocked out of her; she couldn't move out of the coals fast enough to avoid burning her hands.

The white light soon surrounded the two of them.

"Concentrate! Heal her hands."

A healing warmth traveled down Lilian's arms into her hands, and from there, into the girl's wrists and hands. As the two of them watched, the blisters healed, the open wounds closed, the skin fused, until her hands were as perfect as they were before the fall, albeit sooty.

When she finished, she withdrew from the girl's mind and released her wrists. The white aura faded and with it went her strength. She was weak and exhausted, and when she glanced up, became uneasy with everyone staring at her. She staggered to her feet and Matthias reached out to help her, but she waved him off.

Without warning, she was shoved from behind and fell, too weak to try and keep on her feet.

"What did you do to Katherine?" a woman's voice demanded.

Anoria.

Before she could reply, or even try to stand, Matthias scooped her up. She could feel the tension in his body as he held her.

"How dare you lay a hand on her," he snarled at Anoria.

Some of the people moved back a few steps, eyeing Matthias with wariness. Anoria was too angry to notice or care, it seemed. She pressed on.

"What did she do to my sister? How dare she touch her!"

Lilian was too exhausted to even defend herself. She leaned her head against his chest and sighed. At once, Matthias held her closer to him, his stance became protective, possessive, and he gave an audible growl, in warning. Anoria went silent.

Obviously, Anoria's sense of self-preservation is working just fine.

With a glare, Matthias turned and carried her toward the compound's living quarters. People moved out of the way without a word, without looking at Matthias. She noticed they kept their eyes down in deference to his authority, or maybe his anger.

"Matthias," she whispered, "I can walk."

He hesitated and then said, "I know."

"So let me walk."

"No. I like you in my arms, and this way I know you're going to get to where you need to be without someone bothering you. Right now, there are too many questions and you need your rest. You're exhausted. You're pale and you're trembling."

Now that he had pointed it out, she could feel herself shaking.

"They're going to think I'm weak," she argued. "I don't want to be thought of as weak here. Not with you all being Lupine."

"*Lilia mea*, I doubt anyone will think you to be weak, not after what you just did."

She heard the amusement in his tone, and said, "I'd hit you if I wasn't so exhausted."

"You can fight with me later, baby. Right now, I want you to get some rest."

"You're too bossy," she murmured against his neck.

He chuckled and she closed her eyes. She trusted him. She knew he wouldn't allow anything to hurt her while he was near.

Matthias carried her into the large palace-like house and to the guest room appointed to her. Already drifting to sleep, she sputtered a weak protest when he started to undress her. He murmured soft reassurances and tucked her into bed. The covers were placed over her and she snuggled into the softness, allowing herself to fully sleep.

* * * *

Matthias watched over her as she slept. She seemed to be sleeping quiet, nothing in the way of fitful dreams or nightmares.

He knew she was more than she seemed, but either she was good at keeping her secrets, or she didn't know herself. He was aware she was trying to protect herself from him, and protect him from the *Custodes Secreti*, she was his mate. He'd known it from the moment he had kissed her outside the diner.

Every Lupine knew the moment they've met their mate, and he'd suspected it when they had their first encounter, but didn't know it for sure until they kissed. It was a defining moment in a Lupine's life, when they realized their mate was there, for them. He suspected she wouldn't be receptive to the idea, and she'd fight him tooth and nail because of the experiences in her life.

Had Stephan raped her? She didn't seem afraid of him in a sexual way, but again, she *was* rather adept at hiding secrets.

He'd tried to keep things slow and gentle for her, kept their relationship easy to give her time to get used to him. He hadn't wanted to rush her, to frighten her. She was still unsure of him, despite her trust in him.

For her, he would take his time and do what he needed to do to protect her, to keep her safe, until she accepted him as her mate. He hoped, in time, she'd have learned to recognize him as her mate and realize he wasn't going anywhere. It was inevitable, written in the stars, and despite the white stag's protest, she would be his.

She'd already dreamt of it.

* * * *

"So, you're Stephan," the graveled, male voice came from behind him.

Stephan spun around, almost losing his balance as he did so, but could see no one. He scanned the area.

"So?" he asked, belligerent in his reply.

"You're playing in someone else's backyard, boy," said the man. "I want to know why."

"What's it to you?"

Stephan, hit by a ball of black energy, was blasted back a few yards until he hit a tree. He struggled to breathe.

"What it is, to me, is you're encroaching upon what is mine," the man growled, low and sinister. "I do not appreciate your presence here."

Stephan could feel the voice worm its way into his mind, digging, tunneling through his brain, eating at his thoughts, his memories. Stephan struggled harder but could not escape the invisible force holding him against the tree or the worm in his brain.

"Ahh," the voice echoed in his ears and his mind. "You want power over her. To control her. Unfortunately, she is not for you. But, you have a use for me."

"No! She's mine!" Stephan yelled.

The voice laughed and the sound of it grated down Stephan's spine, into his gut. He was sick at hearing it.

"No, she is mine. Her powers will be mine, just as her life will be mine. I have plans for Lilian, plans which do not include you, the Summer King, or the Lupine who sniff about her. No, Stephan, she is mine."

The worm dug in and Stephan screamed with the intense pain. Even when freed from the invisible force, he could not escape from the pain and he fell to the ground, writhing. His fingers curled into claws and he dug into the dirt, as if he could escape the intense pain in his mind. Behind it all, underneath it all, came the sound of laughter.

* * * *

Lilian was rather sick of her dreams being in the woods. She knew this dream wasn't one of the regular nightmares she'd been having, but still, couldn't she at least dream about a castle, or Hawaiian beach, or some tropical locale and *not* a darkened forest?

She looked around, catching sight of the white stag as it walked toward her. She held her ground, refusing to approach and refusing to back away. Another thing she was tired of, being a victim. She was going to start standing up for herself a lot more now.

"*Daughter.*" The white stag bowed its great head toward her.

"Daughter?"

"*I have a story to tell you. Will you listen?*"

"Do I have a choice anymore?" Her tone edged toward bitterness.

The white stag folded its front legs and with a slow, regal manner, lowered itself to the ground, to lie down in the soft grass.

"*Sit, my daughter. I will tell you the story of your life.*"

Lilian sat, facing the stag, and sighed.

The stag's form began to mist and melt away. She watched, unsure whether to be horrified or curious at this point.

What was revealed caused her to gasp. In its place sat a man, dressed in white, with white hair and silver eyes, very much like hers. His clothes made of silken materials gave him an aristocratic appearance, even as he sat on the ground before her. His hair long and loose, his silver eyes bright and clear, held wisdom and experience in them. His ears were pointed, and in the left one, he wore a silver cuff, studded with emerald stones.

"When I called you daughter, I meant it in the literal sense," he said, his voice very much like the white stag's, powerful yet calm.

"You're my father?" Her voice broke a bit in her confusion.

He nodded and she was glad she was sitting because she'd have fallen down if not.

"How do I know you're not just saying that?" she asked, stiffening. She would not allow herself to become a victim again.

"The brand on your palm, the four circles connected, represents the four seasons of the year, the four major courts of the Sidhe. Each year, during the turning of the wheel, that aspect of the court rules for the season. However, the balance has been tipped. The Lord of the Winter Court, the Winter King, has set into motion plans to destroy everything in his bid for complete control. He wishes to become the High King."

"But what does this have to do with me?"

"You are my daughter," he replied. "The daughter of the Summer Court, the Summer King. He seeks your power to add to his own."

Lilian frowned. None of this made sense, and she wasn't sure she believed what she was hearing.

"You have the abilities of telepathy, telekinesis, empathy, and healing. You are sensitive to salt and iron, the bane of the Sidhe. You are standing upon the edge of a great precipice, in which you have a choice. Stay where you are, or to take the step over and embrace what you are."

"Say it." She clenched her hands into fists, her tone fierce and demanding. "Say the words."

He nodded once. "To become Sidhe, fully, as is your heritage, your birthright."

Lilian scrambled to her feet. "No."

He stood as well, although he did it with such grace, it looked as though he skipped the whole process and went from sitting to standing in a moment.

"You do not understand. If you do not, the madness will overtake you. It will drive you insane. Your human mind is not able to withstand the shift in perceptions. You will doubt your senses. It will be a constant battle. You will not know what is real and what is not."

"I almost do that now!" she snapped. "I won't accept this! I'm not a faerie!"

"Not a faerie," he said with a smile. "Sidhe. There is a difference."

Lilian shook her head. "Either way, I'm not one. I'm human."

"No, you're half human."

"Prove it," she demanded.

He grinned.

Lilian's body jerked and she found herself awake, heart pounding. She blinked a few times and sat up. She *was* awake, right? She slid from the bed and grabbed the *peplos* from the nearby chair, pulling it on. It was dark in the room, and she assumed it was the middle of the night.

Outside, there was a loud howl, followed by another, and her heart jumped in her chest. She heard yelling. She didn't wait. She ran to the door, threw it open, and ran down the hall. The shouting grew louder, but she couldn't understand. They were using their native language.

As she reached the courtyard, she bolted for the entryway and out onto the grounds. There, she could see the man from her dreams, surrounded by the Lupine. His arms were behind him and she assumed they were bound.

"He says he's your father," Tiberius said to her.

Lilian looked at Tiberius, lost for words.

The men growled and circled the man with reined in anger. She knew they were territorial, as wolves were, and having a strange male just appear on their land made them uneasy.

"If you are her father, then you are welcome here. If you are not her father, you will be torn apart," Matthias said from behind her.

"No!" She protested as she spun to face Matthias. "Don't hurt him!"

Matthias looked at her, studying her face. "Is he your father?"

"I don't know," she said. "He's the white stag."

Matthias stepped up to her side and reached for her hand, but kept his eyes on the stranger. "Prove it."

The man nodded and lifted his right hand, bringing it around to show them his palm. His left hand fell to his side, holding the rope which had been used to bind him.

The man's palm held the same mark as hers, and glowed with a bluish light.

"My name is Amras, King of the Summer Court. Lilian is my daughter, stolen from me as an infant."

She slipped her hand into Matthias's and held on with a tight grip. He gave it a light squeeze.

"Again, prove it."

Amras nodded. "I met her mother, a human, and fell in love with her. We created a child from our union, but because Emma was human, full human, I could not bring her to my Court, nor could I take her child from her. Her mind would not have been able to comprehend all she would see, and a mother should never be separated from her child unless necessary. So, I visited her as often as I could. Lilian's birth name is Ariella."

Lilian listened with an intense concentration. She could only vaguely remember her time before Jane, the woman she knew as Mama, had taken her in, and those shadowy gaps in her past had always bothered her.

"Your mother was beautiful. She had blond hair and emerald green eyes," Amras said, as he looked at her. He touched his ear cuff. "I wear this in remembrance of her. I have never taken a wife because of my love for her."

Tears prickled in her eyes and she blinked them back. Doing so, she missed Amras's approach and from the reactions around her, so did the others. She jerked back in surprise when she realized he was standing in front of her, looking at her in earnest.

"She was driven insane by my brother, Ulwe, the King of the Winter Court. He is the huntsman in your nightmares. He wants you because you are on the cusp of a great change, your Chrysalis. If he can gain your power before you come into your own, he will have won against the Summer Court and be much closer to taking over as High King. Once he has reached that stage, the mortal world will never be safe from him."

Lilian sensed Amras's earnestness, his pain when he spoke of her mother, and knew without having to use telepathy, this was sheer honesty, spoken from the heart. Still, he could have faked it and she wasn't going to take it on blind faith.

"He convinced her your life was in danger. He used his abilities to drive her insane, made her afraid of every shadow, every noise. He made her believe the Sidhe were evil, demons, and I would come for her, kill her, to take her child. My child. She took you and ran away. I tried to follow, to tell her she was safe, I loved her and you, that I would never harm the two of you, but Emma was too far-gone. Ulwe had fed upon her, played with her mind too much."

"Fed upon her?" Lilian asked, confused.

"The Sidhe are able to feed upon the emotions of those around us. It is a part of the Empathy ability. Have you not experienced it?"

"I'm not sure what you mean."

"When you go into an establishment where there is a group of people, the larger the better, and you feel their emotions so much that they become your emotions. If you went in and were feeling bad, soon you are feeling good. When you go in feeling good, you feel ecstatic. It is the same in the other direction. You become upset when others are upset, sad when others are sad. Yet, underneath it all, you feel more energized, more empowered."

Lilian wanted to deny it, but she couldn't. She knew he was speaking the truth. "You can feed from one person, feed from their energy, although to do this, it is dangerous for the provider. We do not condone the feeding from one person. Ulwe has always disagreed with this law and we suspected he might have been breaking the law, but it was not until I saw Emma when I caught up with her and you that I knew he had."

Lilian frowned. She only had vague recollections of the night he was talking about. Vague images, emotions.

"I lost track of her and you soon after. Until the night your stepfather had killed your surrogate mother I had not a clue as to where you might be, if you were even alive. Your fear and your pain called out to me across time and space, penetrated the Mists, and for a brief moment, I was able to help you."

Lilian gasped and her hand tightened on Matthias's.

"I didn't kill him?" she whispered.

"No, daughter. You were but the instrument of his destruction. I killed him. I wielded the instrument, in order to protect you. Still, even after that brief time, I could not find you again. By the time I arrived, you were gone and it took all these years until we could connect once more, through your dreams."

Lilian wanted to sit down. "You're my father?"

He smiled and when he did, she could feel the rightness to it, the connection. Seeing him, in person, this close, outside of her dreams, she could feel his presence and she knew, *knew* he was telling the truth. He *was* her father. She released Matthias's hand and threw herself into Amras's arms, crying. Amras held her, murmuring in a gentle tone to her in his language. Their language, and while she could not understand the words, she was aware of the meaning behind them, the caring.

She had found a connection to someone who was family, connected by blood, and a piece of her life returned to her. She cried for the loss of her relationship with Amras, cried for the loss of her mother, and cried in relief that she had a family, a past.

"Shh, daughter. You will make yourself ill with these tears. Do not cry for things lost. They are in the past now. Be happy we have found one another."

Lilian sobbed, nodded, and tried to step back and wipe her face. Matthias stepped forward and swept her into his arms.

"Let's go inside and sit down. We can talk some more in private." Matthias tilted her chin up and leaned down to kiss her with a gentle brush of his lips. "Take him to your room. You have a sitting area. I'll bring some food and drink."

Lilian gazed up at Matthias and saw he worried about her. She gave him a soft smile.

"I'll be all right," she whispered. "Thank you."

He leaned down and kissed her lips. It wasn't a gentle kiss like before, but neither was it possessive or aggressive.

It was a promise.

Chapter 7

When Matthias walked into her room bearing a tray of food and drink, Lilian almost didn't notice him. Granted, he could have been butt-naked and she probably wouldn't have noticed as she was so caught up with Amras.

Wait, no, I'd notice that.

She glanced at him just to be sure he was clothed before she returned her attention to her father.

Lilian sat across from him, the table between them, which left only a couple of feet separation. Their eyes were locked on one another, and both were silent.

They were sharing their memories via telepathy and empathy, an easier way to catch up about their lives than talking. Amras held the link, though she had tried to at first, but he had argued he should do the work not to exhaust her any more than she already was. She had to give in to his logic.

Matthias brought a chair over and sat close to her. He took her hand in his and caressed it with a gentle touch, which caused her to automatically reach out with a mental link and connect him to the telepathic conversation.

"He won't be able to keep up," Amras thought.

"He'll do just fine," she replied.

They could both feel Matthias's sense of wonderment and awe at how fast the two of them were communicating. Images and thoughts, memories and snippets of conversations were flying back and forth between them so fast Matthias had no hope of keeping up. Still he tried, and she smiled at his persistence.

"You are meant for better things."

Lilian startled. Amras sent his message along a different sort of path, one which did not include Matthias's participation.

"You are the daughter of a king. You are not meant for the Lupine."

She frowned at her father. "*I wasn't the daughter of a king when I met him, when he saved my life, when he was there when I needed someone to lean on.*"

"*That was then. I am here now.*"

Lilian shook her head, her lips pressed together. "*I don't care. I like him. He's fun to be around and he makes me feel...*"

"*Lust.*" Amras dismissed her words.

She surged upward to stand, startling Matthias.

"Enough. Just because we share genetic material doesn't mean you have the right to tell me who I can see or associate with!"

Amras just lifted a brow. Matthias frowned as he glanced between the two of them.

Seeing Amras's reaction infuriated her even more. Lilian stood, tense and furious at her father. As her anger grew, the air around her began to glow a bluish color, which shifted to a deep red. She lifted her hands up and shoved the air in front of her toward Amras.

Her father's chair went skittering back, and tipped over, but by that time, Amras had gained his feet, grinning.

"Is that all you have, daughter?"

Matthias started to speak, but Amras waved a hand in his direction and Matthias went sliding backward. Lilian saw red. She retaliated. Without thinking of her actions or the consequences, she gathered some of the energy from the red aura around her and formed it into attacks, volleying them at her father. Not only did she use the energy from around her, she also attacked mentally, and with dagger-like thoughts, tried to find the part of his mind in which to weaken him. She slashed at his mental shields again and again, as the physical attacks continued.

Amras held her mental attacks at bay.

Lilian could feel Matthias's confusion and his rage when he realized Amras was the instigator of her fury. She knew he would try to protect her from Amras.

Before she could stop him, Matthias had shifted to his battle form and launched himself at her father. It definitely wasn't like in the movies, where the werewolf writhed in pain as bones broke and skin tore to accommodate the monster's form. No, it had been a seamless change. Matthias seemed to melt into mist and reformed into his battle form.

Amras's grin faded, when he spotted the eight-foot monster flying at him, with teeth bared in a fierce snarl. She knew Matthias was in a battle rage. She could feel, and see, the red haze of his mind and knew he'd kill

Amras without hesitation unless she did something to stop him. So, she threw herself into his path.

Not the brightest of ideas I've had.

When they collided, it was as though a truck had hit her. However, Matthias had the presence of mind to realize she was in his way. He wrapped his arms around her and twisted his body so when they hit the table and the tile floor on the way down, his body cushioned hers, taking the brunt of the damage. Once they were on the floor, he rolled over so she was beneath him, his arms still wrapped around her. His body shifted a bit so he wasn't putting his weight on her, but still shielding, protecting her. Matthias lifted his head and snarled at Amras, his ears pinned flat against his large skull.

Lilian reached up and ran her fingers through the thick, black fur covering his chest, making a physical connection as she used their mental link.

"Matthias. It's all right. He won't hurt me." Amras had provoked her for a reason, but he hadn't hurt her.

The killing rage in Matthias seemed to ease a bit, but the beast was still in control, still possessive and protective of her.

"It's all right, I'm not hurt. He's my father. It's okay."

She kept her tone soft and soothing, as she pet him, allowed him to experience the pleasure she savored when she touched him.

The red haze of his mind began to dissipate. Yet, all the while, he kept his golden eyes on Amras, watching him. Amras, to his credit, kept still and just waited, watched.

"Matthias," she said aloud.

Matthias's ears flicked up, flattened again, and lifted from his head once more. He tilted his head and looked down at her.

"It's okay."

He lowered his head, nuzzled against her arm and sniffed at her chest and neck. The rage in his mind lessened more, releasing him.

Concern for her filled his mind. She could tell anger still possessed him, but it wasn't an all-encompassing rage as before.

"I'm fine."

Amras must have moved because Matthias's body tensed and he snapped his head up to glare at him. Before she could say anything, Matthias gathered himself and stood, picking her up as well. She found herself situated in his large arms, his movements slow and careful. She knew he wouldn't hurt her deliberately. It was in his mind and in the way he handled her, in the way he kept his claws from touching her skin.

"I think I will retire," Amras said.

"You can use this room," she offered, keeping her eyes on Matthias.

"I must return through the Mists, but I will return. I will send a warning ahead."

Lilian nodded. "All right. Good night, Father."

When Amras had gone, Matthias relaxed and looked down at her. He carried her to the bed, shifting back to human form as he did so.

He was still angry, she realized. His body remained tense, his mind a bit hazy.

"Not angry," he said aloud, although his tone was tight and growling.

Lilian lifted a brow.

"Not angry," he repeated.

"Intense then."

"Yes."

"Why?"

He laid her on the bed. She started to ease back but froze when he growled in warning. "Don't move."

Her heart raced and she couldn't help but breathe harder. His eyes were melting her; the way they seemed to burn her with their heat. His hands came up and undid the pins holding the *peplos* closed at the shoulders. Her eyes widened.

"Matthias?" Her voice shook.

"Shh," he said.

She hushed.

His roughened fingers brushed against the sensitive skin of her collarbone as he removed the golden pins. He lowered his head and, with infinite care and gentleness, kissed her lips, light brushes as though testing his welcome. She lifted her hands up to his face, but he captured her wrists and pushed her hands down onto the bed, on either side of her head, holding her in place. Her lips parted in a soft gasp and he deepened the kiss, his tongue moving against her lips and into her mouth.

Breathless, hot, and restless, she twisted her wrists in his hold, just a little as her body moved on the bed with a growing yearning.

He tasted like wine and wildness, something exotic and untamed and she moaned.

Matthias pulled away from her mouth and plied kisses along her jaw, her neck, to her left collarbone. He scraped his teeth against the sensitive skin and she whimpered and shivered. He released her wrists and traced his hand down her arms to the top of the *peplos*, where he began to drag it down, oh so slowly revealing more of her skin to his golden gaze.

As the material moved over her skin, it was a sensual torture; it tickled and caressed. His lips were hot as he traced the path the garment took and his breath made goose bumps rise up on her skin as it cooled the damp trail his lips left.

She arched up from the bed with a soft cry as he took one of her pebbled nipples into his mouth and suckled it, his tongue flicking against the tip. Her gut clenched and her nether region throbbed in response. His hand caressed her other breast, palming it, and she threw back her head in pleasure. He took the opportunity to lower the *peplos* further, and pulled the garment from her body, leaving her naked except for her cream colored panties. Air currents made by his movements caressed her skin and it only added to the erotic experience.

Matthias switched to her other breast and paid homage there before he began to trail damp kisses along her skin, moving downward. The muscles of her stomach jumped and twitched beneath his lips and she couldn't help but to move on the bed, unable to lie still beneath his roving kisses.

When he played around her belly button, she giggled at the ticklish sensation. She felt his lips tilt up into a smile as his tongue dipped into the well before he moved further downwards. His fingers glided against the skin just above the waistband of her panties and she froze.

"Shh," he whispered as he slid her panties down.

"Matthias," she started to protest.

Lilian yearned for him, even as naked as she was. He removed her panties and dropped them over the side of the bed, lifting his head to look at her, splayed before him. She shivered in reaction; the sensations were far beyond what she had ever experienced before, and it made her ache and whimper.

With incredible gentleness, he touched her sex. A finger caressed over her nether lips, wet with the fluids of her arousal, and she jumped from the sensation. His fingers drifted over her clit, causing her to moan and Matthias rumbled his approval. He caressed her clit, rubbing and tickling it with his fingertip. She whimpered and writhed beneath him.

"That's it, baby," he murmured against her stomach, tilting his head a bit in order to watch her expressions play across her face.

Desire rose in her when Matthias looked at her with such hunger in his eyes. He lowered his head, his tongue replacing his finger.

Lilian's legs tried to close in shock, but his body kept her from doing so. No one ever told her how intense oral sex could be.

His tongue flicked against her clit and she cried out. Her body jerked, and her hands clenched the blanket beneath her. He grasped her thighs and opened her legs wider.

She was close, her breathing was ragged and quick, her legs trembled, and the tension building inside of her, like a predator about to pounce.

His tongue moved down to her opening, his thumb coming to rub her clit. A couple more moments and she cried out, her body coming up off the bed in a tight arch. Matthias pressed his mouth to her sex, lapped up her juices, his tongue delving inside of her for more, rumbling and growling with pleasure and hunger.

When she finally collapsed back onto the bed, panting and trembling, he lifted his head and tore at his own clothes, tossing them aside.

It wasn't until his body settled over hers, feeling his heat, the muscles and the hardness of his toned form, she roused enough to open her eyes. His eyes were intense, watching her as one hand reached between them to hold his arousal steady as he placed himself at her opening. She stared up at him, feeling his hunger, causing hers to come alive again. She shifted her body, rubbing against him.

Was it an invitation? Had she done it without conscious thought for more, or had it been her nervousness? She didn't know, and didn't care once he started to press into her, entering her with care.

Her eyes widened in shock, feeling his entrance as a seductive invasion. When Matthias reached her hymen, he leaned down to kiss her, a hungry and demanding kiss, and only when she pressed her hips up toward him did he push through the last barrier of her innocence, taking her and making her his. He was filling her, stretching her, creating sensations she had never imagined could exist.

Lilian's active life ensured the breaching wasn't as painful as it could have been, a mere pinch, a soft gasp, and it was over, but the resulting sensation of the act amazed and astounded her. As Matthias pressed all the way inside of her, he moaned. Even his moan was sensual to her, as she was the cause. She wanted to remember this for all time, every moment of this experience! She moved a bit beneath him and a sense of needing more consumed her.

Bracing his hands on either side of her head, he began to withdraw, and then thrust back inside of her. She whimpered and writhed in reaction, and soon, she moved in time with him, their bodies meeting one another. He leaned down to kiss her jaw, her neck, nipping the sensitive curve there, and along her collarbone.

Her body reacted to the sensations of him inside of her. The strength of his thrusts, the hardness of his arousal, the heat of his body moving above hers, drove her to the edge. Her nostrils flared as she took a deep breath, taking in their scents, their combined arousal and passion. Her body tightened as it journeyed closer to orgasm and he growled.

She moved with increasing need and he bit down on her collarbone, hard enough to sting, to keep her in place, but not to break skin.

Lilian screamed as her orgasm ripped through her. Matthias followed her, and his roar, somewhat muffled by the bite he had on her, was still loud and filled with satisfaction and pleasure.

She lay there, trembling and panting, her mind going a million miles per hour even though her body worn and exhausted by everything. Matthias lay on top of her, although he still braced himself not to crush her.

"*Ever thoughtful and protective,*" she thought with a smile.

"*I am.*"

It startled her, hearing his voice in her head. She tried to withdraw the mental connection, but became even more surprised and confused to learn this connection wasn't done through her telepathy.

"Matthias?"

He slid to one side, bracing his head on a palm, his elbow holding him up as he looked down on her.

"Hmm?" he asked.

His eyes roamed over her exposed body and she blushed.

"Stop it. How is it you can communicate telepathically?"

He grinned and reached out with his free hand to caress her stomach. "Mating."

Lilian's breath caught in a soft gasp at the awakening sensations he caused. "So how many other women can you communicate telepathically with?"

Matthias's eyes widened. "What?"

"You couldn't have been a virgin, so there must have been others," she said.

His hand roamed down toward her sex and she shivered.

"True, I've been with others, but I've never spent myself in them."

Lilian wiggled a little. "I don't understand."

Of course, he wasn't helping her by reawakening desire in her body.

"The mating is caused by spilling my seed inside of you."

His fingers played along her sex, and she moaned. Her hips lifted up to his fingers, wanting more.

"What does it mean?" Her words spoken soft and breathless.

He leaned down to kiss her, but she turned her head away.

"No. Stop trying to distract me and explain what's going on."

He nibbled along her collarbone instead.

"We're a mated couple now. We share the ability to communicate with one another telepathically, much like your ability with others."

Lilian tensed, anger building within her. "Oh, really? And at any moment did you ever, oh, I don't know, stop to think whether or not I *wanted* this?"

He lifted his head to look at her. "You dreamt it."

"I did not!"

"Yes, you did, when you dreamt of the two of us together running as wolves."

Lilian pushed him back and struggled to sit up. "That was a dream, Matthias! You can't just make decisions which affect my life without consulting me!"

"No, it wasn't just a dream. I've known almost from the time I met you."

Lilian punched him in the shoulder. "Move!"

He winced and moved back. She sat up and pulled a sheet over her to cover her nakedness.

"You're so arrogant, you can't see what you did wrong, can you? You made the decision to tie my life with yours without even asking me if it's what I wanted. What makes you any better than Stephan?"

Matthias growled. "I would never hurt you, let alone raise a hand to strike you."

"No, but you're trying to control my life and that makes you just as bad. Is there a way to end it? A divorce?"

"No."

Lilian lifted a brow at his succinct answer.

"No, as in there's not, or no, as in you're not going to tell me?"

At least he had the decency to look a little shamed.

"Hmm. So there is and you aren't going to tell me."

Matthias used his body to push her back down onto the bed so she was beneath him once more. His eyes almost glowed with his anger and possessiveness. Touching his mind, she could tell he didn't want to even consider the idea of them parting ways. She didn't understand the possessiveness in him. They didn't know one another very well, and yet he was so sure they were fated to be together. She hadn't even considered the possibility of being with anyone, not with the *Custodes Secreti* after her.

He kissed her with his pent-up anger, pain, and fear of her leaving him. Feeling his emotions, she wondered how she *could* leave him now. So, she kissed him back as she wrapped her arms around his neck, holding him close.

"*We'll discuss this later.*"

"*Later,*" he repeated.

* * * *

Lilian was sitting outside with Helena, enjoying tea and conversation when Matthias woke.

"*Lilian? Where are you?*" He sounded vexed.

"*Outside, sleepyhead.*" She was amused by his tone.

"*I'd rather wake up with you beside me.*"

"*Yeah, not going to happen if you're such a lazy butt.*"

"*Lazy? Did you just call me lazy after last night and this morning's marathon of sex?*"

"*Stop beating your chest. I need to go to work so hurry up and drive me into town.*"

"*I'm not sure I can drive you into town, being lazy and all.*"

"*You're such a baby. I'll ask Tiberius then.*"

She heard his laughter in her mind. "*Where are you, mate?*"

"*I'm with your mother, telling her all the bad things you did to me.*"

"*Be sure to include that you begged for more and moaned with pleasure while doing so.*"

Lilian choked on the sip of tea she'd just taken and coughed to clear her windpipe. Helena patted her on the back with some bemusement and alarm.

"Are you all right?" Helena asked.

Lilian nodded and used a napkin to wipe her mouth. When she could speak, she replied, "Yes, thank you. Your son."

Helena smiled. "Ahh. I can just imagine."

Lilian shook her head. "Are they all like that?"

"Arrogant and yet like little boys? Yes. Every one of them. It's the Roman and Lupine genetics, I'm afraid."

Matthias rounded the corner and just catching sight of him took her breath away. She watched how he moved, how he smiled when he saw her, and her insides melted.

Helena leaned in to whisper to her. "You're glowing."

Lilian blushed and tore her eyes away from Matthias to sip her tea, and to catch her breath. Helena chuckled.

"Mother," Matthias said in greeting.

Helena nodded to him. "Matthias." She gave him a hard look.

He lifted a brow. "What?"

"You better not let this one slip away," Helena said.

Lilian wondered if it was possible for someone to die of embarrassment. *"What did you tell my mother?"*

"Nothing!"

"Hmm."

"Thank you for the tea, Helena. I need to go to work now." She looked at Matthias. "The truck, not the motorcycle."

He grinned. "She's afraid of the motorcycle."

Helena smiled at her. "I'm not all that keen on it myself, but I'm his mother. It's my job to worry."

Matthias helped Lilian stand after she had put her teacup down.

"Go ahead and I'll be right there," she told Matthias.

Matthias nodded and headed off to get the truck. She turned and looked at Helena.

"The little girl? Is she all right?" she asked.

"The one you healed? Yes, perfectly fine. Her mother will wish to speak with you, to thank you."

Lilian shook her head. "No need. I didn't do it for the gratitude. It was something I had to do."

Helena smiled. "All right."

Lilian turned, and headed off to the parking area. As she rounded the corner, she was shoved from the side. It was only due to her training she managed to stay on her feet and not go sprawling into the dirt. She turned to face her attacker.

Anoria.

Lilian rolled her eyes and blocked Matthias from her thoughts. "What do you want, Anoria?"

"Don't even speak my name," Anoria snarled. "You're nothing more than a *human*, a whore. Do you really think you'll keep him?"

Lilian lifted a brow. "Just because you didn't doesn't mean I won't."

Anoria's eyes darkened in her rage. "I'll kill you!" She launched herself at Lilian.

Anger and aggression kicked in and she dropped into a defensive posture. She was sick of this, and she sure as hell wasn't going to stand here and take it from this bitch.

When Anoria closed in on her, she ducked her body low, and used her legs to thrust her body upward, throwing Anoria up and over her. The woman hit the ground, landing on her back, and shrieked with rage.

Anoria surged to her feet as she took a swipe at Lilian's face, her fingers curled like claws, her nails looking as sharp and dangerous as talons. Lilian lifted her right hand and shoved it, palm out, toward Anoria, throwing her back a few feet. Followed by a thrust of her left palm, which a blast of swirling blue and red energy ball shot out, hitting Anoria and blasting her backward a bit further.

By this time, the noises had drawn a crowd, but they stayed back to watch, curious whether or not the "human" would be able to defend herself against a Lupine. Money changed hands as well, Lilian noticed with wry amusement.

Anoria came at her yet again, this time shifting to her war form as she did so. Not quite as tall or bulky as Matthias's form. Anoria was light colored whereas Matthias was black.

Lilian wasn't used to fighting this form. She hadn't wanted to hurt Anoria, only wanted to protect herself and perhaps teach Anoria she wasn't going to be pushed around, but the rules had changed.

Lilian waved her right hand, palm outwards, from left to right, as though sweeping the air with her hand. Anoria charged at her again, hitting the invisible shield, and it crackled with blue light. Anoria snarled with teeth bared. She tried to use her claws to shred the shield and Lilian knew it was only a matter of time before the shield would fail. She had to stop this!

She raised her left hand, drew it back, and at the same time she dropped the shield, and used her telekinesis as a weapon. She punched the air toward Anoria and hit her square in the mouth with enough force to have broken a few teeth.

Anoria gave a loud bellow of pain and rage and she took the moment to gather some of the energy around her for the next round. However, just as Anoria gathered herself for the next attack, a large, black creature tackled Anoria and drove her down to the dirt.

Before Lilian could catch her breath, Tiberius was at her side, trying to draw her away. She took an instinctive, defensive stance and almost sent him flying before she realized his identity. She gave him a weak, apologetic smile.

"Come on, you need to move away."

"No way," she said.

Tiberius lifted a brow at her, but said nothing else, nor did he try to force her.

The battle between Anoria and Matthias was rather short. He managed to get a grip of her throat and clamp down on it with his teeth. With a shake of his head, he growled aloud in warning, and waited.

Anoria went slack, giving a soft whine of submission. Matthias snarled and released her. He lumbered to his feet and swept the gathered crowd with glaring eyes. They all lowered their heads in submission and he turned toward her.

Lilian's heart raced. Seeing this beast, this creature, as he approached her, fierce and primal, both frightened and excited her at the same time. Before Tiberius could stop her, she burst into a run toward Matthias and threw herself at him, ignoring the gasps from around her.

"*Matthias!*"

Matthias caught her and held her with care, keeping his claws from scoring her skin. He leaned in with his great head and sniffed at her.

"*Are you all right?*" He checked her over as he asked.

"I'm fine," she replied, and touched his muzzle with her fingertips.

He drew her close to his body and shifted back to his human form. Before she could speak, he kissed her, hard and passionately. She had no time to respond; he broke the kiss to look at the gathered crowd.

"Lilian is my mate."

There were soft gasps, and she saw some money changing hands again.

"I expect her to be treated in a manner befitting her station," he continued, as he glared at Anoria.

Anoria said nothing, just lowered her head. He turned and carried Lilian toward the truck, Tiberius on their heels.

She could tell Matthias was still seething inside. She didn't need her telepathic connection with her mate to know. Her empathy picked it up just fine.

"I'm okay," she said. "No harm done."

He set her down beside the truck and exploded.

"What do you mean 'no harm done'? She could have killed you! Do not ever block your mental connection with me. How am I suppose to know if you're dead or alive if I you've blocked me out?"

Lilian blinked at the onslaught of his words, and lifted a brow.

"Just because I've been easy on you, doesn't mean I don't have the means to protect myself, Matthias. I was trained to be a soldier, if you remember."

"Little good it did you with those agents," Matthias sniped.

Lilian gasped. "I can't believe you said that! You're an ass, you know that? I already told you I'd been hiding my abilities, trying not to use them. You and your gang showed up and I wasn't about to put on a show!"

Tiberius got into the driver's seat of the truck, saying nothing, but she was sure he listened in.

"Hmm. Get in the truck, since you're bound and determined to put yourself in danger by going to work."

Lilian bristled. "Well, excuse me. Not everyone can live in a recreated Roman palace and have servants at their beck and call, you arrogant bastard!" She fumed as she spun around and opened the door to the truck.

Matthias grabbed her, spun her back around, and pressed his body against hers, so she was trapped between him and the truck. He kissed her. Hard. Demanding.

As his lips pressed against hers, she realized he had been worried about her, afraid for her, and the bickering had been nothing more than a verbal outlet for his fear.

Truth be told, she rather liked it. She wrapped her arms around his neck and tilted her head for him, kissing him back. He growled and pulled her into him, holding her against him.

"You two going to get in soon or you gonna suck face all day?" Tiberius asked.

Matthias groaned as he broke the kiss. "Tell me again why you're my Beta?"

Lilian laughed, albeit a bit out of breath, and pushed at Matthias. "I have to work, Matthias. Plus, I need to talk to the police."

Matthias let her go and she smiled at his reluctance. They climbed into the truck and were on their way.

* * * *

"Thank goodness you're here!" Maria exclaimed as Lilian entered the diner. "Peggy didn't show up for her shift and we're shorthanded."

Lilian frowned as she grabbed an apron. "That's not like Peggy. Has anyone called her apartment?"

"Yeah, no answer."

Lilian tied the apron around her waist. "*Matthias? Could you go by an apartment and see if Peggy is all right? She waited on us the night my house was vandalized.*"

She sent him the address and reminded him what Peggy looked like.

"*Got it.*"

Lilian smiled and picked up an order pad.

"So, how's that man of yours?" Maria asked.

Lilian blushed. "Good. He's good. We're good."

Maria grinned. "Hmm. Oh! Something was delivered for you. I left it in the office."

Lilian frowned. "When was it delivered?"

"Yesterday, I think. It was left at the back door and I brought it in when I opened. No return address or name. Think you got a secret admirer?"

"If I did, why wait until I'm seeing someone before making themselves known?" she asked, although she mused more to herself than to Maria.

Maria shrugged and went back to cooking. "If it's flowers, they're probably wilted."

Lilian smiled at her and headed off to the office to see what the delivery was.

The office wasn't used much, more of a storage room than anything. It had a small desk, a chair, and shelves which held odds and ends, spare aprons, cookbooks, and the like. Maria used the office to do closing bookwork on occasion, but more often than not, she'd just do it all in the kitchen after everything had been cleaned up.

A white box tied with red ribbon sat on the desk, about the size of a standard shoebox. A card had been tucked into the ribbon, and her first name written on it, nothing else.

Lilian had a sudden sense of foreboding and something told her not to touch the box. Was it from Stephan? What was in it? With shaking hands, she untied the ribbon and set it aside. She removed the lid. White tissue paper covered the contents and she moved it aside to find a small teddy bear staring up at her. She smiled at first and picked it up. It wasn't the teddy bear, however, which caused her to scream. Blood soaked bandages and what looked to be a human tongue and eyeballs were nestled in bandages, hidden beneath the teddy bear.

"*Lilian!*" Matthias called to her.

Maria burst into the office, a large knife in hand, ready to do battle. She wasn't sure which sight was more horrifying, the "presents" or Maria brandishing a butcher knife. It shut her up though.

Maria took one look at her, looked at the box, paled, grabbed her and pulled her out of the office. She released her to shut the door, and herded her into the kitchen.

"Sit down. I'll call the police."

Lilian sat down, trying to keep the nausea from winning.

"*Lilian, what's happened?*" She could hear and feel Matthias's worry.

"*I'm fine, I just...someone left something for me.*"

"*What aren't you telling me?*"

Lilian clenched her eyes closed, not wanting to think about it.

"*Lilian, stay with me.*"

"*It's horrible!*" She shuddered.

Maria was on the phone with the police. She could hear the urgency in her friend's voice, but the words sounded muffled, from a distance.

"*Just breathe, baby. I'm on my way.*"

Maria hung up the phone. "The police are on their way. They said not to touch anything until they get here."

Lilian nodded.

"What's going on, Lil?" Maria whispered.

Lilian opened her eyes and looked at her friend.

"Your house was burned down, now this?" Maria continued.

"Maria, I…" she started, but stopped.

How much should she tell her? How much should she keep secret to protect her?

"I have a stalker," she said.

Maria lifted her brows. "A stalker."

Lilian nodded a bit. "An ex-boyfriend. I ran away from him after I got tired of getting beat up."

"And this is all from your stalker ex-boyfriend?"

She nodded again. "He's psychotic. I don't know how but he's managed to track me down here."

"Then your name really isn't Lilian?" Maria asked.

"It is. My last name isn't Quinn though."

Maria turned away and checked on the steak she was cooking on the kitchen's indoor grill.

Lilian knew she should say more, apologize or reassure her somehow, but no words came to mind. She was spared by the arrival of the police.

She stepped outside to answer some questions while a couple of officers questioned Maria in the kitchen.

What had she been doing before she received the present? Who else might have touched it before her? Did she think it was tied to the arson?

Stupid, stupid questions!

She just wanted to get away, to forget the horrifying sight, but the questions were never ending. She stared at the officer in exasperation.

"*Don't do anything.*" Matthias, the voice of reason.

Lilian took a slow, deep breath to calm herself.

Maria mentioned Peggy being missing. An officer was dispatched to Peggy's apartment, but Lilian knew they wouldn't find her there.

She leaned against the wall of the diner as the officers made notes and moved into the kitchen. Crime scene technicians had arrived and inspected the gruesome present. CSIs were taking prints and other forms of evidence. She had a few minutes to herself to try to just breathe.

A curious, keen, intense sensation oozed into her mind, insidious in its method, slick like oil. She at once slammed down her mental blocks, to keep the intruder from going any further. Whoever it was, was good. The single intrusion branched off into multiple tendrils, each going in different directions, and all trying to breach her mental barriers.

As she concentrated on trapping and destroying the intruder or intruders, she missed the approach of two men.

"There she is," a pale, pasty man said, his voice thick with disdain.

A dark-skinned man smirked and looked down at her. She knew he was the intruder in her mind, trying to gain control.

These were Knights. The agents had failed and *Custodes Secreti* had sent the big guns. So, she struck first, and hard.

Using what little energy she could gather, Lilian attacked the dark man as she bolted for the back door. It was enough to knock his concentration off and his tendrils left her mind.

Mr. Pasty, however, was still a threat. He darted into her path, blocking her from the diner's door. She jerked aside as not to run into him or allow him to get his hands on her.

Mr. Dark had his own tricks. He assailed her mind with what felt like a sword, slicing through the barriers. She cried out from the pain, but would not, could not allow it to distract her. Mr. Pasty came up hard and fast and she spun and jumped, using a roundhouse kick to catch him in the side of the head. Her balance was a little off, her concentration divided, and she fell to her knees when she came down. Mr. Pasty was pissed when he hit the ground and spat curses as he scrambled to his feet.

Lilian was on her feet just as quick. Their anger and hatred was a palpable sensation and she pulled the energy into her, feeding on it, using it to fuel her as she fought them.

"*I'm almost there, baby! Hold on!*" Matthias was near frantic in his need to protect her.

"*I'm capable of fighting my own battles, you know.*"

Mr. Dark came at her then and she blocked everything out of her mind other than her two attackers. He tried to throw a telekinetic punch at her, but she used an energy shield to block it by waving her right hand across the air in front of her. Still, the blow had been hard enough to knock her back a few steps.

Before she could decide her next course of action, Mr. Pasty yelled in pain and both Lilian and Mr. Dark turned to look. Mr. Pasty had a short arrow sticking out of his upper shoulder blade. He dropped to the ground, writhing as he tried to reach for it. When Mr. Dark turned to look for the shooter, she took the moment to attack, firing off a volley of energy bolts at him. With each hit, Mr. Dark wobbled back, but before he could retaliate, a large bird came diving out of nowhere and raked his face with razor sharp talons.

Mr. Dark shrieked with pain, echoed by the bird, a hawk, with its *kee-eeeee-arr* sounding scream.

Mr. Dark managed to knock the bird away and to the ground, his bleeding face marked by gouges caused by the hawk's talons. She was nauseated at seeing the blood, but she put herself between the downed bird and Mr. Dark, sending another volley of attacks his way.

Mr. Pasty got to his feet, favoring his wounded arm, the arrow still protruding from his shoulder blade. When he took off running, Mr. Dark gave her a glare and ran after his partner.

Lilian was weak. The world rocked on its axis, but immediately someone grabbed and held her steady.

"Easy," she heard a masculine voice say.

"*Don't let him take you anywhere!*"

She turned her head to look at her rescuer.

"They were shielding the diner in case you screamed. They didn't want the police to come out. If you cried out now, they'd hear you."

The man was gorgeous. His eyes were dark yet intense, his hair a reddish brown. He looked familiar, but she couldn't place him.

"Your mate will be here in a few moments," he said, smiling.

"Who are you?"

Before he could answer, the screeching of tires could be heard and he released her. With a slight bow, he turned and darted off into the woods, away from the parking lot. She watched him until he was out of sight. She turned to see Matthias jumping out of the moving truck before Tiberius could apply the brakes, to race toward her.

The moment he touched her, she sent everything that had happened into his mind, smiled, and let the soothing arms of unconsciousness take her.

Chapter 8

Well, at least I'm not in the forest again, she thought as she found herself in a bed.

Not just any bed. No, this bed was a scrumptious thing, with an explosion of colored sheets, and contrasting colored, silk covers. Above her head a canopy of material so sheer it looked very much like gauze, yet shimmered like silk. The drapery which surrounded the bed was also the same.

Lilian sat up and checked to make sure she was wearing clothes, and noticed it wasn't what she'd been wearing before. Now, she wore a chemise-like gown, sheer, but not as sheer as the drapery, thank goodness. It was white with silver embroidery along the hem and neckline.

The door opened and she started. Her father walked into the room, smiling.

"Sleep well?"

"I'm still sleeping, so I suppose I am."

Amras chuckled, swept back a side of the drapery, and tied it into place on one of the corner poles.

"I thought perhaps you might like this rather than the usual forest scene."

"Very much, thank you."

He climbed onto the bed and leaned back against the footboard. He stretched his legs out in front of him and watched her.

"What happened?" he asked her.

Lilian sat up and arranged the covers. "What didn't happen? I got jumped by one of Matthias's kind, found a present left for me that contained a tongue and eyeballs, and then I was attacked by the Knights, but saved by a hawk man thing."

Amras sat up straighter, frowning. "What?"

"Which part?"

"The hawk man thing part."

Lilian sighed and brushed his mind with her own, a way of asking permission to enter. If he refused, he would block her entrance. He allowed her in. She flooded his mind with the memory of being attacked at the diner and how aid came in the form of the hawk that had turned into a man.

Amras looked stunned and leaned back.

"What is it?" she asked, worried.

"You felt him to be familiar?"

Lilian nodded. "I couldn't place him and I don't remember ever having met him, but he seemed familiar to me."

"If it is who I think it might be, you are indeed either very lucky or are in more trouble than we previous thought," Amras replied.

Lilian lifted her brows. "What?"

"Let me tell you a story. It is an old story, a legend passed down from parent to child."

Lilian relaxed and listened.

"In the old days, there was but one Court, ruled by one king. The High King. In this way, many of the lords bickered over borderlands and squabbled over power. The High King did nothing to stop them. He believed if the lords were too busy with one another, there'd be no worries of trying to take the crown from him.

"The High King, in his arrogance, did not take into consideration the three sons he had sired. Altis, Talis, and Ionu."

Amras told the story in such a way that if she closed her eyes, she'd be able to see it in her mind.

"These three wished to inherit the throne and become High King, but they knew only one of them could, and so Altis and Ionu began to plot against their own brothers. Talis did not. He chose to study, to speak with the people and learn from them. However, the High King's health quickly faded and the High King knew he had to decide on a course of action. As the days passed, he weakened until finally he told his sons they must fulfill a quest. The one who found the answer to the quest would inherit the throne.

"So, the High King gave each of the princes a purse of gold, a swift horse, a sharp sword, and sent them off with a riddle."

Lilian nodded. Her eyes wide on her father as he told the story, enthralled. "What was the quest?"

Amras smiled. "The High King told his sons to go and use the money to buy what they could to fill a chamber, but they had only seven days to do so."

Lilian frowned. "A chamber? What kind of chamber?"

"A room, much like this."

"Oh."

"So the three princes went in different directions to seek out what could be bought to fill the room.

"Altis was the eldest and thought himself the brightest. More skilled with sword and warfare, he used his money to purchase soldiers, mercenaries, and from there, he pillaged villages for their wealth. This, he took back home to present to his father.

"Ionu, the second son, was not as skilled in warfare, but in herbs and medicines. He went abroad, came across a medicine man, and purchased his wares. He would fill the room with health, and so he, too, returned to his father.

"Talis was the third son. He was skilled in the sword, but not as well as Altis. He was knowledgeable in herbs but not as much as Ionu. What Talis excelled in was strategy. So, after he had ridden out, he made camp in a cave he had come across. He watered and fed his horse, set aside his sword and gathered wood. He set the wood in a makeshift pit and used his flint and steel to start a fire. He sat back, enjoyed the heat and relaxed, knowing the light would drive off the predators which hunted in the night."

Lilian smiled. She had a feeling she knew where this was going, but let Amras tell his story.

"He stayed there for the time he was allotted, pondering the riddle. Then, on the morning of the sixth day, Talis broke camp and returned to his father with his answer. Along the way, he stopped and bought lanterns and candle tapers.

"Altis, being the eldest, presented his answer first. He told his father what he had done and presented the treasures, but while rich and plentiful, it did not fill the chamber. The High King accepted the offering and said nothing.

"Ionu was next and presented his answer, the gift of health with medicinal herbs for all those in the chamber. However, one of the High King's advisors began to sneeze and, of course, this negated Ionu's answer.

"Talis was last. He brought forth the lanterns and the candle tapers. He set the tapers into the lanterns and lit them.

"No one understood his answer. What did candle tapers have to do with the quest? When Talis ordered the drapes closed in the chamber, the answer became obvious.

"Talis had filled the room with the light, purchased from the money his father had given him.

"The High King, impressed with his youngest son, declared him the winner and the next High King. None too soon, for the High King died that evening."

"Sounds suspicious. Maybe he was poisoned by one of his sons."

Amras laughed and lifted a finger to his lips. "Shh. Talis realized he would never rule in peace, not with his two brothers vying for control of the crown, nor the lords still bickering over their borders. Therefore, he created a capitol and divided the kingdom into four parts. The northlands, Winter. The southlands, Summer. East became Spring, and West, Autumn. He chose a ruler for each and they were named after their kingdom. Once a year, they were to meet at the capitol to discuss issues, and the creation and dissolutions of laws. Talis kept himself High King and thus held control, but he was an impartial judge, fair but just."

The two pondered the story in silence for a few minutes before Amras spoke again.

"As you know, the Sidhe are able to shape shift into any form they wish."

Lilian frowned. No, she hadn't been aware of it. Amras lifted a brow at her reaction.

"You did not know?" he asked.

"No. I'd only seen you change into the white stag."

Amras nodded. "Each king has a specific form for their Court, but as Sidhe, we can adopt any form we wish."

"Is the white stag part of the Court or your own preference?"

"Both," he replied with a smile. "The white stag is the symbol for the Summer Court, but it has deeper meaning. In Celtic mythology, deer are magical creatures, able to move between the worlds, through the Mists. The stag stands for solitary nobility, honor and a strong commitment to the protection of the herd. It is a symbol of protection and sexuality and focus on the balance of law, rigid in their thinking on the issues of justice."

"What of the other courts?"

"The Winter Court is symbolized by the white bear, Spring Court is symbolized by the fox, and the Autumn Court is symbolized by the cat."

"And the High King?" she asked.

"The hawk."

Lilian blinked at her father. "The hawk? So the stranger might have been the High King?"

"Not necessarily. Remember, we are able to change our form to any shape we wish. It could have been he needed the hawk form to aid you."

Lilian shook her head. "No, I doubt it. This man was more than that. He was intense. Even in human form, he was intense. Like a hawk. Who is the High King now?"

Amras hesitated.

"What aren't you telling me?" Her eyes narrowed on him.

He gave her a weak smile. "Talis is the High King."

"Talis. As in the same Talis as the legend or one of his descendants?"

Again, he hesitated, but answered. "The same."

"Wait. How old is this legend?" she asked.

Amras smiled and slid from the bed. "Time to wake up."

"Oh, no, don't you dare!"

Lilian scrambled to try and stop him, but he grinned, winked and she found herself waking up in a familiar room, a familiar bed, and with Matthias staring down at her.

"I don't think I like my father very much right now," she announced.

Matthias smiled at her. "Why?"

Lilian sat up. "He was telling me a story, trying to explain something that might have come up, but when I tried to question him on it, he made me wake up."

Matthias frowned. "What came up?"

"The hawk man. Seems as though he just might be the High King."

He blinked. "The Sidhe High King?"

"Yes, but the Sidhe can take on any animal form they want, so his being a hawk might mean nothing."

"His scent was a little strange. Similar to your father's yet different."

"Since you're here," she changed the subject and glared at him. "You can plant your butt down and explain some things to me."

"I had other plans for being in bed with you," he said with a grin.

She pointed at the foot of the bed. "Sit down and start talking about the mating thing. I want to know exactly what it means, how it works, and what it takes to get out of it."

Matthias growled but he took a seat and leaned against the iron railing of the footboard. "I'm not going to tell you how to end our mating, but I will explain other things."

Lilian lifted a brow.

"As I told you before, a mating happens when the male shares his seed with the female. We're not entirely certain how it works, but it creates a bond between the couple. Likewise, a female Lupine can create a bond with a human male if the male spends himself into the female. There's been talk of certain chemical reactions which might cause it, we really do not know and we're not willing to find out either. The risk of our kind being discovered is too great and I will not allow my people to be cut apart in the name of science."

"So, what about biting someone else, like in the movies?"

"Doesn't work. We also don't eat human livers, we don't hunt humans on full moons, and holy water doesn't work on us. Silver, on the other hand, does. It's like an acid in the bloodstream, and if we can't shift through our forms to filter the poison, we'll die. Shifting through the forms also heals wounds, like the gunshot wound I had."

Her gaze dropped down to where the wound would have been and saw he was right. No wound, no scar, nothing.

"Had it of been silver, I would have scarred."

Lilian nodded, and then blinked when a question popped into her mind. "What happens to your clothes when you shift?"

He grinned. "Magic. Whatever we're wearing becomes, well, absorbed, I guess, when we shift. When we shift back, it's there again. We used to explain it as our clothes became our pelt, but even naked, we had a pelt when we shifted, so that explanation went away."

"It must be the same with the Sidhe, because my father was never naked after he shifted and even the hawk man had clothes."

Matthias nodded. "Perhaps. We are magickal creatures after all."

"And so, what does the mating mean? What powers does it give you over me?"

"None, actually. What it does is allow us to communicate together. I think, when it first began, it was meant so the males could better protect the females. At first, all the Lupine were males and so they mated with human females. In this way, the males could keep an eye on the females. We would know when there was trouble and how to protect them. Later, when offspring were produced, females were born. Some were able to shift, some not. Females who could shift were able to mate with humans and become bonded. Females who could not shift mated with Lupine shifters and bonded, but when they mated with human males, they could not bond."

"So it doesn't make them into a Lupine, mating with them?"

"No. You must be born a Lupine."

"You said you knew I was your mate because of my dream. How?"

"You ran with me as a mate in the dream."

"So based on a dream, you figured I'm your mate?" She watched as he tilted his head at her.

"And you did spill the iced tea and water over me."

Lilian blushed. "That was your fault."

He grinned. "It was a nice way of getting to meet you."

"We didn't meet though."

"Close enough."

They were interrupted by a knock at the door. Matthias growled and eased off the bed. The sound came again, though this time, it sounded more urgent. Matthias pulled the door open before the third set could finish out.

Lilian couldn't hear what was going on, or see who it was, but before she could use her mental connection with Matthias to get the information, he communicated with her.

"Baby, you better get dressed. The police are here."

Lilian frowned. *"Why are they here?"*

"They found your friend."

Lilian held her breath. She knew his next words weren't going to be pretty.

"Her body was found on your property."

* * * *

"I'm sorry to have to tell you," Ben started as she and Matthias, followed by Tiberius, approached, "Peggy's body was found on your property near the house."

Lilian gave a stiff nod as she came to a stop, still trying to wrap her mind around what was going on.

"It's believed the tongue and the eyes you received are hers."

Lilian whimpered before she could stop herself and Matthias pulled her into his arms. Tiberius stepped up to her other side and stood there, as if to protect her.

"Her family's been notified," Ben continued as he eyed the two men. "We have an APB on this Stephan guy. Stephan Cavanaugh, right?"

Lilian nodded and pushed back from Matthias enough to turn and face Ben. "Yes, Cavanaugh."

"We found some blood outside the diner. We're checking to see if it was Peggy's, but it looks too fresh to be hers."

Lilian frowned at Ben as his gaze moved over her, as if looking for something. "What is it?"

"We just wanted to make sure it didn't belong to you."

"No, not mine. Trust me, if it'd been mine, I'd be at a hospital. I'm very…" She hesitated, trying to find the right word. "I'm a baby when it comes to blood. Phobic."

Ben smiled at her. "Really? You?"

Matthias tensed, and she stepped into his arms, leaning back against him.

"*Knock it off,*" she thought to Matthias before replying to Ben, "Yeah, it's embarrassing," she said.

"*Stop flirting with him.*" Matthias's tone was matter of fact.

"*I am not flirting with him, you doof.*"

"*Yes, you are. Oh, and if it's my blood, you forget about your phobia.*"

Lilian paused, taken aback by what Matthias had said. Thinking back, she realized it was true.

"It's nothing to be ashamed of," Ben said. "We'll keep you up to date. Just be sure not to go anywhere alone, and if he tries to contact you again, call us right away."

Lilian blinked. "Oh, I will, Ben. Thank you."

Ben touched the brim of his hat and gave her a polite nod. With one last glance at the two men, he turned and headed back to his car.

Matthias waited for Ben to leave before he looked at Tiberius. "I want five of our best trackers on this Stephan. Start at the property and go from there."

Tiberius nodded, gave her a wink, and headed off.

* * * *

Some time later Lilian found herself wandering around the compound, enjoying the scenery. People greeted her with shy curiosity, but respectful of her status as the Alpha's mate. She wasn't sure she liked it and tried to make friends.

The children were much more receptive to her overtures, however, and she loved being with them. They were so playful and accepting of her. They invited her to play, they spoke without concern, and they jostled one another to hold her hands. She loved it.

"*Matthias? Are the children Lupine as well? Can they shift?*"

Lilian knew he was busy with his Alpha duties, meeting with the other Lupines to deal with pack issues, but he had told her to keep in contact with him, to check in often. Sometimes, she could just feel his mental touch and then it was gone, and she knew he was just making sure she was all right without disturbing her. She sort of liked it about him. Protective,

Isobael Liu

possessive, yet respectful of her independence and freedom. Well, most of the time anyway.

"*I caught that.*" He growled.

Lilian grinned.

"*No, shifting doesn't happen until their teens, after the onset of puberty.*"

"*Ouch. Hormones, angst, and shifting.*"

She heard his laughter in her mind and let him go back to his duties.

Just that brief moment of communication helped to ease some of her worry and sadness. Stephan's cruelty had always been a frightening thing, but she had never expected him to take it as far as murdering someone she knew. What about her other friends? What about Maria? Or the children here? They might be surrounded by Lupine family members, but as children, they were still vulnerable. What if her being here meant she was putting them into danger?

Receptive, as well as perceptive, the children stayed close to her, touching her arms and hands constantly. It was as though they tried to reassure her, comfort her in her sadness. She smiled a bit at them and returned their touches with hugs.

When the children suggested a game of Hide and Seek, and scattered with much laughter to hide, she assumed she was "it" as within seconds, she stood there, alone. She chuckled and closed her eyes to count.

At fifty, she opened her eyes and started to go search for the children. With twenty children to find and a large compound to search through, Lilian decided to cheat and opened up her senses. She sent out psychic feelers to pick out the children among the residences.

On the way to the nearest child, she picked up on a child's distress and stopped to try and pinpoint it. The emotions came from someone young and innocent. She turned and hurried in the direction the it came from. She hesitated on entering the woods, but when another wave of distress rolled over her, she pushed on, intent on finding the child.

Lilian knew it was a little girl who had become disoriented when she ran into the woods without thinking of the dangers, only to hide.

She pushed herself harder, jogging along the path, into the forest which bordered the backside of the compound. As Lilian went deeper into the forest, she soon found herself lost as well. She stopped for a bit to catch her breath and get her bearings.

Ten minutes later, there was no child in sight. Her psychic feelers could detect the girl though, picking up on her distress, now amplified.

The girl had to be close. She turned a bit, adjusted her path, and headed off once again.

"It's Lilian!" she called out. "If you can hear me, come toward me!"

There was a burst of elation and then it was gone.

Not just the elation, but also all emotions. She froze in place.

"Come out, come out, wherever you are." The words were spoken in a graveled voice, but the tone seemed to slither and ooze with sinister intention.

Lilian knew that voice. She'd heard it before, in her nightmares.

The huntsman!

The shadowy man who had trapped her in the pit.

"*Lilian? What's wrong?*"

"*Matthias! He's here! The huntsman!*"

Lilian felt the explosion of rage in Matthias, but she had to block it out in order to concentrate on what was going on here and now.

Her palm burned and throbbed, and the baying of the hounds came from a distance. A shudder went through her.

"Tsk, tsk," came the hoarse, harsh toned words. "One should never run into the woods alone, little girl. Don't you know there are bad things which exist?"

"Like you?" she asked as her eyes scanned the area where the voice came from.

A cold touch skittered along the back of her neck and she spun around.

Some yards back stood the shadowy figure of a man, tall and lanky, dressed in black. She couldn't see the details of his face, however.

"Your words are disrespectful," he growled.

Lilian gasped as an onslaught of psychic feelers struck her. She scrambled to block them, but with so many of them, she couldn't devote all of her attention on the mental attack when she was threatened physically as well.

"*We're on our way!*"

The mental attack withdrew and she took a deep breath, shoring up the barriers in her mind.

"Who are you?" she demanded.

Lilian heard the grinding chuckle, followed by the baying of the hounds, closer than before.

"Amras must have told you, dear girl."

Lilian eyed him with wariness. "The Winter King. Ulwe. You're my uncle."

"Do not presume since your father is my brother you can claim a relation to me. You are an abomination, tainted by your human blood. You are nothing more than a vessel, a slave."

She bristled. "I'm not an abomination, and I sure as hell will never be a slave!"

He laughed in his harsh, coarse tone. "That remains to be seen, if you survive."

The hounds were getting closer. She could hear them crashing through the forest on their way. She gathered the energy around her in preparation.

The man moved from his spot, but did not come closer. He skirted the edge of her vision, staying in the shadows. She was sure he used magick of some sort to conceal his features because she should have been able to see him with more detail.

To hell with it, she thought, and launched the first attack.

He must have been expecting something because he was quick to raise a shield to block the telekinetic punch she lobbed at him. She dove for cover behind a small grove of trees.

"Not very nice of you," he growled.

There was a loud explosion and tree bark showered the air around her.

"I was going to kill you, but now I think I will let you live, as my personal slave. I can think of plenty of tortures to repay you for your disrespect."

The tree began to scream in horror, and she covered her ears with her hands to block out the sound. It wasn't the sound, but the pain emanating from the tree which hurt the most.

"*I'm going insane! How can I feel the pain of a tree?*"

The shadow man, Ulwe, barked a laugh. "So close to your Chrysalis! Do you feel its pain?"

He caused the tree next to her to explode and shriek with pain. She cried out in horror as the same sorrowful whine emanated around her. He battered at her mental barriers as well, weakening her further. The onslaught of the attacks and the pain drove her to the ground, onto her knees.

"*Lilian!*"

"*Daughter!*"

Two male voices in her head, both on different mental paths.

She was lifted and shook hard. She looked up into Ulwe's face, seeing him for the first time, without a veil of magick. He ripped her hands from her ears, snarling.

"You are mine, and your powers will be mine!"

Lilian reacted. Not with her powers, not with her magick, but physically.

Lilian brought her knee up, rather hard, connecting it with his groin, and he released her as he exclaimed aloud in pain. She couldn't understand what he said, but it sounded like cursing.

Rather than give him the chance to recover, she followed with a spinning roundhouse kick, aiming for the side of his head. Her heel connected with his jaw; she felt the hard jarring of bone against bone, but rather than knocking him over, he shoved her away from him and she hit a tree behind her, knocking the wind from her.

The hounds were very close, by the sound of their snarling and baying, and she watched as Ulwe grinned a slow, evil smirk at her. He wiped his mouth, smearing black blood across his cheek.

"You will pay for that."

Lilian gasped for air and saw behind Ulwe, there stood the hounds. They looked like wolves, large and dark, with red eyes. They snarled and bared their teeth.

"*Hold on!*"

Lilian tried to stand, but Ulwe waved a hand and pinned her to the tree. As she struggled to free herself, his head jerked up and he stared behind her. With a cold, vicious snarl, he shifted his form, becoming a large black crow. The hounds launched themselves at her, only to be met with the Lupine in their wolf forms before they could reach her.

She found herself freed and she skittered around the other side of the tree for cover as the creatures battled. She could hear the snarling, feel the rage from both sides, and her body sucked in the energy. It filled her, energized her, revitalized her, and she panicked. She tried to bolt away from the battle scene, to put distance between her and the killing rage she was feeding from. Before getting far, she collided with someone and out of instinct, stood her ground and fought.

She heard some words in a foreign tongue, but ignored them and kept fighting. There was too much fear in her mind, too much rage building in her from the battle, for her to comprehend what was going on.

All of a sudden, it was as if someone flipped a switch and her body went still. She was awake and alert, but unable to control her movements, her own body. She was lowered to the ground with gentle care, although still held in someone's arms.

After a bit, someone leaned over into her view and smiled.

The hawk man. Behind him, her father appeared.

"*Keh por et pai?*" Amras asked as he knelt beside her.

The words were odd, yet the tone musical, soothing.

The hawk man smirked and handed her over to her father. *"Ai desore caes thews kalar ti."*

Amras took her into his arms and the hawk man touched her forehead. She was in control of herself once more and exploded with anger.

"How dare you! You can't just…just…"

Hell, what did *he do to me?*

The stranger and Amras looked at one another, grinned, and then back at her, which peeved her off.

"Daughter, this is Talis."

"I don't care if he's…wait, Talis?" She frowned. "The High King?"

Talis bowed to her. "I am."

Lilian would have been horrified if she hadn't been angry.

"Still, you just don't grab someone after they'd just been fighting. You don't sneak up behind someone." Her words sounded more peevish than angry, even to her ears. She sighed.

Talis nodded with feigned seriousness. "I will remember next time."

"Was that the Sidhe language?" she asked. "What you were speaking earlier?"

Amras nodded. "Did you understand?"

"No, but it's beautiful."

"I asked him, 'what did you do to her' and he replied, 'I stopped her from killing me.'"

Lilian's face heated and she glanced at Talis who smiled.

"Lilian?" Matthias was checking on her.

Lilian struggled, broke from her father's arms and scrambled to her feet. The fighting was over, but she could detect pain. There were wounded. She hesitated to go to the battle scene.

"Are you hurt? Everyone all right?"

"We have some wounded but no one from the Lupine died. Go with your father. You don't want to see this."

Lilian frowned. *"Matthias?"*

"It's all right, lilia mea. Go. Take your father back to the palatia. We will be there soon."

Matthias didn't mention Talis. Did it mean he wasn't aware of the stranger or…

"He does not know of my presence," Talis said. "I have kept my presence unknown for obvious reasons."

Lilian looked at him. "How did you know I was thinking of that? Are you in my mind?"

Talis smiled. "Do you have wine?"

Lilian looked at her father, who smiled and winked at her. She sighed. "I'm sure I could find some."

She started back toward the compound and with them following, she muttered, "This ought to be interesting."

Talis laughed.

Chapter 9

Lilian was rather irked Matthias had blocked her from using the connection between mates. Although she could just enter his mind and get the information she wanted, she knew his views on that, and he might see it as her not trusting him. Still, she didn't like this secrecy he had going right now. She worried about him and Tiberius, and not knowing what was happening made her anxious.

She watched as her father and Talis entertained the children and more than a few adults with their magick and antics.

The Sidhe were fun loving creatures, it seemed, and adored children. Watching the two men act like the children they entertained was rather amusing, and she wasn't the only one who laughed as Talis and Amras danced, played tricks, and made the children shriek with joy.

By the time the warriors had returned, Lilian, like most of the adults, was wiping tears of laughter from her eyes, and the children were so wound up, the cacophony was deafening.

Talis and Amras took their bows and were immediately surrounded by the children, all clamoring to get the men's attention.

"What in the world?"

Lilian chuckled at Matthias's confusion. *"My father and Talis were entertaining the children."*

"Entertaining? It sounded like a full fledge battle was going on. Who is Talis?"

She turned and watched her mate approach from the woods. Behind him, she could see the bulk of the group heading off a different route, carrying something between them. *"Talis, the High King. He'd been shielding his presence in the woods."*

"Why?" Matthias sounded suspicious.

"Because I didn't want Ulwe to know of my presence."

Lilian looked at Talis in surprise. He had used the same, private mental path a mated couple used.

Matthias growled in her mind.

"Explanations later," Talis announced.

As Matthias stopped at her side and wrapped an arm around her, Talis and Matthias stared at one another. After a few moments, Matthias nodded and looked at her.

"Are you all right?" he asked.

"I'm fine. How is everyone? No one hurt?"

"All healed, and cleaned up. We should take this into the meeting room."

Lilian didn't like how Matthias looked weary, and yet more dangerous than she'd ever seen him. Something was wrong.

She looked at her father. "If you and Talis would come with us? We're going to have a meeting, it seems."

Amras and Talis both gave a nod and followed as Matthias and Lilian led them into the palatia. Along the way, Matthias called out to a couple of servers in their language. Both bowed their heads and hurried off.

"Food and drink," he said to her in explanation.

Lilian smiled.

The smiled lasted right up until she walked into the meeting room, noted the gathered Lupine warriors, and the captured enemy, a human, chained. She tensed.

"Easy, baby. He's secure. He has some answers."

The prisoner snarled and lunged in her direction, but could not move very far or very well. Even in human form, the prisoner was still very savage in demeanor, wild and vicious. His eyes still red, his ears pointed, and his hair ragged and dirty. His clothes were disgusting, and she could smell him even from the door.

The Lupine, save two, took seats at the long table and Amras and Talis sat down on the far end. She was torn, but opted to sit with her father and Talis. It was also farthest from the prisoner.

Even so, the prisoner continued to struggle within his bindings and glare at her.

"It seems these creatures are targeting Lilian specifically. A room full of potential victims and he concentrates on her alone," Amras said.

Lilian wasn't thrilled. Neither was Matthias, based on his reaction to Amras's words.

"Every one of those 'hounds' as Lilian called them, are Shifters. They are not of the Lupine, neither my clan nor our cousins' clan, the Remus. The bastard children of outsiders perhaps."

Lilian listened as she concentrated on the prisoner. She eased her way into his mind and would have recoiled from the sheer hatred and evil which had poisoned his thoughts, but knew she had to dig deeper, to find out more. She knew the *Custodes Secreti* and the lengths they went through to gain their people, their agents and Knights.

She noticed it was getting much easier to use her abilities. she wasn't sure if it was because of the practice she was getting, or as Ulwe had said, her Chrysalis nearing. She'd have to talk to her father about what the Chrysalis was and what it meant.

The prisoner's mind had become a twisted labyrinth of darkness and pain. She kept seeing a worm in the memories, and the worm was associated with pain. The conversation going on around her died away, became nothing more than background noise, as she concentrated on the prisoner's memories.

Forming a sword of light, her mental self cut away at the evil in the prisoner's mind, bringing light to the darkness, and healing wounds associated with the worm. She could feel the prisoner's rage at first, and confusion, followed by an inkling of hope.

His name was Khayyam, she learned.

Lilian continued to cut through the poison, to reveal the man beneath the monster.

Ulwe had taken him, as a young boy, about ten years of age, and began his training. Khayyam had been an orphan and had nowhere to run when the torture began.

The pain had been excruciating. The mental anguish Ulwe had inflicted was far worse than any physical damage he could have done, but Ulwe needed his body whole. He needed a personal guard, a soldier, and his own elite assassin. Through mental torture, he twisted the boy through the years until Khayyam became the monster he was today.

Not anymore.

Lilian made sure she went through every corner of Khayyam's mind to clear out the shadows, to bring light to the darkness, cutting and slashing through the evil until it retreated, unable to find a hiding place, and when she head Ulwe's howl of rage echoing through Khayyam's mind, she knew she had won.

When she disconnected from his mind, Khayyam was on his knees, sobbing, everyone looked confused, and she was sick, weak with hunger, shaking uncontrollably. She tried to stand, but almost fell over, and would have if Amras and Talis both hadn't moved as quick as they did.

"*What's wrong?*" Three distinctive voices asked her, two on individual paths, the third, Talis's voice, echoed both paths. It was a very strange sensation.

Lilian shook her head and glanced up, toward the prisoner. "His name is Khayyam. Get some food and drink and take the chains off him."

Talis touched her brow and she felt him in her mind. She tried to eject him, but was too weak at the moment, and he too strong in his abilities.

"*You still wouldn't be able to,*" she heard Talis say.

"*What do you mean?*"

"*I am the High King. Until I relinquish the crown, I am the most powerful of our kind. Why do you think Ulwe wishes to unseat me and take the throne?*"

"*What can't you do?*"

There was a long silence in her mind before she heard his reply. "*I can't be free.*"

Lilian considered his answer.

"*I can't have my own life. I must be in charge of everyone. Even outside of the Mists, in the humans' land, I must make decisions for the best of my people. I am tired. Ulwe knows this and uses it to his advantage.*"

Lilian hadn't thought of it like that before. All of a sudden, she realized what he had said. *Until he relinquished the crown.* Did it mean he was looking for a replacement? Was it the reason why he was here instead of in his realm?

"*Let me see what you did.*" Talis went through her memory, like a fleeting and gentle ray of light. If she hadn't been aware of her abilities, and how to use them, she would have never known he was there.

Definitely a far cry from Ulwe's methods on Khayyam.

Of course, following it was an alarming thought. Talis could twist someone's mind in so subtle of ways they wouldn't know it.

Talis burst out into laughter and handed her off to Amras.

"Your daughter has a keen mind and sharp wit about her."

Amras grinned and his eyes twinkled. "Thank you, My Lord."

Talis looked at Matthias, still amused, from what she could see. "Your prisoner won't be a danger now. Do as she says."

Matthias lifted a brow and glanced at her. "What did you do?"

Lilian narrowed her eyes at him. "And what made you think I did something?"

Matthias grinned. "I know you."

Lilian clamped her mouth shut, which caused Matthias to chuckle. He turned and reiterated the order to remove the chains.

"Perhaps Lilian should be allowed to rest," Amras suggested.

"Hell, no." She snorted and tried to sit up on her own. "I'm not leaving."

"I'll speak only to the lady," Khayyam said. His voice was rough from ill use, hoarse and dry, but it held strength and conviction.

Lilian smiled at him in reassurance. "I will be here and they won't hurt you. Speak freely."

There was some grumbling at her words, but she glared at the group and all went silent.

Food was brought in and Khayyam gulped it down as though starving. He kept eyeing them as he ate and she wondered if he expected them to try to steal his food, or punish him for eating it.

With deliberate slowness, she pushed herself up from the chair, straightened her back, and made her way toward Khayyam. Amras and Talis both followed her, ensuring there was no danger, and Matthias stepped up to her side when she passed by him.

Khayyam froze as she approached, watching her with wariness in his haunted eyes. She smiled and extended her hands to him.

"You shouldn't stand to eat, Khayyam. Come sit down. If you're hungry still, we'll get more food. Actually, I'm hungry too." She looked at one of the Lupine and nodded to him.

The Lupine gave one look at Matthias and hurried from the room.

Lilian eased down into a chair and sighed. Khayyam glared at the others around him, and holding his plate close, eased over to a chair next to her. He sat and placed his plate on the table.

"I would share my meal with you, Lady, but you have a mate," Khayyam said with his ill-used voice. "I would not want my throat torn out for offending him with my offering."

Lilian smiled. "I should be the one sharing my food with you, Khayyam. The tortures you lived through at the hands of Ulwe, you deserve to be honored."

The Lupine eased back down into their chairs to listen.

Khayyam shuddered and lowered his gaze.

"Tell us about the *Custodes Secreti*," she said.

Khayyam picked at the food on his dish before looking around. "It's not as you think. There is the public face, there is the private face, and there is a deeper, darker face. You think it is just a group to gather and study those with abilities, but it's far more sinister than that."

Lilian nodded. "I know. I was one too, one of the children, before I escaped."

"No," Khayyam argued. "You don't know. You did not see further down the dark hole, Lady. You were able to escape. Ulwe is creating his own private army, his own legion of creatures, bred to enhance their powers, all under his control."

The Lupine murmured together at his words.

"His hounds are just the beginning. We were experiments to begin with, to see what he could do to us. Then we were bred with others with unique abilities, to create his legion."

"I am not surprised," Talis said. "Ulwe has always been a malcontent. He has never been happy with what he had and always wanted more."

"Ulwe wants you, Lady, because you are close to your Chrysalis. If he can harness your powers as they come, rape them from you, he would become undefeatable."

Khayyam gave her an intense look; fear and pity filled his eyes.

Lilian shook her head. "Don't. I won't go through with whatever the Chrysalis is."

Amras and Talis both protested.

"You do not understand what you are saying, daughter," Amras said. "There will be little choice. You'll be driven into madness if you do not."

Talis shook his head. "Your human mind will not be able to withstand the changes you will be going through. The Chrysalis is a buffer for those changes, protecting you while your mind expands and accepts what you see and hear."

"I heard the trees screaming in pain," she said.

Everyone fell silent and stared at her.

Talis looked at Amras. "*Si Teiralor shor cadael myl.*"

Amras looked at her, worry in his eyes. "*Ai cyrn. Sher mi vaeraraer. Shar tal shi pai?*"

Lilian looked between the two Sidhe. "Don't do that. Don't exclude me when I know it's about me."

Lilian stood. Khayyam surged to his feet, causing quite a few of the Lupine to tense. She looked at the group and shook her head.

"The *Custodes Secreti* is an organization which must be taken down. Starting with the nearest. Word has to go out about them to all other supernatural groups. Warn them about the Agents and the Knights. Warn them to do what they can to destroy any cells of the CS they find and rescue prisoners. Let them know what's going on with the breeding."

Trays of food and drink were marched in and set up along the long table. She sat back down and reached for some fruit, but Khayyam beat her to it. He picked up the fruit and set it on a plate, and offered it to her, serving her.

"You aren't my servant, Khayyam."

"You rescued me from the darkness, Lady. My life is yours. I will serve you, protect you."

Matthias growled.

* * * *

A couple of hours later, she nodded off in the meeting. Matthias scooped her up, startling her, and settled her in his lap as he continued to discuss their plans.

It had been decided messengers would be sent out to the nearest groups of supernaturals to warn them of the dangers within the *Custodes Secreti*, and have them extend the warning out to other groups, and so on. The Sidhe would also be alerted to take great care when crossing the Mists, and Ulwe would be declared a traitor, his kingdom seized.

Talis grumbled about having to find a replacement for the Winter Court as well. It had been the second time Talis made some cryptic mention of some higher purpose for his being here, but he wasn't going to reveal anything more than that, it seemed.

Khayyam protested the separation between them when shown to his own room. He'd been adamant about standing outside her door to guard her, but Matthias used his Alpha position to enforce his word. Khayyam capitulated, but said it had been under duress and he didn't feel comfortable being so far from his Lady, even if she was with her mate.

She heard Matthias mutter beneath his breath, something along the lines of "overzealous hero worshipping puppies" as he tried to herd her away from Khayyam's door.

"Hero worship? I'm a hero now?" she asked, amused.

"He seems to think you are," he grumbled.

She chuckled. "Better than trying to kill me, don't you think?"

Matthias took her to his room. "Infinitely better. Still, he *is* a Lupine. I don't like the way he fawns over you. The wolf in me snarls and tests my control when he's near you. Lupines are possessive of our mates, protective."

Lilian shook her head. "Wow, and I thought the Romans were historic. I never realized they were pre-historic."

He looked at her in surprise, and then narrowed his eyes at her. She knew it wasn't from anger. He was feigning insult.

"Are you calling me old?" He began to stalk her across the room.

Lilian batted her lashes at him as she backed away. "A Roman Neanderthal."

Matthias gave a playful growl and pounced, capturing her in his arms. She laughed, and kissed him, which resulted in heated kissing, and the fastest recorded time for removing clothes, followed by several rounds of lovemaking.

However, afterward, when Matthias had slipped off to sleep, snuggled up against her, she had time to think, to be alone in her mind. She was able to ponder the problems without distractions, without worries and fears, and without being bombarded with others' fears and worries.

As she watched him sleep, she thought about everything that had happened from the moment she met him.

Could I lose him? Will I lose him?

Pain sliced through her heart at the very thought, brought tears to her eyes and fear gripped her tight.

She loved him. She was in love with Matthias. When realization hit her, she had to fight back the shock before it woke Matthias. Even so, he shifted uneasily in his sleep and gathered her closer to him.

I love him.

Repeating the words in her mind, they felt right.

And it terrified her beyond reason.

Lilian had never thought to fall in love, or even have a meaningful relationship. She'd been on the run, hiding, and with the constant threat of the *Custodes Secreti*, she hadn't wanted to risk anyone else's lives because of her. So, she'd buried away any thoughts of a love life, or a family.

"*Your distress carries even to me.*"

Talis's voice echoed in her mind.

"*I'm sorry. I'm just realizing a few things.*"

There was a fluttering at the open window and she turned her head to look. A white owl perched on the sill and watched her.

"*You should be more concerned about what will happen if you refuse the Chrysalis.*"

Lilian sighed.

"*Come with me,*" Talis coaxed. "*Let me show you.*"

"*Turn away,*" she thought as she made a shooing motion toward Talis in the owl form.

Talis laughed in her mind and turned his head away. She extricated herself from Matthias's body, careful not to wake him, and pulled on her clothes. When she was dressed, she approached the window and Talis looked back at her. His eyes captured hers, and she fell still as he pulled her consciousness from her mind, into his.

Soon, they were flying as he launched the owl's body into the pre-dawn air.

"*This is what it is like to be Sidhe.*"

All at once, she saw the world as he saw it. Beauty beyond imagining made her gasp. Colors, even in the semi-lit world, were brighter and more intense. Sounds of the world touched her consciousness. She could hear the Earth and the plants created a harmony that wove together the song of life.

Even in the mind of the owl, she could feel the air, cool and wet, and she saw the mist rising from the lowlands as they flew overhead. Night was giving way to dawn and the world waking. No stars shone, nor the moon visible. It smelled cool and crisp, with the faint scent of sweetness in the moisture-laden air.

Lilian took a deep breath, and without thought, she concentrated, focusing her senses on the view. Her eyesight sharpened. Her sense of smell picked out sweet lavender, pine, and the deep, ancient scent of the Earth.

Concentrating even more, she could feel the pulse of life coming from the Earth, and hear the whispers of the faint breeze, tickling the inner reaches of her mind with pagan, primal music. It made her heart race and her breathing quicken. It was a seductive song—an invitation.

She took control of the owl. Talis's surprise was palpable. He retreated far enough to allow her control, remaining alert in case he was needed.

Lilian flew through the air, the wind caressing her, as if encouraging her to move, to explore. She glided as though she was a current of the wind itself, or a part of the night, and it was freedom.

Yes! She was a part of the night, and the night a part of her. She surged through it as it through her. The wind whispered in her ear as they moved through time and space, telling her secrets of life, of death, of existence, of nonexistence. It told her of peace, and war, history and the future. She took it all in until it filled her mind and body, and she glowed with the knowledge of it.

Lilian was not who she had been anymore, not now. Here, she was… nothing and everything, a mere speck of dust, and the universe itself. She was freedom incarnate and moved through the world unchained and unbound.

This is what life should be! A gnawing ache in her gut woke and stretched its wings, reveling in the freedom. It embraced her and she accepted it, and they soared through the night as one.

The world sang for her, the night sang in harmony, and she floated on the eddies of a song with no words, no tune, no rhythm. Yet, music still filled her senses and her soul. It drove her forward, and comforted her in its peaceful movement. The chorus warmed her, the stanzas made her shiver with delight. Sensual, primal, angelic, demonic, life moved on, the thread spun, the weaver wove, and death was there, waiting to cut the thread.

The darkness was filled with nothing, and everything, and she was not alone, even in her solitude.

Lilian hummed along, joining the tune, creating a three-point harmony. Her heart beat the time, and her blood coursed through her veins in a pounding rhythm as she moved with the universe, as though she was the universe in miniature.

She moved with pent-up energy as every beat of her heart caused a surge of tangible evidence that life continued.

Time slowed, sped up, and then stopped. She watched it within her mind's eye, experienced it with every cell of her being, tasted it on every taste bud, every pore.

She lived, she died, and she lived again. She was joy, and pain, and rage, and love. She was and she was not.

"*Do you understand now? How can you turn this down? Do you know what you will go through if you do not accept the Chrysalis?*"

Talis's tone was seductive. She tried to shake his voice from her mind. "*Do you want to know?*"

She had no choice. Talis ripped away her control and closed the wings of the owl until they plummeted toward earth in a free fall dive. She screamed and tried to wrestle back control, to open the wings and keep from colliding with the fast approaching rocks below, but Talis would not let her win.

The Earth screamed. Whispers upon whispers upon whispers as well as the cries of pain and the screams of terror, all created a cacophonic bombardment of noise. She saw horrific monsters wandering about without destination, nightmares given life by those who dreamt of them and released them into the world.

Every cry of pain, every tear shed, ripped at her soul. The world tasted like garbage, the smells were of death and decay. The colors were dark, somber, and the overall aura was of an evil so pronounced, she wanted to vomit.

"This is what you will see and hear until you are driven into complete madness. This is what you will live through until you are driven into ending it by taking your own life, if your mind could survive long enough to reach that state. When the time for your Chrysalis comes and you deny it, there are no more chances. You cannot change your mind. You must *go through the Chrysalis, Lilian. You* must!*"*

She cried out in pain, in fear, in protest of Talis's words, and he released her from the owl's mind, jettisoning her back into her own body and mind. She wobbled, her equilibrium off. Instead of catching herself, Lilian fell to her knees and cried.

* * * *

Lilian was somber and quiet the next day. She had risen early and wandered the quiet compound as the others slept. Amras and Talis had gone back through the Mists, returning to Jhal os Tor, Land of Mists, or as Amras called it, The Kingdoms.

They would not have stayed the night here, preferring to return to their own lands. Probably best, too, considering she was irate with Talis for last night's "journey".

Lilian had returned to bed after she cried, snuggling up against Matthias. In the early morning, he woke and made love to her and she had reveled in it. She was also careful to keep her thoughts to herself. She didn't want Matthias to know her feelings for him, not yet at least.

She'd gotten up when Matthias had slipped back to sleep, and cleansed in the bathing pool, dressed, and went to wander the grounds in the peaceful dawn.

If she went through the Chrysalis, how much of it would change her? Would she be herself anymore or something else? Would she have to go live with her father in their land, or would she be able to stay here? Would she lose her abilities or gain others, or both?

"Lilian?" she heard a female from behind her call out, soft and almost shy.

Lilian blinked, and turned, only to be surprised to see Anoria. She tensed in readiness, just in case.

"Lilian, if I'm not disturbing you, would it be all right to talk to you?" Anoria asked.

This Anoria was different. The Anoria from before wouldn't have asked for permission. She wouldn't have cared if Lilian wanted to be alone with her thoughts. She wasn't sure how to take this version of Anoria and so she just touched upon Anoria's surface thoughts.

Please, let me apologize. Please don't turn away from me. Let me explain. Hope Matthias doesn't get pissed off at me. Maybe I can talk to her.

Lilian smiled. "Of course, Anoria. I don't hate you, you know."

Anoria flicked her gaze up toward her, and away again, down to the ground. "I'm sorry I tried to hurt you."

Lilian walked again and Anoria fell in step alongside.

"I'm not angry, Anoria. I don't believe in holding grudges. You made a mistake and it's done."

Anoria sighed. "I felt threatened by your presence. I didn't know Matthias was serious about you, and I thought if I could drive you off, I could console him."

"What you did for my sister, healing her like that, thank you. Helena told my mother you didn't wish for anything in return, not even gratitude."

"I didn't do it to make myself look better to the pack, or for gifts. I healed her because she was in pain and I had to do it."

Lilian avoided the woods as they walked, skirting along the forest edge until they reached the front drive.

Anoria kept beside her.

"He isn't too rough with you, is he? I mean, it's none of my business but you aren't Lupine."

Lilian frowned. "He's fine with me, Anoria, and yes, it is none of your business."

"I'm sorry," Anoria was quick to interject. "No offense. I just…well, you're human."

For how much longer, she wondered.

"What's it like having your abilities?"

Lilian pondered for a few moments, then smiled. "It's not easy. Sometimes, you have to use them. Sometimes, you know using them will make it that much easier to be found."

"The *Custodes Secreti*?" Anoria asked.

"Yes, they have people like me who can detect when abilities are used, and track them down."

Anoria glanced around before looking at her. "It must have been difficult."

Lilian nodded. "When I escaped, I buried it deep down, didn't use any of them, but they still managed to find me."

As they walked toward the gate, they saw it open and Anoria frowned. "Something's wrong."

Anoria hurried toward the gate and she hesitated for a moment before she followed. Anoria slipped out through the large gate and around the corner. When she neared, she saw Anoria kneeling beside a prone figure of one of the guards.

"He's alive, just unconscious," Anoria said.

Lilian went to the other guard, kneeling down checking for a pulse, and found him to be the same. "Same here."

Lilian heard a noise behind her and turned. Anoria's blow caught her in the side of the head, hard enough to knock her unconscious.

* * * *

When she came to, she found herself in the forest again. Unfortunately, it wasn't a dream. She was on the ground; her hands tied behind her, she was gagged, and lying on her side.

The pounding pain in her head kept her from hearing much, but she could tell there were two people talking somewhere close by, a male's voice and a female's. As the pain faded to a dull throb, the voices became clearer. She knew the female was Anoria, but the male she couldn't recognize.

Anoria walked toward her and knelt beside her.

"You really thought I'd beg your forgiveness?" she sneered. "You're nothing more than a human."

She stood up and kicked her in the stomach, hard enough to knock the wind from her.

"Pathetic."

Anoria didn't pay any mind to the man coming up behind her and she couldn't see who it was from her position on the ground.

The silver glint of the knife was the only warning before it slid across Anoria's throat, slicing through flesh and windpipe. Lilian heard the cry of pain, and looked up, only to watch in mute horror as the man gripped Anoria's head and yanked it back, slashing her again and again, until he decapitated her. Bound and gagged, she could do nothing to help.

The blood was horrible! It seemed to spill out of Anoria as though it would never stop, falling onto the ground so near her that she tried to wriggle back from it. She could smell the coppery scent mixing with the loamy aroma of the earth, and she heard muffled screaming, but was confused as to where it was coming from.

"She shouldn't have kicked you. I might have let her live. No one's allowed to hurt you except me."

Lilian looked up and stared in horror. It was Stephan, and yet, wasn't. This Stephan was in horrible shape, gaunt with yellowish pallor, and his eyes wide and crazed. He let Anoria's body fall, her head hitting the ground after the body had. Blood covered Stephan's arms and hands, the knife drenched in it, and as he held it at his side, blood dripped.

When Stephan came toward her, she tried to scream, only to realize it had been her screams she'd been hearing. He knelt down and tried to reach for her, but she struggled back, away from him. Infuriated, he grabbed her with his bloodied hands and dragged her closer to him. She could feel the metal of the knife in his hand, but he wasn't trying to cut her. Yet.

"*Lilian! Where are you?*" Matthias sounded frantic. "*Try to use your abilities! We're coming to find you!*"

Lilian tried to connect her mind with Stephan's, to force him to release her, but found herself blocked. Someone else had tampered with his mind already.

Stephan struck her with a bloodied fist. "Don't you dare, you bitch! Get out of my head!"

Pain flooded her, followed by disgust, as she knew her face now had Anoria's blood on it from his fist. She bit back the cry, not wanting to give him the satisfaction. She would not beg, not like before.

Stephan jerked her up from the ground, leaving blood on her upper arms. He dragged her away from Anoria's body.

"The bitch shouldn't have touched you. Treacherous whore. I'm the only one allowed to hurt you," Stephan muttered in an inane tone of voice.

Lilian tried again to reach his mind, but he screamed and jerked her around, slapping her face again and again. She tried to struggle from his hold, but he was too strong this time. Something or someone was in control now.

"Get out of my head! Only the worm is allowed! Only the worm!"

"*Lilian, don't aggravate him any further. Go with him. We'll find you. Don't do anything to make him hurt you!*"

Lilian went limp, closing her eyes. She'd fake unconsciousness. "*I don't think I'd have to do anything. He's crazy, Matthias. He killed Anoria. Please...hurry.*"

She unloaded her memory into Matthias's mind, showing him what had happened. Matthias howled.

The sound was in stereo. She could hear it in her mind and outside of it, and knew they were still near the compound.

Stephan grabbed her, threw her over his shoulder, and carried her off, hurrying. The branches and low-lying limbs of the trees scratched and slapped at her, but she made no noise, did not move. After a minute or two, or perhaps longer, Stephan dumped her off his shoulder without warning. She hit a floor of some sort and groaned in pain. She opened her eyes and saw Stephan's crazed, gleeful look as he slammed the door to a cargo van, leaving her in darkness.

Chapter 10

"I'm in a van of some sort. I'm not sure where we're going."

Lilian's voice was shaky and she trembled. Even with the gag, her teeth rattled in her head. She dragged ragged lungfuls of air into her flared nostrils.

"We're coming after you. Just hold on." Matthias tried to sound brave, in charge, but she sensed his worry and the rage he held inside of him.

"Don't do anything stupid," she warned.

"Exactly how did you mean that?"

Lilian smiled behind the gag, though it was weak. *"Well, you know. You're a man so you can't be accused of doing anything smart."*

He was offended at first, which was followed by amusement when he realized her intention.

"I'm not the one who goes off half-cocked and tries to kick ass like a little Super-Woman."

"Hah."

Lilian closed her eyes and allowed the swaying of the vehicle to relax her muscles. Every fiber in her told her she'd need her strength against Stephan at some point.

Inside her mind, she heard the soft twinkling sounds of music, very faint and soothing. It helped to relax her further, yet not put her to sleep.

Before long, the van slowed and stopped. The door slid open, and she cringed back from the sudden glare of sunlight pouring in and blinding her. She was grabbed and dragged out of the van. When she hit the pavement, she grunted.

"Take her and lock her up. The Master will want to speak with her."

Two men, who wore the distinctive *Custodes Secreti* uniforms, carried out Stephan's order. She was lifted, bundled through a metal door, and down a darkened hall.

The combined scents pervading the building were very familiar and very terrifying for her. She could feel her heart beating faster and faster and her breathing came in ragged draws through her nostrils. The scent of medicine, fear, and pain combined and drifted through the building.

"*Easy, remain calm. Do not let terror fill your mind.*"

Her father's voice filled her mind, and soothed her fears. She tried to take deeper, slower breaths, to ease the panic.

"*Lilian. Stay with me. We're coming.*"

She was set down on a gurney, and untied, only to be strapped to it.

Screams filled her mind, screams of pain and of horror. Her eyes snapped open to look around, frantic, only to be met with visions of monsters. They rode on the shoulders of the guards, and they floated through the air, monsters of all shapes and sizes, with dripping fangs and burning eyes.

The guards were oblivious to them as they continued with their orders. But Stephan saw them. He swatted at the air, and muttered about the "damn creatures".

Madness! She struggled in the bindings, but could not free herself. Stephan watched and cackled, his eyes wide on her.

"The Master said I could have you when he's done with you!" He came toward her, still holding the bloody knife he had used to kill Anoria. Stephan waved it at her, punctuating his words and causing flecks of the crimson liquid to splatter.

"You're mine, you know. You shouldn't have run away! You'll have to be punished, of course."

He brought the knife in and started to saw through her clothes.

"The Master is going to be pleased," he sneered. "I hope he lets me help."

Lilian closed her eyes and held very still, afraid Stephan would cut her as he sliced the clothes from her, baring her body.

"Oh, pretty kitten," he smirked. "The Master is going to love you." He pulled the gag from her mouth and touched where he'd struck her face earlier, causing her to flinch in pain.

She heard Matthias's roar in her mind. Red rage filled her. Her eyes snapped open and she glared at Stephan. He shrieked and immediately slashed at her, but the guards dragged him out before he could wound her. Her own shrieks of were loud and piercing in the small room.

The nightmare creatures swam about, forward and away, taunting her by landing on her, gnashing their teeth, but they did not hurt her.

Yet.

Still, the sounds filling her mind drove her toward desperation, and she fought the bindings until her wrists became bruised and bloody.

It went on and on until even Matthias's voice in her mind became nothing more than just noise. Amras and Talis tried to call her from the edge of madness, to no avail. She fought them, fought herself, and fought the insanity threatening to take control.

* * * *

Matthias's rage was all consuming. He had to get to his mate. He had to help her. He could feel her mind fracturing in her terror and confusion, fed by his seething anger. Their connection was too strong for him to block his emotions from her and it sped along the mental path to her.

"*It just might help her,*" he heard Talis in his mind.

Matthias snarled back in reply, in no mood for false hope.

The first wave of the rescue group hit the *Custodes Secreti* compound and the guards hard and fast. It was an awesome sight to see, as wolves rushed the guards, and before colliding with them, shifted to their war forms. Anyone who did not submit was eliminated. Gunfire rang out and an alarm tripped inside the compound. Their sensitive ears could hear it.

Damage control is going to be a bitch, he thought.

Talis laughed in Matthias's mind. "*I have it taken care of.*"

Matthias wasn't sure how, nor did he want to know. He launched himself at one of the guards, who fired at him. The bullets connected with his body and caused Matthias to jerk and stumble, but he caught himself and continued on, colliding with the guard. Teeth snapped on the man's collarbone and broke it as claws shredded flesh from bone. The man screamed and fell still as he died.

Matthias let the body fall to the ground and looked around. His ears swiveled, taking in the sounds of battle and the constant noise of his people as they kept in contact with one another. He could also hear the roaring of the hounds from inside the compound and knew another round of fighting was close.

The doors to the compound opened and a surge of hounds rushed out, about twenty in total. They, too, were in their war forms, and with a howl, Matthias rallied his people to meet the onslaught.

It hurt Matthias to have to kill his own kind. Their numbers were not great, but he knew he had a duty to destroy the evil. He didn't know if Lilian had pulled a miracle out of her hat when she saved Khayyam, or if she could do it again, but he wished saving them was an option.

Claws raked his midsection, and he roared in rage. Retaliating in kind, he swiped his claws at the face of a red-eyed Hound in war form. Teeth met with flesh and the two combatants fought it out like titans.

All around them, the chaos intermingled with the turmoil of his emotions and his mind. He could feel Lilian's growing madness and it pushed his control even further toward the breaking point. His own upheaval was feeding hers and amplifying it until he wasn't sure her human mind could withstand it.

His enemies fell, one by one, as he made his way to the compound entrance. When his people had made their way there, they entered en masse.

* * * *

Lilian could hear the screaming in her ears and in her mind, her own, and others. The coppery stench of blood was strong in the air, emanating from her skin and her clothes, left by Stephan, and from outside the room.

She could see within her mind the scenes of death and destruction, followed by the nightmarish monsters as they fought amongst one another and attacked the fallen bodies, consuming what looked to be the last vestiges of energy, or souls of the fallen.

The rage and terror reached a critical level and as the pain of it crested, she let out a scream, long and shrill. Objects in the room began to fly, spinning around her as though in a tornado with her as the eye of the storm. Glass shattered and her bindings fell apart, releasing her.

Even as her scream died away, everything continued to move in what seemed to be controlled chaos. She scrambled up on the gurney to crouch there, her head lowered, eyes closed. Her hair tickled as it hung about her face.

"*Lilian?*" The query came in her mind, but she ignored it. It wasn't important, the voice unrecognized.

The door opened and Ulwe stepped in, followed by Stephan. Even with her eyes closed, she knew who had entered from the energy they radiated around them and she didn't need to open her eyes to know where to aim her attack. She sent a blast of telekinetic energy, hitting the two of them and sending them backward into a wall.

Ulwe laughed. His harsh, coarse tone grated on her and she snarled.

"The Madness has taken control!"

Lilian lifted her head and opened her eyes. His dark eyes glittered with uncontrolled glee. The objects around her began to spin faster.

Stephan eyed the room in wariness, his movements jerky.

Ulwe pushed forward and when she sent another blast, he waved a hand to block it. She snarled with rage and shifted her weight on the gurney.

"That's it," Ulwe growled. "Let the Madness control you."

"*Lilian! Fight it! Control it!*"

The voices she heard in her mind warred with the ones she heard outside of it. She could see the nightmares hovering and flying around Ulwe, as they fed on Stephan's energy.

"*We're losing her.*"

"*No, she's stronger than you realize.*"

Lilian screamed in rage and curled her hands into claws.

Ulwe launched a mental attack and she met it without hesitation. He dug in and shredded at her barriers, but she was stronger than even he realized in her current state. She ejected him, slashing at his barriers as she did so.

He snarled with anger and tried again, this time hitting her harder. The two battled mentally. Each time, she managed to eject him, striking damage at his mind even as he damaged hers with each attempt.

When Stephan moved to approach, she lifted a hand and swept her arm across the air. The brand on her right palm glowed as Stephan went flying through the room to hit a far wall. He hung there, unable to struggle, and fighting just to breathe.

She caught a moment of weakness, an opening, in Ulwe, when he realized how great her power had become and she struck hard and fast. She had become a feral beast, a cornered predator now, pushed to the limits, and she fought back.

Ulwe found himself in his own mind, in a courtyard made of stone. She stood across from him, wearing white armor, a sword, glowing silver, in her hand. She gave him very little time to fashion a weapon before she attacked him.

At first, she fought him with just the sword. In her mind, she was adept with the bladed weapon, slashing and slicing at Ulwe, driving him back. Still, she hadn't been trained for this type of battle, fighting on an astral level. To her, the battle was physical, not mental, and so she gave herself the same limitations she expected to have as though in the physical world.

No! I can do this!

It had been Ulwe, infiltrating and insinuating his darkness into her mind, undermining her thoughts to try and weaken her, make her doubt herself.

Lilian snarled as she struck at him, using both sword and telekinetic abilities. He braced himself, fought against the onslaught of her attack, pushing her back.

She kept his mind busy, and with his concentration on her, in their mental battle, he was unaware of what was going on outside of his body. With her mental fracturing, in the Madness, she could use both mental and physical abilities at the same time. She released Stephan from his pin against the wall, and she crept across the gurney toward Ulwe's form.

The nightmare creatures shrieked with rage and dived at her, but she ignored them as she moved closer to her enemy. Stephan cursed and tried to attack her, but when flying objects bombarded him, he tucked tail and ran from the room. She heard his shrieking down the hall, adding to the cacophony of screams which had become her world.

Ulwe's sword clashed against her mental shield. Her previous battle with her father had taught her to create shields and she used the newly developed ability now. She could see Ulwe's surprise in his eyes, but he only sneered at her and renewed his attacks.

Even in the astral plane, their fighting caused wounds and she tired from the mental exertion. Ulwe was, as well, from what she could see. His brow was beaded with sweat, and he was bleeding from various cuts made by her sword. She used everything she knew in order to keep Ulwe from realizing what she was doing outside their minds.

His evil radiated from him like an aura of sickness and it drove her mind closer and closer to the edge of insanity, to Madness. She used this to her advantage. As her mind fractured even further, it gave her the strength to separate her mind, to shield her physical body as it moved ever closer to his. To end this battle she would kill him. There could be no other choice in the matter.

"I will use your shell as my slave," he said with a grin. "You will obey my every desire, my every command. I will feed from your soul and fuck every orifice.

"I will enslave your Lupine mate and use him for breeding my own soldiers, my private knights. I will rule as High King after I destroy Talis."

Lilian snarled and sliced at his throat with her sword, but he managed to dance back out of the way.

"Touched a nerve? What about your father? Should he remain alive to witness your fall? I shall keep him chained and he can watch as I take you, rape you every night."

Lilian's physical body reached out and grabbed a shard of glass, broken from the window. She held it with such a tight grip, her flesh sliced open and blood spilled from her hand.

"Perhaps I will force you to seduce him, your own father!"

Lilian screamed in rage. "I'll kill you!"

Her palm glowed red, lighting up the glass in her hand, and as her astral self spun, the sword sliced through the air toward Ulwe's throat, her physical body spun and the glass shard sliced through the air. His astral self managed to avoid the sword, but his physical body hadn't expected an attack and did not move. She opened his throat in a bloody gash.

Ulwe screamed, in his mind and out loud. He tried to eject her from his mind, but she renewed her attack, keeping him busy as her physical body kept slashing and cutting at Ulwe, opening deep cuts and slices in his flesh.

Furious, Ulwe hacked at her with his sword, driving her back. When she stumbled, her control wavered, and it was enough for him to shove her out. Both in control of their physical bodies now, he attacked and tackled her. They fell to the floor as the shrieks and screams of the nightmare creatures flew about them.

The glass shard in her hand penetrated Ulwe when he fell atop her. In her Madness, she instinctively jerked the shard upward, slicing through innards, and twisted her hand, creating more damage to the both of them. Ulwe shrieked in pain and rage, and jerked himself backward, off her. He pulled the glass shard from his gut and stabbed at her with it. She raised her arms to protect herself, but he slashed at them, opening flesh and with one lucky shot, sliced deep enough to open veins and arteries.

With the last ounce of her strength, Lilian raised her energy until she glowed, pulsating blue and fiery red, and shot it at Ulwe. The energy ball exploded on impact, and he, with a look of shock and horror, fell to the ground, writhing in pain. His growling voice groaned and then fell still and silent. The nightmare creatures shrieked in delight, attacking his body and one another in their attempt to feed from the dying energy and his soul.

Lilian could only watch, feeling disconnected from everything around her as she lay dying. Her blood pumped out of her open wounds onto the floor beneath her and the maelstrom created in her Madness soon died, objects fell from their riotous orbit to the floor. She closed her eyes and let go.

* * * *

Matthias and Amras found her first. They had almost overlooked the room; a cursory glance inside yielded only bodies, but it was Amras who recognized Ulwe first. He jerked back and hurried into the room. Matthias followed.

Matthias roared when he saw his mate lying in her own blood, her skin pale . He threw himself down onto the floor beside her, gathered her up, and tried to staunch the bleeding.

"Lilian!" he yelled. "Don't you dare die!"

Her eyelids fluttered and opened. A weak smile hovered at her lips.

"*Always the bossy one,*" she thought to him. Even her mind was weak and sluggish.

"She must go through the Chrysalis or she'll die!" Amras said.

"*I could die even then,*" she sent.

"I won't let you die," Matthias said.

"*I don't want to do it.*"

"*You don't have a choice.*" Talis, with his strong words and his will unbendable. "*You will not die now. You will go through the Chrysalis. As High King, I demand it.*"

It was odd to feel Talis in his mind on the same mental channel reserved for mates. Matthias certainly didn't like it, but at the moment, it was a minor problem.

"Not my king," she protested in a weak voice.

She was cold. Matthias could feel her trembling and tried to gather her closer, to use his body heat to warm her, but he could feel her slipping further away.

Matthias was torn. He knew she didn't want to go through the Chrysalis, but he didn't want her to die either. Still, to force her through something she didn't want, he couldn't do it, even if it could save her.

The room rolled with energy and the hair on Matthias's arms and the back of his neck stood on end. Everything fell silent, shielded from the outside's continual battle.

Talis appeared in the room, dressed for battle, sword in hand.

He motioned toward Lilian and Matthias watched as her body stirred and lift on its own.

"She has no say in the matter, her mind weakened. I invoke the right of kings. She will go through the Chrysalis as I demand it."

Her body floated in midair. Matthias got to his feet, worried and unsure. As he watched, her body began to glow a pale blue, and soon concealed in a shield of energy. Even the shield glowed, pulsating with silvers and blues.

Without warning, both Talis and Lilian disappeared.

* * * *

Lilian was floating on a cloud. The world was a soft blue in color, with flickers of pastel pinks, purples, and greens. It was peaceful and calm. She loved it.

Pictures floated by her, scenes of her life.

Am I dead? Did Ulwe kill me?

If so, she seemed rather at peace with the idea.

What is going on?

The lights flickered around her, creating a psychedelic light show in her mind. It was so beautiful.

Until she began to feel...

At first, she was aware of a growing heat inside of her. The sensation intensified, and the warmth turned hot, and then scalding.

She tried to take deep breaths and found in doing so, her lungs burned. She whimpered in pain and tried to move, but could not.

The pain ebbed. It gave her time to catch her breath, only to crest again, building in strength and pain, and for it to ebb yet again.

Time lost all meaning. Life lost all definition. She only knew what was happening to her body.

It was as though she lay on a bed of flames, the mounting heat licked her body and she ached as the power within her restructured her, forming a place in which to reside.

Lilian screamed, yet made no sound. She fought, but did not move. She cried, but shed no tears.

On and on it went until all she knew was this ebb and flow of pain.

* * * *

Matthias prowled the grounds, snarling. His sense of responsibility was eating at him, as well as his worry for his mate, not knowing where she'd been taken, or if she was all right. He knew she was alive, he could feel that much. He paced as he snapped off orders. The cleanup effort was going well, regardless.

Tiberius had prisoners broken into two groups, Bad Guys and Good Guys. Amras had lifted a brow at that, but Tiberius just grinned and shrugged.

Bad Guys were Agents, Knights, and others involved in the capturing, subjugating, and torturing of innocent people. The Good Guys were, of course, innocents who had been captured, subjugated, and tortured.

Many of the Good Guys were terrified of them, to such a degree they would not even look or speak to the Lupine. Several were women and children as well.

Bad Guys were dealt with in the only way possible—executed. Most were too mentally unfit to do anything with, and twisted supernatural creatures would only create more problems later.

Things were going well though. At least, up until Matthias dropped to the ground and roared with pain. His hands came up and pressed into his temples, and his body rocked. Amras and Tiberius came running, but when Matthias lifted his head and gave a roar of rage, Amras stayed back.

"What's going on?" Tiberius demanded.

When Tiberius tried to help him up, Matthias sent him flying backward with an explosion of light.

"Impossible…" Amras sounded stunned.

Matthias dropped onto the ground, his body writhing in pain.

Amras gathered a ball of energy and aimed it at Matthias. He spoke in his language as he fired the ball at the prone Matthias. "*Maer paer eil vaer shaer!*"

Matthias was struck by the energy and knocked unconscious.

When Amras glanced up, he saw a young woman, one of the prisoners rescued from the compound. Her hair a bright white, not the platinum of his own or Lilian's but white, as pure as fresh fallen snow, and eyes the color of the badi stones of the Jhal os Tor, a bluish green color which seemed neither just blue, nor just green, but changed as he watched. He could tell she was special. She gave off a feeling of magick, an aura of… well, he wasn't sure. He just knew there was something about her.

Amras took a step toward her, but she turned and ran and before he could give chase, Tiberius drew his attention away from the young woman when he stepped up to Amras and asked, "What the hell just happened?"

* * * *

The mood of the Lupine compound was noticeably somber and quiet. Even the children walked about subdued and sad.

Everyone was on vigil, waiting to learn of their Alpha and his mate's fate. Bonfires were lit, herbs burnt, and they waited.

After Amras had sent Matthias to sleep, the group finished up and headed back to the compound. Talis had taken Lilian back and deposited her in her room, the Chrysalis still surrounding her, still glowing in pulsating colors. Amras had Matthias placed in the room as well, next to her. Although not surrounded in a Chrysalis, it was obvious something similar was happening to him.

Talis had taken the news with some surprise. This was unheard of and he left to search through their libraries for references to any other similar instances.

Tiberius had the rescued prisoners brought back as well. Many of them had families they could contact and return to. Some did not, and they would be remaining with the Lupine until homes could be found for them.

Amras offered to take a few across the Mists if they wanted. They would be given homes and a chance to make a living for themselves there. He kept his eyes out for the young woman, but she remained elusive.

* * * *

Maressë watched the going of the Wolf Shifters from afar. They were somber despite having freed the prisoners of the *Custodes Secreti*, and having lost only two of their people. She was aware they kept watch over another two, a human and another of their kind, but Maressë knew better than to get involved. She had a secret she needed to keep.

Maressë was a magickal creature, a supernatural creature as they were termed, and while she was safe here, with the Lupine rescuers, she couldn't stay. Therefore, when no one watched, Maressë slipped off into the woods.

* * * *

Matthias woke first. He ached everywhere; every muscle in his body protested when he moved, and he had one hellacious headache. He lifted a hand and rubbed at his brow.

How the hell did I get here? He tried to remember what had happened. The last thing he could remember was cleaning up after the battle and rescue attempt.

"*You decided to share the Chrysalis with Lilian.*"

Matthias jerked into a sitting position at Talis's words, and then flinched as pain raced through his body.

"*Easy does it. You'll wake her.*"

Matthias looked around but the only person present was Lilian, still sleeping. Better yet, there was no glowing energy field around her. He rolled over and looked at her.

If it had been possible for her to have grown more beautiful, she did and yet, nothing about her appearance had changed all that much. She still had her platinum blond hair, and her pale skin. Matthias wasn't sure what it was, but she had changed, grown more, well, something.

He watched as she came awake in gradual increments; the way her breasts rose as she inhaled a slow, deep breath, followed by an exhale, the way her eyes moved behind the lids, the way she slowly stretched as she moved from sleep to waking.

"Am I dead?"

"Open your eyes and see," he replied.

"You're so serious. I can feel your emotions."

"You're so beautiful. There's something about you, more than before."

Lilian opened her eyes and turned her head to look at him. Her silver eyes were like mercury, liquid and bright.

"There's a change to you," he whispered as he realized what it was. "An aura of magick around you."

Like her father, and like Talis, she emanated an aura of magick, of sensuality, of being more in touch with life, yet moved through it as though apart from it.

He rolled over and stood up, anxious.

"What's wrong?" she asked.

"Nothing. I need a shower. I feel like I was run over by a train."

"Were you wounded?" The concern was obvious in her tone.

"No, I went through the Chrysalis with you, according to Talis," he replied.

He made his way to the door. She touched his mind, but he blocked her, as difficult as it was. Mates were not meant to deny one another access to their thoughts, but he knew until he got his head straight and figured out what was different, he wouldn't, couldn't, let her in.

* * * *

The rejection was a sharp pain in her heart and she hated it.

She had suspected her going through the Chrysalis would be trouble and mere seconds after waking, it was proving to be true.

Climbing out of bed, she stretched and reveled in the feeling of her body. Before, a stretch had been just a stretch and while it had always felt good, this time, it was amazing. Every fiber of her being rejoiced at the sensation of muscles pulling, as blood flowed through her veins, and her heart beat in a tempo which went far beyond just a heartbeat, but even to the beat of life itself.

Movement itself was a sensual act. Air passed over her skin and kissed her with a gentle caress, and she smiled.

Nevertheless, even so, deeper down, she ached with emotional pain.

"The Sidhe feel much more keenly than humans," Amras said.

"You know, Talis could have told me that before he forced this on me," she sniped back.

Lilian changed into fresh clothes. Let Matthias have the bath alone, she would see how things were going and find something to eat. She was starving!

"How do you feel?" Amras asked.

"Alive," she replied.

"It was a close call, daughter. You were severely wounded. You would have died."

"Yes, well, I'm still deciding whether it's worth it."

Amras met her in the hall. Khayyam was with him and seeing her, his eyes lit up, the worry faded from his face.

"My Lady!"

Lilian smiled. "Khayyam. How are you?"

"Better now that I've seen you well and whole. They refused to allow me in."

Amras rolled his eyes. "The man camped outside your door the whole time you were in your Chrysalis."

"How long?" she asked.

Amras offered her his arm and she took it. The trio walked toward the kitchen.

"Three days and nights."

Lilian looked surprised. "No wonder I'm starving."

"Matthias must be hungry as well," Amras said.

Lilian tensed. "He knows where to find food."

Amras looked at her and she shook her head.

"Give him time, daughter. He almost lost you."

"Give him time?" she snapped. "I almost died and when I do finally wake up, he leaves me alone? How is that giving him time? He makes some odd comment about me being different and then walks away, blocking me from his mind."

Khayyam and Amras glanced at one another, then away again.

"Maybe some distance might be good," Amras said. "Come with me to the Summer Court. You can learn about your heritage."

Lilian's mind brushed against Matthias's but he still had her blocked. The result pang of rejection made up her mind.

"All right," she said.

Khayyam looked worried. "Lady?"

"Yes," she said. "You may go."

Khayyam's smile lit his face and her answering laughter floated down the hall.

After an hour, during which the three of them ate and talked together, she was back in her room with Matthias nowhere to be found. She sat down and wrote a letter to him.

> *Matthias,*
> *I've gone with my father back to his Court.*
> *I think the distance will be good for us. We can get our thoughts in order, figure out if this is the best course of action, and decide if we really want to be together.*
> *Amras wants to show me my heritage and to teach me more about what it is that I am now. He's promised I could return whenever I wish and you're able to come through the Mists if you choose.*
> *Until then, I have Khayyam with me. He'll serve as bodyguard, although I doubt I'll need one.*
> *Goodbye.*

Lilian folded the letter and wrote his name on the outside. She carried it to the bed where she propped it on her pillow for Matthias to see.

She took nothing with her; Amras promised she would have everything she'd need there.

Lilian turned and walked out of the room without looking back.

Chapter 11

When Amras talked about The Mists, Lilian had assumed he used the term as a flowery metaphor, as though "The Mists" was a fancy name for portal, or doorway. She expected some cave with a shimmering door into the Sidhe kingdom, or some form of standing stones in which her father would recite some strange yet beautiful words in his language to open the gateway to his world.

However, as they stood outside the bank of fog in the woods, her brows lifted in surprise.

"It's fog," she said.

Amras glanced at her. "The Mists, yes."

"It's *fog*," she reiterated.

He grinned. "If that is how you wish to think of it."

"I hate to tell you this, Dad, but this is fog. *Just* fog."

Khayyam cleared his throat, but she detected his amusement and knew he tried to cover the laughter which threatened to spill out.

"Dad?" Amras asked. His brow furrowed in confusion.

Khayyam coughed and spoke up. "Dad is a shortened term for Father. It's a more familiar term. Father is more formal."

Amras pondered Khayyam's explanation and shook his head. "The Mists are just as you see. Have you ever walked into The Mists and as it enclosed you from the surrounding world, you knew you were not alone? If you listened closely, you could hear the whispers of the Wild, and if careful to keep watch, you would see the shadowy figures of those who came and gone through The Mists?"

"Okay, now you're just freaking me out," she said, exasperated.

Khayyam snorted and grinned.

Amras looked at her and frowned. "You are in what the humans call 'a snit.'"

Lilian gasped. "I am not. I just expected something a bit more magical than fog. I expected magic words and fancy gateways or maybe some music. Not...*fog*."

Amras lifted a brow at her and pushed her into said fog. She heard Khayyam's burst of laughter just before everything went silent.

Lilian shivered and glanced around. As Amras had said, there were shadows which moved amongst the fog, and around her faint traces of whispers could be heard, although she couldn't pick out any one conversation. She couldn't even pick out specific words, but she could hear the soft whispering sounds as though many people spoke all at once in such a soft tone, that she wanted to yell out, "Speak up!"

It was very eerie and she didn't like it, but before she could turn around and go back the way she had come, Amras and Khayyam stepped into the fog beside her.

"*Do you understand now?*" Amras asked as he took her arm and led her and Khayyam through the Mists.

"*Yes, and I don't like it. It's frightening.*"

"*You, who faced Ulwe and the Madness, who just survived your Chrysalis, are frightened of the Mists?*"

Lilian tried to explain. "*It's eerie. I don't like not knowing what's out there. I don't like the feeling here, the way it feels when it brushes against my skin.*"

"*You're more sensitive than I realized,*" Amras said. "*Perhaps your abilities give you a heightened sensitivity.*"

Before she could reply, they were through. They stepped out into a world she had only dreamed about. She saw even Khayyam was taken aback by the sheer beauty and intensity of this world, and she smiled.

"Welcome home, my daughter," Amras said.

Lilian laughed. "It's amazing! The colors are so bright, and it smells so clean and fresh here!"

Amras led her along a path and Khayyam followed behind them.

The path widened and soon became a cobblestone road. When they rounded the corner, she could see what Amras meant by kingdom.

Just like out of a movie, she saw a town square. People seemed to be setting up for market, dressed like they had stepped back in time, or into a Renaissance Faire. Either way, she was awed.

The cobblestone road was lined with shops and homes, decorated with bright, colored ribbons and the sound of bells and chimes.

"My Lord," someone called out in greeting.

Soon, everyone was looking at them, greeting Amras and staring at her and Khayyam.

Amras waved and returned their greetings. As they walked on, they were stopped often, everyone wanting to speak to Amras. After moving no more than halfway down the road in ten minutes, the sound of hoofbeats approached and people moved out of the way.

Men in matching clothing and riding white horses approached, one without a rider. As they neared, they slowed and the lead man jumped down from his mount to approach.

"*Os Condraer,*" he said, giving a bow.

"Calawe," Amras said with a smile. "Calawe, this is my daughter, the Princess Lilian." Amras spoke in English.

She startled and looked at her father with a faint frown. "*I'm not going to claim any such title.*"

Amras grinned.

Lilian looked at Calawe and noticed his casual perusal of her. She lifted a brow at him.

"Nice to meet you, Calawe."

Calawe blinked and bowed. "Highness."

Amras motioned the rider-less horse to be brought forward and when done so, he mounted and offered his hand to her.

Lilian shook her head. "Oh, no. I'm not riding on that thing."

"It is safe," Amras said.

"If it bucks, and I go flying off, I'm going home."

Amras laughed and pulled her up in front of him, though she sat sideways. Calawe mounted his own horse.

"You're going to need clothes, maids, and you should learn Sidhe. Calawe, you will help tutor my daughter in our language."

Calawe looked at her. "If that is your wish, My Lord."

Lilian narrowed her eyes on him. While handsome, Calawe had an arrogant look to him. His blond hair was long and tied back into a ponytail, and he had emerald green eyes women would melt over, but focused on her, as hard as the stone they were named after.

He did not like her here.

She smiled at him and he looked away, his jaw set in a stubborn line.

When Khayyam shifted to his wolf form to walk beside Amras and Lilian's horse, the guards, four besides Calawe, were shocked and drew their swords.

"You strike him in any way and there'll be hell to pay," she snapped at them.

The men eyed her, glanced at Amras, and nodded their heads as they sheathed their swords once more.

"Who is this wolf man?" Calawe asked Amras, not bothering to look at her. "He is not Sidhe."

"His name is Khayyam, and he's my bodyguard," she said in reply.

Calawe flicked a glance at her and said nothing more.

The ride to the castle would have been in silence had Amras not filled it with snippets of information about the area. She paid close attention to what she both saw and heard.

"*Khayyam, be sure to remember how to get back to the Mists,*" she sent him.

The russet colored wolf huffed and nodded his head once in reply.

The castle, or Court Seat, as Amras called it, wasn't what she expected either. Books and movies, and even photographs of castles in Europe, had them large, made of gray stone, and rather daunting. Not so here, it seemed. In fact, it looked more like a villa to her than a castle, shaped in a horseshoe configuration. In the center was a large open courtyard, the far end held a large stone chair with smaller ones on either side, the whole area raised up on a dais to be higher than the rest of the courtyard. To either side were benches, three deep, and a red carpet which ran the full length of the courtyard from entrance to throne. They dismounted out front and Amras led the way toward the throne, and behind it where there was a set of double doors. Guards saluted and opened the doors for them, although they gave her curious looks and smiles.

Khayyam gave a low growl before passing through the doors after her. Behind her, she heard Calawe and the guards talking in Sidhe. While she'd love to slip into Calawe's mind to see what they were talking about, she decided against it. He was already rather ambivalent toward her, why make it worse?

"*He is a good man,*" Amras thought to her. "*He was in training to become king.*"

"*Was?*"

"*Now that you are here, you would be in line to inherit.*"

"*Uh. That's not something we've discussed. I don't know if I'll even be staying here.*"

Amras said nothing in reply as they were inundated with people. A large group had come en masse to welcome their king home and spotting her, she found herself the center of attention. She tried to move back, out of the way, but Amras took a hold of her arm.

"This is my daughter, Lilian," he announced to the crowd. "She has only just recently gone through the Chrysalis."

Silence filled the room. A flutter of nervousness went through her, but when her eyes met Calawe's and she saw the smirk on his face, anger rose in her. She straightened. Khayyam, still in wolf form, stood beside her, tense and ready.

"Hello. It's nice to meet all of you. Give me some time to get to know everyone's names."

There was a soft murmur in Sidhe amongst the group, and a young woman stepped forward and gave a deep curtsy.

"Highness, my name is Elena."

Elena had russet brown hair with red highlights which glittered in the light. Her skin was a pale ivory and a smattering of freckles along her cheekbones. She looked young, maybe a little younger than Lilian herself, and despite her formal manners, she could see a spark of mischief in Elena's hazel eyes.

Lilian smiled and extended her hands to Elena. "Thank you. Call me Lilian."

Elena looked shocked and with a hesitant motion took her hands. A slow smile appeared on Elena's face.

"Now, Amras has declared I must have new clothing and I know nothing about Sidhe style of dress. I hope you can help me and Khayyam."

"Khayyam, Highness...err...Lilian?"

Lilian looked down at the wolf at her side. "Khayyam?"

Khayyam glanced up and shifted to his human form. Elena gasped and her hands tightened on hers.

"He is not Sidhe!"

Lilian grinned, very much enjoying the shock value. "No, he's a Lupine. Khayyam is my trusted bodyguard."

"Not that you will need one here, daughter. No one would dare to hurt you."

Lilian looked at her father. "Ulwe tried."

There was another murmur amongst the Sidhe.

"Calawe? Tomorrow we'll start those lessons," she said. "After lunch."

"Lunch, milady?" he asked.

"Midday meal?"

"Ahh. I will endeavor to rearrange my schedule for you, milady."

The words were polite and accommodating, but it was obvious he was a bit perturbed. *Good.*

She smiled oh so sweetly at Calawe before looking back at her father. "Could I be shown to my room?"

Elena piped in. "My Lord? Let me show her to her room? I know the perfect one for her...the Blue Room."

Amras smiled. "Excellent, Elena. Have two maids appointed to her. Oh, and have the dressmaker come out and measure her for some gowns."

"Nothing too over the top, I'm not staying very long," Lilian reminded her father.

Amras leaned in and placed a light kiss on her forehead, grinned and strolled off. Many followed him, but a couple stayed behind.

"Is it true you battled the Winter King?" one asked her.

Lilian drew a slow, deep breath. She didn't want to talk about it.

"Yes. He was going to kill me, so I protected myself." Her tone made it clear she wasn't going to elaborate.

Elena pulled her along. "Come. I'll show you to your room, and then we'll see about getting you some clothing befitting your station."

Lilian grinned. "My station?"

"As a princess," Elena replied.

Khayyam followed behind the women, close enough to be a deterrent, but far enough away to be circumspect. Elena kept glancing back at him, curious and shy.

"Would you like to meet him?" Lilian asked in a whisper.

Elena looked at her in surprise, and blushed, giving herself a soft glow.

Lilian stopped and turned, motioning for Khayyam. When he stepped closer, she took his arm.

"Khayyam, this is Elena. Elena, Khayyam."

Khayyam gave Elena a slight bow. "Miss."

Elena blushed even more and dropped into a curtsy. "Khayyam."

Lilian just grinned.

Khayyam looked a little unsure of himself and glanced at Lilian. She took pity of the two of them and with Khayyam on one side and Elena on the other side, she linked arms with both and started walking.

"Khayyam will want a room near mine," she said.

"Are the two of you..." Elena started to ask.

"We're friends. I have a mate," she said.

Elena looked hopeful at first only to hurry and cover it up. "A mate?"

"He's Lupine."

"Why did he not come with you?"

Lilian smiled a bit. "One, he doesn't know I left, and two, because he's being a typical, pig headed male. Present company excluded, of course, Khayyam."

Khayyam grinned.

* * * *

Elena had shown Lilian to her room, appointed two maids, and already ordered a bath to be brought before she could even take a deep breath. It was rather obvious Elena knew what to do and how to do it, and for a young woman, she had a definite knack for taking charge of things. She liked her.

Khayyam was given a room next to hers, and the only other room on this level would be given to the maids to share.

"We need to find you some clothes," Elena said. "I can summon the dressmakers, we can take measurements. Until then, I'm sure we can find someone similar to your size."

"Can't I wear something like the men do? Pants and a shirt, something easy to move in?"

Elena stared at her as if she was insane.

"I don't suppose that's a yes?"

"Ladies do not wear men's clothing," Elena announced.

"Who made up that law?"

"It's not a law…"

"So then I could," she said with a grin.

"But it's just not done," Elena protested.

"And a sword. I want a sword."

Elena sighed. "Is this truly what you want?"

Lilian nodded. "Oh, yes. Definitely."

"I'm not even sure how to get you a sword."

"Get me the clothes and show me where to get the sword. I'll pick one out myself."

Three hours later, to Elena's amusement, after much grumbling by her, and threats by the dressmakers, they finished. After a wonderful soak in a bathtub, which could fit three people, and she preferred not to get the details from Elena on *why* the bathtub was so large, Lilian was dressed in a lord's finery, with silken breeches and a black tunic, belted with a silver sash. Her hair was braided back and black, soled slippers were found to fit her feet.

"Your father is not going to be pleased," Elena said.

"My father will just laugh."

Lilian eyed herself in the mirror. The clothing fit well and accentuated her curves without making her look trashy. There would be no mistaking her for a man despite it being a man's outfit. The breeches came down to just below her knees and exposed her feminine calves. She pursed her lips. She needed anklets.

She looked up to her face. The black of the clothing set off the silver of her eyes, but she needed earrings, she decided. Maybe a cuff like her father wore. She eyed her ears. They weren't pointed like the Sidhes', although they had a slight point to them. Would the point develop as she aged or would they remain the same because she wasn't fully Sidhe?

"Sword," she said, to shake herself from her ponderings.

Elena gave an ever-suffering sigh and followed her out of the dressing room. Khayyam eyed her as she stepped into the receiving room and nodded his approval. She grinned and headed for the door.

Khayyam might have approved, but the resulting wave of shock both astounded and amused her. Servants collided with one another, the Ladies of the court had to pick up their jaws from the marble floor, and the Lords, well, their shock was a different sort altogether. Khayyam had to ensure they kept their distance and didn't get too close.

Poor Khayyam, she mused.

Lilian received an invitation to the midday meal, another wanted to take her on a picnic, one of the bards wanted to write a ballad to her, and two others couldn't even speak, they just followed like lost puppies.

"What are you doing to my Court?"

Amras sounded very much amused and exasperated.

"Nothing," she replied with such innocence in her tone that Amras snorted.

Elena looked either mortified or amused; it was hard to tell as she tried to hide it from her.

Khayyam leaned in and whispered, "It'll be the fashion in a couple of days. You watch."

Lilian laughed. "I can't wait."

Elena led her to the weapons room, where they kept spare weaponry of all sorts. Only the guards and soldiers wore weapons, and non-military wore a small dagger used for personal protection and eating. The servants in charge of keeping the weapons polished and rust-free jumped to their feet when they walked in. Their eyes widened when they recognized her and hurried to make their bows.

"I'm looking for a sword," she said. "I hope you can help me find one."

The servants looked at one another and back at her. One piped up. "What kind of sword, milady?"

"Small and light for my hand."

"But you're a Lady," another stuttered.

Elena nodded in agreement.

"Yes, but does it exclude me from having a sword?"

Their shoulders drooped and in resignation, they showed her the swords. She grinned.

Two hours passed as she went through the selection. Khayyam had propped himself against a wall and Elena had taken over an abandoned chair as they waited for her to make up her mind.

Lilian couldn't though. None of the swords had been made for a woman's hand and not a single one connected with her. She wanted the one like she had conjured in her astral battle with Ulwe, but what had been created mentally didn't always mean there'd be one in reality.

One of the servants offered her a long dirk. It was a slender thing, sharp on both edges, with a delicate look to the hilt and a weight more suited to her hand. It wasn't what she hoped for, but she loved it.

The servants found a scabbard for it, showed her how to loop her sash through the belt slide and retied it for her. They looked her over, grinned, and sent her on her way.

Of course, having had time to get over their initial shock of her style of dress, everyone was shocked a second time when they saw her armed with a dirk. Elena just sighed and led her through the castle to the back portion, where other rooms were located.

"I need to get cleaned up and ready for the evening meal," Elena said. "You can wait for me and I'll show you the way."

Lilian nodded. "All right."

"More than likely, His Highness will have some entertainment for you. Maybe some music and dancing." Elena grinned at the thought.

"Dear Lord, I hope not," she gasped.

"You aren't planning any surprises for the evening meal, are you?"

Amras chuckled.

Lilian groaned. "Oh, no. He is."

Elena looked at her as they arrived at a set of doors. "Of course, he is. You're his daughter. He'd want to introduce you to his people."

"I hope he doesn't think he's going to convince me to stay," she said as they walked into Elena's receiving room.

Elena made her way to the dressing chamber of her suite. "Perhaps he does. I do know he was very happy to have found you."

"It was a surprise to me."

"I can imagine," Elena called out.

Lilian noticed Khayyam's attention remained centered on the door where Elena was changing and she grinned.

It didn't take very long for Elena to change into a different gown and come back out. It was burgundy with matching slippers and fit her form very well. Khayyam seemed to approve by the way he looked at her, which caused Elena to blush.

The three of them made a rather grand appearance into the dining hall. Amras stood with a few of his lords, conversing, but when she walked in, the resulting wave of silence had him turning to see what had caused such a disturbance with the crowd. Upon seeing her, his brows lifted and burst into laughter.

"*I see you are going to be a handful, daughter.*"

Lilian grinned. "*Of course, I'm your daughter after all.*"

He motioned her over and Elena gave her arm a light squeeze before wandering off to her friends. She was sure they would interrogate Elena about her, but she had faith in Elena's restraint.

Lilian made her way over to her father, Khayyam following behind her. Silence followed them; many of the people stared in shock at her clothing and the weapon she carried.

"*I'm not changing and I'm not removing the dirk,*" she stated, defiant.

Amras smiled. "*No one's demanded you to. If it makes you feel safer, then carry it.*"

Tears prickled in her eyes. Amras understood her reasons for needing to make herself feel safe.

He held an arm out to her and when she neared, drew her in, holding her in a one-armed hug.

"This is my daughter, Lilian. I hope you treat her with respect."

The men bowed, although they never once looked away from her.

"She is your daughter, King Amras. She looks just like you," one said. The other agreed with the speaker.

"I would hope she is prettier," Amras said in a wry tone, and chuckled.

"You've recently gone through your Chrysalis?" one asked her.

"Lord Gaeris," Amras said.

Lilian nodded. "Yes."

"So you still need guidance," Gaeris said.

"I believe Calawe was appointed to be my tutor," she said.

The group glanced toward Calawe, who must have felt himself being watched because he looked up and around until he found the source. Seeing her, his brows lifted in shock.

"Oh, this will be fun," Amras said under his breath, amused, although she detected a hint of sarcasm in his tone.

Lilian looked away from Calawe and toward her father.

"*Excuse me?*" She folded her arms. "*You aren't planning anything, or hoping anything will happen between him and I, are you? I am mated, remember.*"

"*That remains to be seen, but until then, you can still have fun.*"

"*Fun? What kind of fun? Please tell me you don't think I'd just...have sex...with others?*" The heat from a blush came over her face and she glared at Amras, blaming him.

Amras burst into laughter and led her to where they would sit for the meal. He was still laughing when he seated her and took his seat beside her. Khayyam sat at a lower table, but kept her in close proximity and within eyesight.

Once settled, everyone else followed suit, and the meal was served. She was awed by the amount and different types of food offered. Fruits like she'd never seen came in on platters, large bowls of soups, trenchers of meats, everything anyone could imagine, and it was there. Her father kept watching her reactions, smiling, until she glared at him.

"If I didn't know any better, I'd say you were doing this on purpose."

He blinked oh so innocently. "Doing what on purpose?"

She gestured to the display. "Trying to impress me."

"Me? How could you think such a thing?"

Lilian lifted a brow and he laughed.

"I will admit to this," he replied. "I wanted to show you everything about my home."

"It's wasteful, this much food," she whispered.

"Nothing goes to waste here. What does not get served to the Court is served to the servants. They are allowed to take what they wish home to their families. The bones are cooked for soup stocks. Fruits are cooked into desserts, vegetables added to soups. Nothing is wasted. Or, very little is."

Lilian was a little relieved at partaking in such a huge affair after it had been explained, and allowed herself to enjoy the meal.

Conversations flowed around her and even though she couldn't pretend to know anything in order to join in, she enjoyed listening to her father as he dealt with the people of his kingdom.

After the food was cleared away, she began to tire. The excitement of coming here with her father, and the adrenaline rush of being in a new place, seeing how his people, their people, lived had carried her up until now, but it had faded and exhaustion set in.

Music began to play and tables were moved back to open up the floor for dancing. Khayyam came up to stand behind her as she watched, relaxing as the music soaked into her mind and her body.

Calawe approached and spoke with her father, but she ignored him. She didn't feel up pretending to be polite to him, but was startled out of her drifting when he stepped in front of her and bowed. "Would you care to dance?" He didn't sound as though he had wanted to ask.

Lilian blinked at him. "I don't know how to dance."

"A perfect time to learn," Amras said.

Ahh. Her father had put him up to it. *Figures.*

Lilian sighed and stood up. Calawe walked around to meet her at the end of the table and offered her his hand. She took it and he led her to the open floor, where in a polite but succinct tone, showed her the position, and began to explain the steps.

"*You know, you don't have to do this,*" she thought to him.

He looked surprised and lifted his brow. "*I have no idea what you mean.*"

Lilian snorted. "*You're a liar and not a very good one at that. Look, I know you don't approve of me being here and I don't care. I'm here because my father asked me to come.*"

Lilian detected a wave of derision come from Calawe before he replied.

"*You don't care about the kingdom or the people therein. You're just here because you thought being a princess might be fun and then you'll go back to wherever it is you came from,*" he accused.

Lilian bristled. "*You know nothing about me. From the way you've treated me, I don't care for you to know me. I have a mate in my world. I'm not here for anything but my father and to learn about this part of who I am and where my father came from. If you don't like it, then you can go sit and spin.*"

"*You assume I want to get to know you, Highness.*" She could feel the disgust of his having to use the title in regards to her.

Enough was enough. Without thinking, she reached up and touched his temple. Before he could jerk back from her, she sent him her memories of her recent past and the battle with Ulwe. She sent him her emotions, the physical and mental pain of the attack, of the battle, and what she had gone through with the Chrysalis, although in a watered down form. She then jerked her hand away.

"Don't you ever presume to judge me. Until you've walked a few miles in my shoes, you will never understand what I've been through, nor will you ever get the chance to!"

Lilian pushed him away from her and with one final glare, turned to walk back to her father. She saw Khayyam frowning, unsure if he should intervene, but he remained where he stood, leaving it to her to indicate if she needed or wanted his help.

A hand settled on her shoulder. "Highness…"

She didn't let him get any farther. She reached up with the hand opposite of the shoulder he had touched, grabbed Calawe by the wrist, spun and jerked, which pulled him through a flip over her shoulder. He landed on his back on the marble floor with a loud *thud*.

"If you ever touch me again, you'll be sorry," she snapped at him.

She noticed the music had stopped and silence had fallen in the room. She straightened, smoothed down her tunic, glanced around, and headed back to her father.

"Dare I ask?"

"You can dare but I'll probably just tell you off."

Amras laughed.

"I'm tired. I'd like to go to bed now."

Amras stood and came around the table to her. "Come." He offered her his arm and she took it, grateful for the support. She could still feel everyone staring at her and she was too drained to put up a positive demeanor.

With Khayyam following behind, Amras led her out of the Hall.

* * * *

Matthias showered and returned to his room to dress. When he stopped by Lilian's room on the way out, she had already gone. He debated on going to find her, but decided against it. He needed the time away from her in order to think. He blocked her out of his mind as well, to keep his own thoughts to himself.

Matthias was confused and scattered, and he needed to think without her present. He spent the next few hours being with his people, doing his Alpha duties. He consoled those who had lost someone and visited with the wounded to ensure they were healing or, in some cases, already healed. Matthias gave his thanks and his praise to the warriors that fought with him and for him. The bodies of two fallen warriors burned on the funerary pyre, Matthias gave eulogies and honored their sacrifice.

Quite a few people asked after his mate and guilt wormed its way further into his gut. Perhaps he had been a bit harsh with her. After all, she had nearly died and forced to undergo the Chrysalis against her will. She was still his mate. He made a mental note to speak with her during lunch.

When she hadn't shown up for lunch, he figured she was with her father, sequestered away for privacy. He paced, undecided on whether to interrupt or give them more time alone. They both needed some time and if she was with Amras, they were probably talking Sidhe business. So, he let her be.

However, by the evening meal and still no sign of her, Matthias became concerned. He tried to reach her through their mental connection, but there was nothing. Frowning, he headed to her room, expecting to see Khayyam camped outside the door, but when he approached, there was no one.

He knocked on her door and received no answer. He knocked again, and when he heard no reply, he opened the door and stepped in. Worry gripped his stomach and held tight as he looked around, but nothing was out of place.

Where could she be?

When his eyes fell across the bed, he saw the envelope propped up on her pillow.

Matthias had a sinking feeling in his gut when he walked toward the envelope and saw his name across the front.

No, please.

He opened the envelope and pulled out the letter. As he read it, his heart jolted as though it would stop.

She left me. Lilian's left me.

Pain gave way to rage as it exploded and burned like wildfire. It took hold and spread through his mind. He lifted his head and roared out his anger and his pain.

* * * *

Lilian jolted awake with a stabbing pain in her heart. Her heart beat too fast in her chest, like a panic attack. Was it fear? Anger? Was she in danger? She rolled over and grabbed the dirk she had set beside her on the bed and waited.

Nothing.

She sent out psychic tendrils, to try and feel for any danger, but found nothing.

After a bit, she collapsed back onto the bed and tried to even her breathing, to slow it down to a normal pace so she didn't feel like her heart would jump out of her chest.

What had woken her?

She surged upward, worried. *Matthias? Was it Matthias?*

Lilian tried to contact him but their connection was weak. What she could feel was muted, but she picked up on his rage and his pain. Had he found her letter?

"Leave it be, daughter."

"Father, he's hurting. He still cares."

"Let him come to you, if he does. Let him show it."

Lilian lay back down, frowning.

"Trust me."

It took some time before she fell back to sleep.

The next morning, her two maids woke her, opened the drapery, wrestled her for the covers, and got her out of bed, bathed, and dressed. During which she grumbled, cursed, and threatened, to no avail.

She heard Khayyam's muffled laughter as the maids stuffed her into a corset and gown with her commentary, but when she walked out of the room and into view, no sign of amusement remained on his face.

"Lady, I'm going to have to beat the men off you now."

It might have been a compliment, but the way he said it made it sound as though he was resigned to the future battles he'd have to fight.

Lilian blushed, but waved off his words, only to invite him to eat with her. He joined her with no hesitation.

Before leaving her room, she was quite adamant about wearing the dirk. With great reluctance, the maids helped her wrap the sash.

She was quite lucky to have worn it. Without it, she would have taken a tumble down the stairs if Khayyam hadn't grabbed the sash and kept her upright.

Lilian cursed the gown, the corset, and anything having to do with being a princess. Amras's burst of laughter could be heard coming from one of the meeting rooms nearby.

The first lesson of the day was deportment. She found out she had to learn how to walk in a gown, to move with grace and elegance. Personally, she thought she walked just fine, but she supposed being a princess meant she had to walk in a different way than normal.

"If I have to wave, I'm rebelling."

"Wave?"

"You know, parade princess waves."

Amras was confused; she could feel it in his response, and so she showed him. He burst into laughter.

"*No, no waving.*"

The second lesson of the day was curtsying. She all but rolled her eyes at the thought.

"I'm not curtsying."

"But you must learn how. Each title has a certain bow and while you'll only have to curtsy to your father and the High King, you should still learn."

"Okay, but I'm wearing a corset and it's not exactly the best thing for bending the back."

"You aren't supposed to bend."

Lilian sent the mental image of strangling her father to him.

The third lesson was her language lessons with Calawe.

The moment he walked in, she stiffened and her eyes narrowed.

He bowed to her. "Princess."

She heard no sense of derision, no disgust in his tone.

Hmm.

"Our language is difficult to learn if you are not Sidhe," he began as he motioned at the chairs. "Please sit down, Princess."

Lilian was too glad to sit. One could only learn to glide as if floating, and curtsy without bending for so long before one had to just give it a rest.

"Fortunately, as you have been through the Chrysalis, the language is there, in your mind, sleeping. It only needs to be awakened."

Lilian eyed him. "You are not getting into my head."

Calawe nodded once, although there was a glint of amusement in his eyes.

"I mean it, Calawe."

"I believe you, Princess. You must do it yourself then."

"Where would I find it?"

Calawe shrugged. "I do not know. Each person is different."

She glanced at Khayyam and back at Calawe. "You know what I can do. Don't mess with me."

Calawe smiled. "It would be an honor to die by your hand."

Lilian wasn't sure how to take his words, so she ignored it. Without closing her eyes, she went within.

To her delight, she found it much easier than before.

There was a brushing at her mind, a knock of sorts. Calawe was trying to speak with her. She let him in only at the surface and no further.

"*Have you found it yet?*"

"I just started."

"Look through your memories. Sift through it for something not there before. It will feel as though it belongs, but you will not remember ever seeing it before."

Lilian began the search, while keeping Calawe at the center of her attention. He might find it amusing, but she didn't trust him yet.

"Nothing."

"Look deeper."

Lilian frowned and resumed her search. Her concentration was broken when she saw Calawe move. Well, saw wasn't the right term. She *felt* his movement as ripples in a current of air and she shoved him out of her mind as she surged up, furious.

Calawe laughed, his eyes twinkling. "You are too sensitive. Sit down and try again."

Lilian glared at him. "Don't play with me, Calawe. I have no problem with blasting you through a wall. After Ulwe, I don't trust anyone in my head."

Calawe shook his head. "If anyone has the right to distrust, it's me. You are newly Sidhe and you come here, a princess. What are your intentions?"

"I already told you."

Calawe motioned her to sit again. "Let us try another way. I will teach you a few words. After which, go within and see if you can find where the memory is being stored."

Lilian eased back down in the chair and sighed. "All right."

Calawe pointed to the table. *"Tardi."*

She repeated the word.

"Jhyli," he said as he pointed to a chair.

On and on, he gave her words, tested her memory by having her repeat them. She stumbled, she gave the wrong word, she mispronounced them, but he drove her on until she had them down and she gave the right answers with the right pronunciation.

"Now, look for it."

Lilian nodded and went within again. She searched through her memories, tracing and tracking.

"Let me help."

"No."

"I know what to look for."

"Thank you, but no."

Calawe's exasperation and anger at her refusal was tangible, but she wasn't going to allow him to run around in her mind. She heard the knock at the door and the ripples of movement caused her to hesitate in her search. Her physical body waited, a part of her mental awareness surfaced so she could determine if there was a threat to her.

Khayyam had moved to the door and answered the knock. He nodded and strolled toward Calawe where he leaned down and whispered. Khayyam straightened as Calawe stood and made his way to the door.

There was a flurry of Sidhe, none of which she understood.

"*We do not have time for your reticence, Lilian.*"

Before she could gather herself, Calawe stormed her mind.

"*How dare you!*" She was furious and the energy around her began to pulsate.

She attacked Calawe mentally, trying to eject him from her mind, but he was quick and agile, able to dodge the attacks. He kept her busy, antagonizing her. Being focused on him in her mind, she was unable to use her physical attacks to wound him.

Lilian realized she was stronger with her abilities, but he was better trained in using them. She quieted, watching him with wariness. Calawe also quieted and watched her. He did nothing else.

"*Now, let us look for this genetic memory together,*" he instructed in a calm, even tone.

Her fury remained, along with her distrust of him being in her mind. After her battle with Ulwe, she held an innate suspicion for anyone invading her mind.

"*It is good to be cautious, but do you think your father would have appointed me to help you if he did not trust me? Do you think he would not have already been through my mind to determine if I could be trusted?*"

"*It's too soon after Ulwe. I'm still raw from it.*"

"*It is because of Ulwe again we must hurry this lesson. His Court has decided to investigate his death and wish to question you.*"

Lilian frowned and sought her father. "*Is this true?*"

"*Yes, it is so. It is a formality, so a returning former king cannot dethrone the next Winter King.*"

Damn it, she thought, causing Calawe to chuckle in her mind.

"*Fine, let's get this over with. I want to be able to understand everything they're accusing me of.*"

Calawe nodded and they began.

Together.

Chapter 12

"Who pissed in Matthias's corn flakes this morning?" asked Tiberius as Matthias snarled at a few of the pack members for not moving fast enough.

"Lilian's gone," someone whispered in reply.

Tiberius looked surprised. "What? Why?"

The young pack mate shrugged and gave a wary glance toward Matthias before whispering, "Don't know, but her father and Khayyam are gone too."

Tiberius shook his head.

Matthias turned on them and snarled. "You got anything better to do than to gossip about me and my mate?"

Tiberius lifted a brow. "Keep it up and she won't be the only one who leaves." He walked away.

Matthias bristled with pent-up anger, but didn't pursue Tiberius. His concentration centered on why she left him.

He stormed off, and then burst into a run toward the woods. He shifted to his wolf form as he hit the border and like a dark shadow, was gone from sight. He stretched out his muscular form as his paws ate up the ground, tearing through the brush as though he could escape from the pain and the anger, but try as he might, he couldn't outrun his loneliness, or his heartache.

It only got worse as the day went on. The longer he went without a touch, a word, anything from his mate, the more his mood and temper became darker and enraged. He snapped at anyone who approached, and caused children to burst into tears from his dark glares. Soon, people avoided him and he was glad of it.

Matthias saw his mother approaching, and from the look on her face, he knew he was in for some ranting. He turned to face her fully, bracing himself.

"I want you to pack up and get out," she said, her tone even and quiet despite the storm he could see raging in her eyes.

"What?" Being kicked out of his pack by his mother was not what he expected.

"I said get out. Pack your things and leave. Tiberius can run the pack until you get your head screwed back on straight."

"I beg your pardon?" Matthias asked, growing angry.

"I mean it. No one wants you here and if you don't leave, the rest of us will. We're sick of your temper."

"Do you even know why I'm pissed?"

"Yes. Lilian left you. She went with her father to learn about her heritage and probably to think about things, considering she just went through a kidnapping, a major battle, almost dying, and then being forced to go through the Chrysalis to survive her injuries despite having not wanting to. Knowing you, you didn't bother to consider any of it before you walked away from her first."

Matthias growled. "I just needed some time to think about things."

"About what? The fact she's Sidhe now? The fact she's more powerful than she was before? Or maybe because she's a princess, the daughter of a king? Which is it?"

"Mother, you're a pain."

"And I'm going to get even worse because I meant what I said. Either you get out or we will."

Matthias ran a hand through his hair, frustrated.

"Do you love her?" Helena asked, her tone softening.

Matthias pondered the question and when he found the answer, he nodded. "I do. I almost lost her before. I don't want to lose her now."

"Did you think it was going to be easy, especially for her? She's mated to a Lupine. She's not what she was before. She's going to be confused and your walking away from her was stupid, Matthias. How insensitive could you be? She just woke up from everything that happened to her and you walk away to think. What about her? A woman likes to be reassured of things, especially when she almost died." Helena shook her head. "I can't believe you're my son sometimes. You're just like your father."

Helena glared at him and with a final hmph, she turned and walked away, leaving Matthias standing there, stunned.

* * * *

It had taken two more hours for them to find the seed of memory in her mind and awaken the language in her. Calawe had seemed perplexed, but once the seed was found, together, they had planted it in her mind and made it grow, blossom and bloom so it opened even more of her mind to her.

Lilian was an unstoppable force when she realized she could understand and converse in Sidhe. She demanded Calawe to speak only in Sidhe to her so she could further her knowledge. She was able to pick up the nuances as quick as he could talk and soon, she rambled on and on about absolutely nothing just so she could hear herself talk in the lilting language.

"*I don't want anyone to know,*" she warned Calawe.

He looked a bit intrigued. "Oh?"

She nodded. "Let them think I don't understand. They'll be more apt to speak if they think I don't know what they're talking about."

Calawe grinned. "Such as making accusation with no merit."

"Exactly. Let them say whatever they want."

Calawe nodded. "Be careful. The Winter Court can be cruel. They take the game of politics very seriously, and with Ulwe gone, they will want to put their bids in for the crown."

Lilian stood, wincing. She stretched, and replied, "I think I know exactly what they're capable of, but thank you for your concern. Be careful though, someone might think you actually like me."

She grinned at his abashed look and strolled for the door, Khayyam following behind her.

Lilian was starving, but she didn't make it halfway to her room before armed guards surrounded her.

"What is going on?" she demanded.

Khayyam tried to push his way through, but the guards kept him from her.

"You are being summoned to Court, Highness. An Inquiry has been brought forth regarding the death of the Winter King."

"*Father?*"

"*A formality. It's all right. You'll be better protected this way should the Winter Court decide on stupidity.*"

"*Stupidity was letting Ulwe be the king in the first place.*"

She detected his amusement in her mind as the guards escorted her to the horseshoe shaped outer Courtyard. There, Amras was seated on the throne, and the courtyard filled with people. The lucky ones were able to get a seat before the benches ran out.

"Wow, just because of me?" she murmured.

One of the guards snickered under his breath and whispered, "You're a bit of a celebrity."

"And how do you know what a celebrity is?" she whispered back in amusement.

"I do take vacations on the mortal side."

Lilian tried to picture the Sidhe tourist industry and just couldn't.

The guards escorted her to an empty chair to the right of Amras and she sat down. Khayyam took his place behind and to the right of her.

As soon as she was seated, a group of four men approached. They were all dressed in somber colors, with pale skin and dark hair and eyes.

"*Northlanders,*" her father explained.

Winter Court.

They bowed to Amras who nodded in return. They gave her a brief glance before they launched into a rambling preamble.

"*Shi cali tysti sai ailmondrai eil orolor ailesia ail vaendreas sail lali 'm. Shi pai byr shaeloli si Ulwe tys myr shi ailylaer eir shi talyr aezaes eil aistasor bedi ail sor taraes.*"

Lilian translated the speech from Sidhe to English. *We have come to instigate an official inquiry in regards to Ulwe's death. We do not believe the Summer Court should be involved, as we cannot expect an impartial judge in this matter.*

It was followed by a diatribe of complaints against her and the Summer Court in regards to the death of their king. She was hard pressed to pretend she didn't understand the language when she wanted to beat them with her chair for the accusations they came up with.

Amras narrowed his eyes on the group, but before he could reply, she leaned in and whispered, "Is this going to take long? I'm starving. Calawe kept me from the midday meal."

Those of the Summer Court and close enough to hear her whisper had to cover their snickers of amusement.

Lilian glanced at the group of accusers. "Oh, am I interrupting something *important*?"

The four glanced at one another, and then glared at her. "You do not speak Sidhe? We were under the impression you've been through your Chrysalis."

"Oh, yes. I awoke from it yesterday morning. I'm still trying to figure things out."

Amras glanced at her, at Calawe, and back at the group. She knew Calawe would explain things to her father.

"We're here to find out what happened which resulted in Ulwe's death," the spokesman for the group said.

Lilian gave a shudder. "Horrible man. He had me kidnapped and tried to torture and kill me. I had to protect myself."

They weren't buying it, it seemed.

"You won't mind then if we look into your memories."

Lilian bristled. "I do mind, actually. I had enough of Ulwe's mental raping. You think I'm going to let someone else try it? If you want to know, I'll tell you what you want to know, but you aren't going to go dancing through my head."

One of the men started to smile, but contained it before his companions could detect the tilting of his lips. She eyed him before looking back at the spokesman.

"How do we know you wouldn't edit out the necessary information?" he asked.

His tone was already accusing her of doing so.

"Lilian, do you remember after we first met, we sat together and shared our memories to catch up on our lives? It would be like so," Amras explained.

Lilian was adamant. "No."

It was more than just giving strangers free reign of her memories, and it was more than reliving Ulwe's torture. In case they could not be trusted, she didn't want them to know what she was capable of, what her strengths and weaknesses were. She would not allow herself to be used against her father and his kingdom, against the Lupines, or even her own people.

Well, former people.

The men turned and spoke with one another. As she suspected they would, they switched to their native tongue. Still, she did understand and it about killed her to not react to their suggestion. They wanted to force her to relive the memory!

Amras spoke up. "No. She was already put through enough torture by Ulwe, I will not have her forced to go through it again with your bungling."

Lilian surged upward, sending a silent thanks to her father for his words so she could react, and react she did.

"Anyone who forces me into anything will get the worse beat down they've ever gotten. I don't care what you are or who you are, I won't be forced to go through it again!"

Just before everything could erupt into mayhem, Calawe spoke up. "If I may suggest something?" he asked as he stepped forward.

Amras nodded his permission.

"This matter will never be fully resolved unless the princess allows her memories to be accessed in regards to Ulwe's alleged treachery," he began.

Lilian noticed he had injected just enough derision in using her title to catch the Northlanders' attention.

"Perhaps, if a chaperone was present in her mind, the chaperone could ensure only the memories regarding this specific matter were accessed and nothing else."

Amras nodded in contemplation. "It is a good idea."

"I only trust my father in my mind," she said, shaking her head.

"Then there is a problem, Highness, because we cannot trust you only on your word nor can we dismiss the idea your father would show leniency or favoritism toward you."

Lilian lifted her chin, and glared with anger at the small group. Around her, the air seemed to shimmer and a few soft gasps were heard.

"After what Ulwe did to me, I ought to instigate an inquiry on the Winter Court. What kind of kingdom would allow a king like that to rule? For your information, he was not only after me, but also involved in breeding other supernatural creatures in order to create a personal army so he could take over this world, and then mine. So, exactly *what* did *I* do wrong?"

"Perhaps the princess would allow Calawe to chaperone?"

Lilian looked surprised. The Northlander in the back of the group, the one who had tried not to smile, spoke up. He watched her as he said it, gauging her reaction. She frowned and straightened her shoulders. "No."

Calawe shook his head as well. "I would rather not."

He said it in such a way she was reminded of how much of an arrogant ass he could be. She lifted a brow and turned to look at him.

"Oh? And just how did you mean that?"

Calawe gave her a practiced smile, one she wasn't buying.

"I would rather not subject you to my presence in your mind as you do not trust me."

Lilian narrowed her eyes on him. He was much too smooth. She wasn't sure which side he was on.

"I'd rather not have you in my head anyway. I don't trust you. You're too schmoozey."

A term none of them seemed familiar with, as they looked rather confused and tried to confide with others to determine the meaning of "schmoozey".

Calawe lifted a brow. "Did you just insult me?"

"Did I?" She smirked.

"In that case," he said and turned to Amras, who watched with some amused interest. "Your Highness, I will chaperone as they search her memory."

Lilian sucked in a breath. This was *not* how she had planned this to turn out. In fact, she had planned no one getting into her head!

"I refuse!" she snapped.

Amras touched her mind with a sense of apology, as well as affection. She realized she was fighting a losing battle. She knew what he would decide and while it hurt, she understood he had very little choice. She understood, she just didn't like the reasons.

"I accept Calawe as the chaperone. Lilian, you will allow them access to the memories beginning when Stephan took you and ending when you woke from the Chrysalis."

She looked at her father. "*All* of those memories?"

Amras's smile grew slowly on his lips. "Yes."

Lilian didn't allow herself to smile. "Yes, My Lord." She turned to the group.

Calawe stepped up to her and laid a hand on her arm. She gave a faint nod, but didn't look at him. When he brushed against her mind, she allowed his entrance and nodded to the Northlanders.

They didn't ask for permission, they slid in like hot knives through soft butter. She hissed beneath her breath at the sensation, and made sure they were aware of her disgust at their presence.

Without warning, she opened the floodgates to her memories for that specific time. She allowed them to see her memories, making sure they experienced what she went through. When they tried to exit, she blocked them from leaving.

"*You wanted to know, so you'll know everything that happened!*"

Every moment of terror, pain, desperation, and Madness, she bombarded them with it. It was as if they had been there themselves instead of her.

Even Calawe had been caught in the memories. Although he had witnessed a portion before, this was an unedited, unadulterated version and he experienced it just as the others did.

When it was over, Lilian threw them out of her mind. They looked pallid and all bore a horrified expression. She herself trembled, but the air around her vibrated with power which crackled in the silence.

"I hope your curiosity is sufficiently satisfied," she said in a soft tone.

Her world tilted at an awkward angle, and she had the sinking feeling she was going to pass out.

They bowed. "Yes. We withdraw the Inquiry."

"Good, because if you don't mind…" And she fainted.

* * * *

When she came to, she lay on her bed. Her father sat in a chair, Calawe stood behind him, and Khayyam stood at the door, watching. Her two maids hovered nearby.

"Ahh, you're awake," Amras said, sitting up.

"What is everyone doing in my room?" She started to sit up.

Amras moved in to help her. "You fainted and Calawe caught you. I had him carry you to your room."

"Okay, so why is he still in my room?" she asked. "You know Matthias is going to freak out when he hears he's in here and personally I don't want to be responsible for Calawe getting killed, or at the very least, maimed."

Amras chuckled. "Don't worry about it. Now, we brought you a meal and then you need to get ready."

"Ready for what?"

"The Ball," he replied.

"Oh, hell, no. I don't want to be paraded around at a Ball."

Amras leaned in and kissed her on the forehead. "I'll come up and escort you when it's time."

Lilian grabbed a pillow and threw it at her father as he turned and headed for the door. Her target was intercepted as Calawe stepped in behind her father and the pillow collided with the back of his head instead of Amras's. Calawe turned and looked at her, a brow arching.

"Don't even," she said, lifting a finger to point at him. "Just don't."

He winked at her before he followed Amras out of the room.

The maids brought a tray of food, fruits and breads, as well as cheese and a pitcher of soft mead, a honey beverage which contained no alcohol.

Lilian thought she deserved some alcohol, having put up with everything she had over the past few days.

After eating, she took a long soak in the tub, reveling in the large size, and once she had stepped out, the maids went to work on her.

They had her dressed, her hair done, and ready in record time. Her hair was swept up into a chignon, with soft tendrils left loose to frame her face. The dreaded corset was worn for the evening's gown, although she was very happy to learn it didn't need to be tied so tight. Of course, the various petticoats she wore were enough to make her want to kill someone from the sheer weight of it. However, the gown took her breath away. It was made of a shimmering silver material, and cut to accentuate every curve, without showing too much skin in the front. An off-the-shoulder number, short sleeved, and dipped low in the back. The expanse of skin revealed in the back concerned her, but her maids swore it was in the best of taste. The neckline and the hem of the gown had been embroidered in black scrollwork. A black sash was added too, in order to accommodate her dirk. Silver slippers completed the outfit.

When Amras came to collect her, she saw he had dressed to compliment her, in opposite. He wore a majority of black with silver highlights.

Her father was a rather dashing man, she thought.

Khayyam had even been given clothing to wear to the Ball. He was clad in black with red highlights. She smiled at him, approving of his look.

Elena seemed to approve as well. When she spotted her, Elena was staring at Khayyam with obvious appreciation.

Hmm, maybe a romance there? She grinned.

A fanfare played when Amras and Lilian stepped out onto the Court's floor followed by music. Amras danced the first dance with her, guiding her steps, as she'd never danced like this before.

"Tell me this isn't an often thing," she whispered to her father.

"What do you mean?"

"Feasts, Balls, those sorts of things. They don't happen often, do they?"

Amras chuckled. "No. Only on special occasions."

"Good, because I wouldn't be able to handle it all the time."

As soon as Amras finished dancing with her, Calawe asked her to dance. She eyed him, but accepted. He seemed different now. Not so arrogant toward her and instead, softer. She wasn't sure which she disliked more.

"Don't you pity me," she whispered. "I'd rather you dislike me than pity me."

"I do not pity you, Highness."

"Stop calling me that. It's Lilian."

He smiled. "Lilian then, when we're not being formal."

They fell into silence once more.

"I think the Northlanders got their butts handed to them," she said, trying to keep a conversation going.

The silence bothered her along with the way he watched her.

"I doubt they will be spreading any lies about what happened to Ulwe after what you accomplished."

Lilian studied Calawe's face. There was an odd note to his tone. Awe?

A strange feeling hit her in the gut, and she stumbled on the dance steps.

"Something wrong?" he asked.

Lilian lifted her head and glanced around. When she spotted her father, he was whispering to one of the servants and the servant hurried off.

"*What's going on?*"

"*What do you mean?*" Amras asked.

"*Something happened.*"

Amras looked at her, studying her. "*What did you feel?*"

"*I don't know. It was just a strange feeling. It almost reminded me of when I was in the Mists. Eerie. It felt like the tickling of a spider web.*"

Amras smiled at her. "*Someone coming through the Mists into our kingdom. You're very sensitive.*"

"*Did you feel it?*"

Amras nodded. "*I always feel when someone is entering the kingdom.*"

"Lilian?" Calawe said.

She glanced back at Calawe. "Sorry. Was talking to Amras."

"Is something the matter?"

"Oh, no. I guess I can feel when someone enters the Mists into the kingdom, like he does."

Calawe looked a bit surprised. "Really?"

Lilian nodded. "Amras thinks it's because I'm more sensitive than others."

"Perhaps."

He took her for another turn about the dance floor.

* * * *

Matthias wasn't sure how he knew how to find his errant mate, but he did. He brought five of his best warriors, Tiberius among them, and headed into the woods to the bank of fog which always seemed to exist near the river.

The connection to her was still weak, but when he stood by the fog, the tug was stronger. Was this the Mists Talis and Amras were always speaking of? It didn't seem like it'd be a gateway to anything other than a quick dunk into the river on the other side of the fog. Still, he could feel the pull of it, the pull of his mate, and knew this fog was a step toward her.

He stepped in. What was just a light wispy bank on the outside was nothing compared to the inside. It was thick inside the Mists, eerie. Shadows moved in the corner of his eyes but when he turned his head to look, he saw nothing. He heard whispers and yet couldn't understand a word spoken. He couldn't even tell what language was spoken.

The hair on the back of his neck tingled as it stood up and he growled. His men were antsy, nervous, and kept glancing around as they made their way after Matthias.

Once in the Mists, Matthias became unsure of where to go, how to proceed. He stopped and looked around, but saw nothing other than the drifting fog.

Without warning, four men appeared out of the shadows, dressed in matching clothing. Each bore a sword at their waist.

"We're here to take you to King Amras," one said.

His voice seemed to float and echo in the Mists, and Matthias wondered if the whispers they heard were just people conversing on their way to and from.

"Good."

The guards opened their ranks and made sure the Lupine were guided through and into the kingdom.

When they stepped out of the Mists and onto a cobblestone path, the spokesman of the guards explained there was a Ball in honor of the princess. He told them about the Inquiry earlier in the day and how the princess had acquitted herself.

"Does she know we've come?" Matthias asked.

"Not that I'm aware of, sir."

Matthias reached through their mental connection to touch her mind, careful not to alert her. He wanted to surprise her with his coming here and so checked to see if she was aware of his presence.

At the moment, she was unaware. He smiled.

The smile didn't remain on his face when they arrived and he saw what was going on.

Lilian sat next to her father, but around her hovered quite a few young men.

Even a couple of older looking men.

Aggravation pricked at him. He watched as her head jerked up and she looked around. Amras too glanced around, probably having picked it up from Lilian.

When her gaze fell on Matthias, he could have sworn the ground shifted beneath his feet. Their eyes locked. All conversation, music, movement, and even the world, melted away until there was only his mate.

"*What are you doing here?*"

Her voice touched his mind and he shivered.

"*I've come to bring you home,*" he replied.

"*Why?*"

"*Because you belong with me. You're my mate.*"

Lilian looked away and returned to her conversation with the men around her.

Matthias strolled toward the group, his eyes on her.

"Lilian, it's time to go." Matthias's annoyed tone carried over the music, over the noises in the Courtyard.

People fell silent to listen and watch the latest drama unfolding revolving around their newest member. Even the music fell silent.

"Go where?" she replied.

"Home. Your visit is done. I want you home."

"I'll be done when I decide I'm done," she replied.

"You're my mate," he growled, and glared at the men.

They hurried to move off, except one, who took a seat beside her, smiling.

Matthias's eyes narrowed at the man.

"Really? Are you sure?" she asked.

Matthias looked back at her. "What do you mean am I sure? Of course I'm sure!"

Lilian arched a brow at him. "How are you sure?"

Matthias started to get angry. "We still have our connection as mates."

"Is that all?"

"And you belong with me."

Lilian sighed and looked at the man beside her. "Want to dance?"

Amras tried not to laugh, but Calawe looked a little unsure as Matthias was glaring holes through him.

"Lilian, you need to come with me."

"No, I don't."

Matthias bristled. Khayyam stepped up to her side, watching Matthias. Even the guards watched him. Matthias snarled and walked away.

He didn't understand why she was acting like she was. She knew they were still mates, even he could feel their connection, her emotions. Pain and dejection.

Wait. Pain and dejection?

He turned to look at her but she had already turned away. His eyes narrowed.

Matthias motioned to his men and whispered amongst them, giving instructions. Once everyone was clear on what was to be done, Matthias turned and headed back to her.

"Dance with me," he said in a seductive tone.

Lilian looked at him, her brow furrowed. "Dance with you?"

Matthias held a hand out to her. "Or are you afraid to dance with me?"

He used their connection to swamp her with feelings of wanting and desire. Her face went pink, and she fidgeted in her chair.

"Dance with me, *Lilia mea*," he said in a coaxing manner.

Lilian stood and took his hand. "One dance and then I'm retiring for the evening."

Matthias helped her down from the dais and out onto the floor. The music started back up again, although a bit halting at first before it continued. He took her into his arms, held her closer than what was polite, but he didn't care. Having her in his arms was all that mattered to him.

"*Lilian, come home with me.*"

"*Why should I?*"

"*Because I need you with me.*"

"*Why?*"

"*Because my mother threatened to kick me out of the pack if I didn't bring you home. Because I can't sleep without you near, even if you aren't sharing my bed. Because, if you don't, I'll throw you over my shoulder and carry you out, kicking and screaming and then make love to you for hours until you agree to come home with me.*"

He heard her breath catch. They were both silent as they danced. He waited for her to say something, to agree to come home.

"No."

* * * *

He's here! Matthias is here!

It took everything in her to keep the joy from showing in her eyes and on her face. All she wanted to do was launch herself at him, tackle him, and hope she made it to the floor before him!

Until he opened his mouth.

He was so arrogant. Matthias never once thought about what she might have wanted when he walked away. He wasn't thinking beyond himself at this point.

So, what *was* she, just a warm body, and a convenient mate? Didn't he feel anything toward her other than lust?

And lust it was.

It radiated from him until she was breathless and shaking. As he held her, she could feel his arousal pressing into her thigh and she couldn't think.

Still, there were no words of love or affection, so she said, "no."

His shock was tangible. He tensed with anger and his golden eyed hardened. She wasn't afraid though because she knew he wouldn't ever hurt her.

Yet, he continued to dance with her, swamping her with desire, his desire. She was breathless, weak in the knees, and flushed. She tried to put some distance between them, but he refused to let her go, and held her tight against him. Memories of their lovemaking kept her unaware of the world around them. All she could think of was Matthias and all she could feel was Matthias. Even the ripples of movement around them failed to draw her attention until it was too late.

In a flurry of movement, she found herself lifted up and thrown over Matthias's shoulder. She gasped in shock and all hell broke loose. The guards noticed Matthias's action. Khayyam snarled and jumped over chairs and benches on his way to help her. Amras and Calawe were on their feet.

Lilian struggled to free herself from his hold, kicking and beating on his back. She tried to wrangle the dirk from its scabbard, but Matthias was quick to remove it from her and tossed it aside.

Matthias's pack members had maneuvered themselves into position to protect Matthias and her from the guards. They were just as quick to move in to block the guards' way, shifting to their war forms, causing shrieks of alarm from the women, and even the guards themselves hesitated.

"Matthias put me down! How dare you?" she demanded.

The gown was not the best of garments for struggling. The petticoats and gown caught her legs and made it much more difficult to move in this position. The corset itself was a detriment as he just bounced her on his shoulder and knocked the wind from her.

"I am taking my mate home," Matthias announced to Amras.

Amras lifted a brow. "No, you're not. She does not wish to leave with you."

"Yes, she does. She just doesn't know it yet."

"How dare you! Put me down, Matthi...eek!"

Was that a hand sliding up along her inner thigh? He wouldn't!

"Matthias!"

She went red and looked around, hoping no one could see what he was doing. She struggled again, trying to avoid his roaming hand, to no avail. His fingers slid along her damp sex and she gasped as her body jerked.

"You're wet for me, aren't you? You want me."

Lilian whimpered with frustration and desire. *"Please, Matthias, don't do this to me."*

"Admit you want me."

His fingers slid into her sex and stroked against her clit. She bit back the cry and her hands clenched onto the back of his shirt. Another look around and from what she could see, the Lupines were doing an adequate job of keeping the guards back. No one was trying to kill one another, but there was some definite combat going on. Khayyam had shifted to his war form and engaging on one or two of the Lupines.

Matthias kept teasing her, teasing her sex to keep her wanting him. She didn't refuse him from a lack of wanting him. She wanted the words. She wanted to hear she was more than just a mate.

"I didn't leave because I stopped wanting you, Matthias!"

His fingers stopped, and she wriggled with frustration.

"Why did you leave?"

"Because you shut me out. Because I almost died. I woke up from three days of sheer torture and wasn't sure about anything and you walked out. You shut me out! What was I suppose to think!"

All of a sudden, Matthias put her back on her feet. She had the distinct feeling she was about to faint from the sudden blood rush out of her head, and was glad he held on to her.

All around them scuffles and fighting were going on, but they were so focused on one another, they didn't seem to notice or care.

"Lilian, I just needed time to think! You were different. I'd almost lost you and then you're alive and so different. I had to be alone, to think things through. I was afraid you wouldn't want me anymore because you weren't human. You were Sidhe, and your father a king. Hell, I wouldn't have wanted me if I had that going on for me."

His eyes were blazing hot, melting her to the very core.

"When you left, I nearly went insane. I just about drove everyone away. My own mother finally told me to get the fuck out if I couldn't get my act together. I realized what I had done when I thought I lost you and what it meant."

What did it mean? Say it!

Lilian stared up at him, daring him to say the words, but he didn't. She shook her head and started to push him away from her.

"Let go of me."

"Lilian, I…"

"No, Matthias. Don't try to explain anything, don't try to backpedal."

His eyes hardened and he pulled her back to him.

"You're my mate."

A sword was placed at Matthias's throat. "I think, perhaps, you should release her."

Calawe.

"Stay out of it. This isn't your concern," Matthias growled.

"She is the daughter of my king, therefore my concern. You will release her."

Lilian watched the two men. She wouldn't allow Calawe to hurt Matthias, but she also didn't want Matthias to hurt Calawe for doing his duty.

Without warning, the ground rolled and there was a loud crackle of energy around them. She grabbed onto Matthias to steady herself and he held onto her to protect her. Calawe stumbled, but caught himself, while the combatants around them stumbled and fell.

"What in the name of Cernunnos is going on in here?" a loud, booming voice demanded.

They looked over to find Talis standing on the dais beside Amras. He looked furious.

All at once, everyone but her, Matthias, and the Lupine dropped into deep bows or curtsies to the High King.

Chapter 13

Even from half a hall away, she felt the rage emanating from Talis. It was time for some damage control.

She started to step away from Matthias, but he grabbed her by the elbow and pulled her back. She tried to pull away again, and Talis turned his glare toward them.

"Release her!" he snapped.

Matthias wasn't having any of it. His back straightened and he squared his shoulders as if preparing for battle.

"Matthias, please."

Matthias growled under his breath, and she knew he debated a refusal. In the end, he released her.

"Now, if someone would be so kind as to tell me what is going on?" Talis said, folding his arms as he glared around him.

"Talis," she said. "Matthias came for me."

"And?" Talis said.

"She refuses to leave," Matthias replied before she could.

Talis looked between the two of them, and slowly eased down into her vacated chair. "Hmm. Why?"

"Because Matthias is stubborn!"

"*Me* stubborn? Hah! You're the one who refuses to come home."

She turned to snap at Matthias. "You only want me there so your mother doesn't kick you out of the pack."

"You know that's bullshit."

"Do I? I haven't heard you say anything otherwise. Oh, wait, yes. You also miss me and miss making love to me."

"All valid and very true reasons." He nodded.

"It's not enough for me! Why can't you tell me the words?"

Talis looked at Amras who grinned and shrugged. A servant came forward and offered the two smirking kings chalices of mead as the drama continued.

"Why do you need the words? You can easily read them from my mind!"

Lilian clenched her hands into fists at her sides and stomped a foot in anger. "Because I want to hear the words, you idiot. Because I shouldn't have to go looking for them. Because no one should *have* to go looking for them!"

Matthias leaned toward her, eyes blazing. "And what about you? You haven't exactly been up front and verbal about the words!"

"Oh, for the love of…" Talis snorted. "Get it over with, you two."

Lilian and Matthias both turned and snapped, "Stay out of it!"

The gasps of shock around them were ignored as they looked back at one another.

"I don't think they'll get to it," Amras said.

"They had better. I want to attend the wedding," Talis replied.

Lilian was distracted by their conversation and glanced over at them. "What wedding?" she demanded.

"Yours. Now, carry on." Talis gestured toward her and Matthias.

"There's no wedding."

"There will be," Amras replied.

"No, there won't be," she argued. "Not unless you have someone else in mind because I'm not getting married."

Matthias was silent as she argued with Amras and Talis. She refused to read his mind, to see what he was feeling or thinking. She wanted him to tell her.

Lilian was about to storm off, frustrated and angry, when Matthias grabbed a hold of her hand. He pulled her around to face him, and lowered down to one knee. She sucked in a soft gasp.

"Lilian, *Lilia mea*. I may be arrogant and a jerk, but…" He paused as he tried to find the right words.

Lilian waited, holding her breath.

"I want to marry you. I want you to be the mother of my children, and I want you as my mate. I don't want to lose you. I love you."

Lilian threw herself at him, almost bowling him over, as she hugged him tight. He held her just as tightly to him as his lips met hers, kissing her with pent-up hunger.

Amras looked at Talis. "Do you think that was a yes?"

Talis burst into laughter and raised his chalice. "I do believe we're going to have a wedding!"

The roar of applause was deafening, but she barely heard it and she knew Matthias couldn't have cared less.

* * * *

Amras refused to allow them to sleep together. Matthias was given a room on the other side of the castle and she was placed under Elena's watchful eye. The castle was abuzz with talk and activity as everyone readied for the wedding.

Tiberius stayed with Matthias but the rest of the entourage was guided back through The Mists to spread word of the wedding to the rest of the pack. Those who wished to attend were invited and the guides would bring them back through The Mists.

Lilian found the numbers of women who flirted with Tiberius vastly amusing. Many of them competed for his attention by bringing him food and little treats to "try".

That night, she couldn't sleep. The wedding was set for the next day and she was too nervous and excited to close her eyes and rest. Matthias couldn't sleep either it seemed and he checked in on her every few minutes.

"*Are you sleeping?*"

"*No.*" She turned over onto her side and snuggled with her pillow.

"*Why not?*"

"*I'm too nervous.*"

"*I could sneak in and help you sleep.*"

Lilian laughed. "*My father had guards posted outside the door, so you wouldn't be able to sneak in.*"

He slipped into her mind and began to awaken her desire with memories of the two of them together. She whimpered.

"*Matthias, I'll never get to sleep!*"

He laughed in her mind, a sensual chuckle causing her to shiver from the mere sound of it.

"*Tomorrow,*" he promised. "*Tomorrow they won't be able to stop me.*"

"*Talis could. He's the High King.*"

Matthias snarled at the thought and she laughed.

In their minds, they were together, despite the distance of their bodies. They drifted off to sleep, dreaming of one another and the promise of tomorrow.

* * * *

Lilian was awakened by a troupe of women, her maids, and lots and lots of laughter. Her drapes were pulled back, and sunlight shone in, blinding her. She grumbled and rolled over, pulling the covers over her head. Elena laughed and grabbed at them, which resulted in a tug of war. She almost won until the maids jumped in to help.

The resulting laughter brought the rest of the women in from her receiving room and it became a losing battle from then on.

Lilian was carried into the bathroom to bathe. She was allowed to soak in scented water, before the torture began. She feigned outrage and put up a token struggle but the women had their way and scrubbed her clean until she was as smooth as a baby's butt.

The women weren't too sure about the phrase, but when she explained, they loved it and everything—the silk covers, the soap—were as smooth as a baby's butt.

Soon, someone brought up male body parts and it resulted in much laughter and stomach holding, as well as wiping tears from their eyes.

"*I hope you're having as much fun as I am.*" Matthias spoke to her, his tone wry.

"*Why? What are they doing to you?*"

"*What aren't they doing? I've been shaved, dunked in a cold river, scrubbed raw, measured, and I'm being strangled in the getup they want me to wear.*"

Lilian laughed in her mind. "*I introduced the term 'as smooth as a baby's butt' and we've digressed to male body parts and whether or not they are as smooth as a baby's butt.*"

Matthias purred in her mind. "*You can find out later how smooth I am.*"

Lilian's face heated and the women, catching sight of her blush, laughed. They assumed it was their joking which caused the blush. She didn't bother to correct them.

Lilian was dressed, her hair done, and led downstairs to meet her groom. She wore silver with black accents. She did not wear her sash or dirk, but she carried a wreath of woven flowers and herbs in her hands.

The Court Hall had been decorated for the wedding. Colored swaths of material were hung from tall poles to make a ceiling, which still allowed light in, yet provided shade for those beneath. All the benches had been removed, so it was standing room only in the great hall.

Matthias stood by the dais, dressed in gold and black. Black breeches and a black tunic with gold accents along the hem and neck, as well as along the wrists and leg openings. He wore a gold sash and a sword as well.

Khayyam, who was dressed in black, although without the added decoration, escorted her halfway down the aisle, where her father waited. He kept a somber expression on his face, walked tall and proud, but when his duty was done, he looked at her with twinkling eyes and winked before he moved to stand beside Elena. Amras greeted her with a kiss on her cheek and then offered his arm to her. When she took it, he led her the rest of the way, to where her mate stood, waiting. Her father lifted her hand to his lips and kissed the back of it before offering it to Matthias. Matthias took her hand and nodded once to the king.

The Sidhe were dressed in their many-colored finery, and Matthias's people wore their own traditional finery, which gave the wedding an exotic feel. She thought everyone and everything looked beautiful. When she caught Helena's gaze, she saw tears shimmering in the woman's eyes and the smile on her lips. She had to look away and blink back her own tears.

The thrones on the raised dais the night before had been removed and a long table set in their place. In the center of the table stood the statue of a man's form dressed in robes with no facial features, and atop his head he wore the antlers of a stag. Beside him stood the statue of a woman dressed in robes and having no facial features. On her head, she wore a crown of the moon.

In front of the statues were three candles, a chalice filled with water, a bowl of water, a censer already burning with incense, a small bowl of earth, ribbons of white, gold, and silver braided into a cord, and a pillow on which were two rings.

Talis stepped onto the dais, dressed in dark green robes which shimmered as though shot through with gold and silver, and a large crown atop his head. Through the crown rose the antlers of a stag, majestic and tall.

Lilian wondered how he could wear the crown. It must have weighed a ton! Amras snorted and pretended to cough to conceal it.

Talis spoke and his voice carried through the space.

"Before us stand two that would be joined as one. There is magick to be done here then, the magick of love, and we call the Lord and the Lady to bear witness to this joining, in this place."

Talis gestured toward her and Matthias with his hands, palms upward.

"It has been said that you both wish this marriage. Is this so?"

Both she and Matthias nodded and answered, "Yes."

Talis laid his hands atop their heads.

"In the names of the Lord, The Horned One, Pan, Cernunnos, I give you the magick of the forest creatures, the wonders of the stars, the desire to fire your soul. In the name of the Lady, Arionrhod, Rhiannon, Cerridwen, I give you the magick of the moon, dreams to rule your destiny, and you shall learn the secrets of the tides."

He removed his hands from their heads. "Kneel."

Lilian knelt with Matthias's help and watched as her mate knelt beside her. Talis took the wreath from her hand and held it over her, touching the top of her head.

"You are the star that rises from the sea. You shall bring the tides to the souls of men, the tides that ebb and flow. You are the magick that moves in the moon and in the sea. You shall hold these secrets, for as woman, they belong to you. You are the eternal woman. The tides of all men's souls belong to you."

Talis moved the wreath and touched the top of Matthias's head.

"You are the Lord of the Forests, and in you, he returns to earth again. Hear the ancient call, for you are the shepherd of wild things and you lead the lost flock from darkness into day. Open the door of dreams so that men may come to you and through you to the Lord of the Wood."

He moved back to the table and placed the wreath over the two statues so the woven wreath bound the statues together. Next, he picked up the rings from the little pillow and turned to them once more.

"Above you are the stars, below you are the stones. As time passes, remember that like a star should your love be constant, like the earth should your love be firm. As each one is individual in their own magick and their own strengths and weaknesses, together they complement one another. Be understanding, be kind, and be trustworthy. Hide not from one another for as you are individual, your love brings you together to complement one another.

"Have patience each with the other, for storms will come, but they will go quickly. Be free in giving of affection and of warmth. Have no fear, and let not the ways or words of the unenlightened give you unease. For the Old Gods are with you, now and always!

"Lilian, daughter to Amras, formerly of the Human, newly born into the way of the Sidhe, is it your wish to become one with this man?"

Lilian smiled. "It is."

Talis turned to Matthias. "Matthias of the Romulus clan, of the Lupine, sons and daughters of Rhiannon, is it your wish to become one with this woman?"

Matthias nodded. "It is."

Talis offered a ring to Matthias, who kissed it before he gave it to her.

Lilian took the ring and slipped it over her thumb first, then index finger, then middle finger, before sliding it over her ring finger. With Talis's guidance, she recited the vows. "In the name of the Cernunnos and Cerridwen, I pledge to love and cherish you, Matthias, through this lifetime. To love you and lend you aid and protection by the power of the starry heavens, the wooded forests, the tides of the seas, and beyond the imaginable reaches of time and knowledge."

Talis offered the second ring to her, who took the ring, kissed it, and gave it to Matthias.

Matthias took the ring from her and repeated her action and pledge, although putting his own beliefs into the vows. "In the name of Lupa, the Mother of the Lupine, I pledge to love and cherish you, Lilian, through this lifetime. To love you and lend you aid and protection by the power of the starry heavens, the wooded forests, the tides of the seas, and beyond the imaginable reaches of time and knowledge."

Talis picked up the braided ribbon cord and joined their hands together, wrapping it around their wrists.

"Then as we all bear witness, and as High King, I proclaim you man and wife. Joined are your hands, two are now one. Know that it is by your pledge that you are united, blessed by the Lord of the Wood and Lady of the Earth and Sky. May your lives be joined as long as your love shall last."

A broom was brought forth by Elena and Khayyam, each holding one end as they lowered it to about a foot off the ground.

Talis gestured toward them. "Jump, for jumping symbolizes your jump from one life to another."

Lilian and Matthias, still bound by the cord, jumped over the broom, together. Elena took the broom and offered it to Talis, bowing her head. Talis took the broom with a nod to the young woman, placed it before the statues, and spoke again.

"Fate has brought these two together. Their lives have converged and shall now be united. It is in our hope that their path be pleasant and their sky fair. With clasped hands and hearts united, may they share it together with joy."

With that, Talis turned the two to face the crowd as the hall erupted in applause.

Lilian grinned at Matthias, and Talis leaned toward them. "This is the part where you kiss," he whispered.

Matthias grinned. "Don't need to tell me twice!"

He pulled her close and kissed her with all the love and passion he had for her.

The guests erupted with thunderous approval.

Later, as they sat down to eat, she and Matthias learned the cord, which united them, had to stay on until they consummated their marriage. Matthias was more than willing to take care of it right away, but Amras and Talis laughed and told them they had to wait. She shook her head at the look of disappointment on Matthias's face.

The problem of being tied together was solved by the sharing of duties they needed done. They fed one another from a shared plate. They held the chalice up to one another's mouths to drink. They kissed away any lingering drops of mead from each other's lips.

There was much laughter and fun all afternoon and into the evening.

Toward the end of the evening, Talis stood up and motioned for quiet. Once the noise died down he raised his chalice.

"Blessings to the wedded couple."

There was a cheer of agreement. "King Amras was blessed with a beautiful and intelligent daughter," Talis said. "She was dealt a harsh blow early in life and yet grew to be honorable, strong, and talented. In all of my years, I have never known anyone to have such inner strength as a human. I am only glad to be able to say I am proud to call her one of our own."

Lilian blushed and nodded to Talis. Matthias leaned in and nuzzled her neck.

"That is why I am making the following announcement," Talis continued. "It is time for me to step down as High King. In order to do so, someone must take my place and I have chosen Amras."

Lilian looked at her father in surprise. Amras himself looked shocked.

"My Lord?" Amras asked. "You honor me well but—"

Talis shook his head. "You have proven to be a good king, a fair and just king, and I have heard no complaints about your rule. Even when it included your daughter, you showed no favoritism and thought of what was right first."

Lilian frowned. "You mean the whole thing had been a test?"

"Not necessarily," Talis replied. "I used it as a test. The Summer Court will need a ruler. I have chosen you."

Lilian gasped. "Oh, no. Not me."

Talis smiled. "Why not you? You did well during the Inquiry. You showed strength of character and honor. You did what was right even as you disliked it. You were fair but made your point."

Lilian looked at Matthias. Matthias shook his head. "It is your decision, wife. If you choose to be Queen, we'll have to work out something with the pack."

Lilian looked amongst the Lupine. Many were showing signs of worry, unsure of what was going to happen.

Would she be willing to live here, she wondered. What about Matthias? He was Alpha. He couldn't give it up just for her. Would his family be willing to move here?

She looked at Calawe. He'd been training for years to take over for Amras. Her presence here had disrupted something he had known for most of his life. Could she rip that away from him? He was not looking at her and his expression carefully blank with only a polite smile on his lips.

Lilian smiled and looked back at Talis.

"I must politely decline the honor. As you said, I am newly awakened to this life. I cannot disrupt my mate's family and friends by uprooting them from their home to move here. I cannot nor would I expect my mate to give up his position. I cannot disrupt my new friends here by trying to take over my father's years of rule. However, by refusing, I know that I am leaving a hole and would like to recommend Calawe as the new Summer King." She looked at Calawe.

Calawe had turned toward her as he listened to her refusal, so she was able to catch his surprised expression when he heard her recommend him as king.

"Don't think I didn't know my being here was a slap in the face for you. I told you I did not intend to do anything other than learn about my father's people."

Calawe smiled at her.

Lilian blinked back tears and looked back at Talis.

Talis's smile was bright with respect and approval.

"Wise words, Princess. I still have an opening for the Winter Court if you're interested. It seems they need someone who might be able to straighten them out."

Lilian shook her head. "No, thank you," she replied, her tone quite emphatic, and he laughed.

"I will have to see what they have to offer."

"Actually, there is someone…" she said and smiled.

Talis lifted a brow and she sent him the image of the one Northlander who had tried to hide his smile during the Inquiry. He nodded.

Lilian had a feeling the Winter Court was going to get some changes, which were going to shake them up a bit. She grinned.

* * * *

Matthias was not going to be put off much longer, she noticed. They had been escorted to her room by the people of the Summer Court, all those who could fit in the hall and up the stairs. By the time they arrived at her room, everyone had stopped and congratulated them, gave advice, and reminisced about their weddings and first nights, Matthias was about ready to throw her over his shoulder and make a mad dash for the nearest window. She laughed and teased him.

Once the doors were closed, in the faces of her father and Talis, Matthias turned to her and let out a sigh of relief, exaggerated though it was. She grinned, but gave a shriek when he yanked her toward him and took her into his arms.

"I have waited for this for far too long," he growled.

Lilian sighed with pleasure as their bodies pressed against one another.

"Me too," she whispered.

Their lips pressed together, their kisses hungry and demanding.

Matthias growled under his breath, the vibrations reverberating through his chest and into her. She moaned as he wrapped his arms around her, pulling her against him as he turned to the nearest wall. He pressed her back against it, his body pinning her firmly.

Lilian whimpered with need, feeling his arousal against her, causing oh so familiar feelings to course through her body, her veins. His tongue delved into her mouth, hot and demanding, and she opened for him, gave in.

"*Lilian, Lilia mea, mine.*"

She shivered at the seductive, possessive tone he used as she heard his words in her mind.

"Matthias, I need…"

"*Yes, baby. I do too,*" came his response.

His lips left hers and trailed down her jaw, pausing to suckle at various sensitive spots, causing her to shiver and gasp with delight.

When one of his hands slid up along her waist, she wanted the beautiful gown she wore off her body.

"*Tear it off if you have to,*" she demanded.

He chuckled, but when her free hand started pulling at the sash he wore, the chuckle ended in a growl.

"*Damn it! Damn cord! We've already consummated before. Untie us so I can touch you!*" She was only a little horrified at her demanding. The rest of her was very much in agreement with her words.

Matthias must have agreed too because the cord which bound their hands together fell to the floor and their hands were all over each other.

"That's it, baby. Touch me. I need you to touch me," he pleaded.

She needed it too she discovered, and when her hands were able to slide under his shirt and find skin, She purred with satisfaction. His skin was hot, muscular, and felt wonderful beneath her fingertips. She traced his chest, reacquainting herself with the feel of his body, and every muscle and bone, every dip and valley, every muscular bulge, and she committed them to memory.

His hands weren't still either. He tore at the fragile material of her gown, and the lacings of her corset, until he pulled away the offending material and exposed her skin beneath. His hands touched her, caressing. She whimpered and shifted against him; the rough calluses on his fingers causing goose bumps to rise, and a shiver to run down her spine.

"You're like silk, baby. Your skin is so hot and smooth."

"As smooth as a baby's butt?" Amusement colored her tone.

Matthias growled and lifted his head to capture her lips once more in a deep kiss and there was no more amusement in her mind.

"I'm going to lift you, wrap your legs around me."

Lilian's brow furrowed in bemusement. When Matthias lifted her up, she wrapped her legs around his waist, causing both of them to moan as her nether region pressed against his arousal. The barrier of their clothing did nothing to suppress what both of them experienced; fire, pure, unadulterated fire, raced through their veins, leaving behind a driving need for more.

Matthias carried her further into the room, toward the bed. Every movement made their bodies rub together, keeping both of them high on the sensations of passion.

Lilian was drowning in it all, unable to think, only feel. Each step caused a deeper need within her, a driving need, bordering on pain. She gasped as they fell together onto the bed, his weight pressing into her, causing even more interesting and familiar sensations. She squirmed beneath him. He growled, adjusted his body, and sat up until he straddled her hips.

He looked down on her, hunger blazing in his golden eyes, and his nostrils flared as he scented the air.

He was gorgeous. Those eyes, his hair, the way he looked at her, combined to take her breath away, and she knew she'd never be able to forget this, or forget him. Every time she looked at him, she'd feel this way. His hands settled on her waist and finished tearing off her gown and the petticoats until she was nude beneath him.

Matthias whispered in his language to her, leaning down so his mouth could trace kisses over the skin of her abdomen. She didn't understand the words, but guessed the sentiment from his tone.

Lilian gasped and shivered. He moved down her body, his hands caressed and stroked, and made her squirm. His lips tickled her sensitive skin.

His breath caressed the insides of her thighs and her eyes clenched closed. Anticipation and embarrassment battled for supremacy. She knew what he was going to do, and she wanted him to do it.

"Reach up and hold onto the headboard," he murmured, his lips brushing over her nether lips, teasing her.

Lilian's hips jumped beneath his mouth even as she did as he instructed. She reached over her head to grasp onto the bars of the headboard. It stretched her out and made her breasts lift, her nipples hardened and jutted upward. He massaged first one, then the other, causing her back to arch and push her breasts into his hands.

She cried out when his tongue delved between her nether lips and brush against her clit, causing her hips to lift off the bed. He subdued her, pressing her back onto the bed with one arm across her hips, his tongue not letting up. He teased her clit with light touches, before he used his free hand to open her up to him, exposing her most private parts to his eyes, and licked her again, using long, slow strokes.

Lilian whimpered and writhed beneath his mouth, her hands clenching into fists on the headboard's frame. His tongue was like fire on her clit, and yet the burning wasn't a painful burn, but a yearning one. When he captured her clit with his lips and suckled in a slow, gentle manner, she nearly bucked him off.

He took his time, suckling and using his tongue to tease, pushing her to the edge of her control. With occasional forays of his tongue, he would lap at her opening, tasting her sexual fluids, and return to her clit. She could feel the tightness coiling within her, like a spring about to explode, coiled too tightly, kept too tense.

Still, Matthias would not let her go. He would back off as she neared orgasm, and when her body had eased its torturous pleasure, he would resume his attack. She cried and pleaded with him, to no avail.

There was a brief moment where it seemed he gave her a respite, yet she wanted more, needed him. She sobbed his name and he returned, this time renewing his attack on her clit, driving her to the edge and then over.

She screamed out her pleasure as she arched from the bed, shaking with the intensity of it. He continued to lick at her, lap her fluids up, tasting her pleasure, driving her to another orgasm even before she could come down from the first.

Matthias moved up her body. She could feel his arousal, hard and hot against her inner thigh. She opened her eyes to look at him, his skin brushing against hers just before he settled atop of her. She wanted him inside of her...needed him inside of her.

His eyes were narrowed on hers, the golden color burning like the sun. He reached down between them and took a hold of his manhood, guiding it to her opening. He stroked himself against her slickness, brushing against her over-sensitive clit, causing her to gasp and whimper. He smiled.

"*Lilia mea,*" he whispered. "My mate, my wife."

"Yes," she replied, her voice shaky with need.

"Say my name," he growled, as he held himself at her opening and started to push himself in.

"Matthias," she murmured, moving with restless energy beneath him.

"You belong to me," he growled. "Say it."

He pressed further into her and she whimpered as he stretched her. She could feel Matthias filling her and was tempted to let go of the headboard to take a hold of him.

"*Matthias,*" she thought to him.

He paused, giving her a moment to collect herself.

"*Yes...*" she moaned.

He plunged inside her, and she released the headboard. She wrapped her arms around his neck, to keep him from moving away, from leaving her body. Matthias growled again and began to move, slow, shallow strokes at first.

"You're so tight, so hot."

Lilian moaned with pleasure, the intimate sensation of the slick friction inside of her caused her to lift her legs up and clasp him by the hips. He must have taken it as permission to continue because he lifted up a bit, bracing himself on his hands, staring down at her as he deepened the strokes, until he was almost leaving her body, only to plunge back inside, deep and hard.

She could feel not only the deep strokes of his manhood within her, touching what seemed like a million, billion over-sensitive nerve endings within her sheath, but her clit was stimulated as well, and before she knew it, she was riding along a knife's edge, ready to plunge over once more.

He wouldn't let her though, again taking control. When she felt her insides start to tighten and flutter, he slowed until he was just moving within her. She protested with a sharp cry and thrust her hips up, trying to entice more of him, but he only chuckled. He kept her on the edge, on the peak, but refused to let her over.

"Who do you belong to?" he growled at her.

Lilian whimpered, writhing beneath him.

"Lilian! Who do you belong to? Who is your mate?"

"You! Matthias! Please!"

Matthias snarled and thrust himself inside of her, moving hard and fast, and the only noises were their harsh breathing and the slapping of flesh against flesh. She screamed as her orgasm washed over her like a tidal wave, sweeping away reality and her world became nothing but feeling and sensations. Pleasure built, and even the slight pain from his near brutal thrusts became bliss.

He thrust once more, and came, and she felt his manhood swell within her, she thought perhaps he would tear her, split her in half. His arousal twitched and jumped as he exploded deep within. His mouth roamed her neck and collarbone, nipping skin. She could feel the sharp bites, but was too far-gone to care or react to it.

As the two of them lay together, still joined, their hands stayed in motion. Even as they caught their breath, they continued to touch and caress one another. She murmured a protest when he slipped from her body and moved off to keep from crushing her, but he gathered her up and drew her close. Their limbs entwined so neither of them knew where one ended or the other began.

"*I love you.*"

"*I love you too.*"

Chapter 14

The room was long and dark and candles were the only light source.

At the center, and taking up much of the space, was a black table made of ebony, finished with a high gloss shine. At the head of the table sat an empty chair. Seated were ten men on each side, with a final man at the opposite end. Before the men sat a document folder marked with the *Custodes Secreti* insignia.

The man at the far end of the table spoke.

"We are here tonight, my brothers, because we are in need of a new leader. Our former Master's death has left a hole in our infrastructure and it is up to us to fill this hole."

The other men murmured amongst one another in response.

"We are at war, gentlemen, with the forces of darkness. They must be destroyed, stamped out, eliminated for the greater glory of man. We must use them for their strength to build our numbers, so that we will win the war against these creatures of darkness. For this, we must have a strong and able leader, a general of generals."

"But who do we know would fit this bill?" one asked.

"Me."

A figure stepped out of the shadows and caused the board members to jump. They began to murmur with nervousness.

He smiled, his fangs flashing in the glittering candlelight.

"Welcome to the new vision of *Custodes Secreti*."

Meet the Author

If there's a few things you can count on about Isobael, it's the fact that she's never without a notebook to write in, a book to read, or a library card to various libraries. And ideas. Oh, the ideas…

With two rather interesting heritages, Scottish on her father's side and Taiwanese on her mother's, you can guarantee Isobael has a lot of interesting ideas. With both heritages steeped in supernatural lore, Isobael grew up hearing lots of stories and a firm belief in things unseen. It didn't help living in haunted places, either.

Give it all a good shake and you're guaranteed a place where magick dances in the moonlight and wild things come to play.

Author's Website:
http://isobael.webs.com
Reader eMail:
Isobael.Liu@gmail.com